EBF

This book should be returned to any branch of the Lancashire County Library on or before the date shown

-7 MAR 2016

01 JUL 2016

FORT

22 MAY 2018

22 JUN 2018

16 FEB 2019

27 APR 2019

-6 JUN 2019

AFC

Lancashire County Library
Bowran Street
Preston PR1 2UX

www.lancashire.gov.uk/libraries

LL1(A)

CLOSING THE DISTANCE

'I want you to find someone,' Deborah said. 'And who would that be?' I asked. 'Me,' she said. 'I want you to find me.' The distinction between right and wrong is embedded deep in Bristol private eye Jack Shepherd. Deborah Thorne employs Shepherd to find her and promptly disappears. Who is she hiding from? Then a body surfaces in the mud of the Severn Estuary and is identified as Deborah's therapist and a former client of Shepherd. Suddenly the search takes a much darker turn, sucking him into a sinister and brutal vortex which might see him pay the biggest price of all.

CLOSING THE DISTANCE

CLOSING THE DISTANCE

by

Jeff Dowson

Magna Large Print Books
Long Preston, North Yorkshire,
BD23 4ND, England.

British Library Cataloguing in Publication Data.

Dowson, Jeff
Closing the distance.

A catalogue record of this book is
available from the British Library

ISBN 978-0-7505-4085-8

First published in Great Britain in 2014 by Acorn Books

Copyright © 2014 Jeff Dowson

Cover illustration © Marcus Appelt by arrangement with Arcangel Images

The right of Jeff Dowson to be identified as the author of this work has been asserted by him in accordance with the Copyright, Designs and Patents Act, 1988

Published in Large Print 2015 by arrangement with Rupert Crew Limited

All Rights reserved. No part of this publication may be reproduced, stored in a retrieval system, or transmitted in any form or by any means, electronic, mechanical, photocopying, recording or otherwise without the prior permission of the Copyright owner.

11861341

Magna Large Print is an imprint of Library Magna Books Ltd.

Printed and bound in Great Britain by
T.J. (International) Ltd., Cornwall, PL28 8RW

All characters appearing in this work are fictitious. Any resemblance to real persons, living or dead, is purely coincidental.

Contents

Dedication

To Mary

Acknowledgments

Thanks to...

Caroline Montgomery, who turned a screenwriter into a novelist.

Inspectors and staff at the RSPCA in Bristol; for the work they do and for their assistance with this book.

All the places in the West Country and East Anglia, whose names and locations the story has plundered.

Prelude

Kosovo is an impoverished, desperate place. The haves have it all; the peasants, mostly ethnic Albanians who make up ninety percent of the population, have what they stand up in.

It has been this way since the days of the Ottoman Empire. The years of Serb control between World Wars 1 and 2, did nothing to relieve the tension between the ethnic groups. Absorbed into the Federal Republic of Yugoslavia in 1945, the country existed in a Balkan limbo. Tito's police cracked down hard on nationalists throughout all Yugoslavia's provinces, whose constitutional autonomy meant very little in practice. Slobodan Milosevic's vision of a 'Greater Serbia' plunged the Balkans into civil war, brutal ethnic cleansing and NATO bombing raids.

In the summer of 1999, the United Nations took control. A mass exodus of Serbs followed, in the wake of revenge attacks by what was left of the Kosovan Liberation Army. Serbian police and Albanian militants kept up the regimen of reaction and reprisal, despite the UN peace keeping forces insisting there was a cease fire in place.

2000

The white Mercedes truck had a red cross painted on each side of the body and a plastic strip across the top of the windscreen which read *Médecines Sans Frontières*. It had travelled one hundred and forty kilometres northwest from the Macedonia border. As it crested the hill, the left front wheel dropped into a hole and bounced out again. The truck swerved to the left, as the driver attempted to keep the rear wheel from doing the same, fishtailed sideways and slid to a halt.

Inside the cab, the driver looked across to his passenger. The young man had been thrown sideways by the truck slide. His head had thumped into the right hand side window. Dazed, he sat upright, leaned back against the seat headrest, raised his right hand and gently prodded at his temple.

'Are you alright?' the driver asked, in heavily accented English.

He was Albanian. In his mid fifties and a little overweight, with heavily tanned skin, close cropped hair and dark eyes. The passenger was English. Early twenties, white faced by comparison, with a mass of thick brown hair which dropped over his forehead. He was thin and unshaven and tired. He closed his eyes, massaged them with his thumb and forefinger, opened them again and squinted ahead of him.

'I'm seeing stars,' he said.

The driver apologised. 'We will go slowly down the hill.'

He found first gear, changed up into second and let the engine revs act as a brake. The truck trundled down the hill, into the village of Donjica.

Or rather, what was left of it.

The road in to the square was lined with stone skeletons which had once been houses. Jagged holes blown out of the walls by mortars, splintered sections of roof timbers, blackened by fire. What must have been some kind of memorial in the centre of the square, was now a pile of rubble. The driver navigated his way around it and stopped the truck. He climbed down from the cab, knelt by the front wheel, dropped his head to the ground and looked under the engine. He rolled over, lay on the ground and shuffled backwards. The passenger walked around the front of the truck and looked down at the driver's legs. There was a muffled curse and the driver shuffled forwards again. He reappeared, with oil smeared across his forehead.

'There is a leak,' he said. 'Somewhere along the road, we hit the sump.'

'Will we get home?'

'Maybe. As long as we keep filling it up.'

He wiped his forehead with the back of his right hand and got to his feet.

'We need to find a garage.'

The two men turned and surveyed the scene. Donjica was a tiny place. Only a dot on the largest scale map. Where they stood had once been the heart of the village. It was now blasted to pieces. The work of Serb security police. The small mosque was the only recognisable building left. Arranged in front of it was a line of bodies, each one covered by a blanket, bed sheet, piece of tarpaulin – whatever had been to hand. Two old men, well into their seventies, were doing the best they could, to give this row of shapes in the road as much dignity as possible.

Moving towards the truck, from the opposite side of the square, was another man. Late forties, tall and slim; dressed in a dark suit, the left sleeve torn at the elbow and the rest of it coated with dust. The driver took a couple of steps forward. The man spoke to him in Albanian. The driver translated for the benefit of his passenger.

'I'm a doctor,' the man said. 'Have you got medicines in the truck?'

The driver shook his head.

'It's empty. Everything in it was delivered to Brazda refugee camp, over the border in Macedonia. We're on our way back to Pec.'

'That's a pity,' the doctor said. Then he lifted his arms and spread them wide. 'At least, you can be witness to this. And the rest. Let me show you.'

He led the driver and the passenger to the line of bodies. He knelt down by one of them, pulled back a bed sheet crusted with dirt and revealed the head and shoulders of a middle aged man. The top of the man's head had been blown off.

Further along the line, the old men were going on with their work as if the driver and passenger were not there. The doctor pointed to one of them.

'He says, that this man…' He pointed to the bloody mess at his feet. '…Adem Mehmeti, was dragged out of his house by three Serb policemen, pushed to his knees in the street and shot.'

Gently, the doctor drew the sheet back over the man's head. He pulled a blanket off the next person in the line. The driver looked at the body and instantly turned away. His passenger, steadfastly, stuck to the purpose.

The doctor looked at him and switched to remarkably fluent English.

'This is Sadik Hajirizi,' he said. 'Those wounds were made by an assault rifle. I know this, because the bullet I took out of the back of his neck is a 7.62mm calibre. Probably from an AK-47. I have seen them before. The Serbs are supplied with old Soviet army guns.'

The passenger looked at the doctor. Mute. Stunned into silence.

'You must write this down,' the doctor said. 'Be a witness. To all ... to all of this. I will take you round the village. There is more, much more.'

The passenger remained rooted to the spot. The doctor went on.

'You work for *MSF*, yes?'

The passenger nodded.

'Then you are in a position to talk with people. Please help.'

The passenger finally found his voice. He pointed across the square.

'That's just a truck. I just help out. I'm not important.'

'Yes of course. But you can tell what you see.'

The passenger nodded.

'Yes. I can do that.'

He turned away from the row of bodies. Walked swiftly back to the truck. Opened the passenger door. Dragged a battered holdall out from behind his seat. Found a ring-bound notebook in a side pocket. Dug deeper and found a pen. Pushed the holdall back into place, straightened up and shut the truck door.

The doctor moved to his shoulder.

'Are you ready?' he asked.

'Yes.'

Chapter One

2012

Marvin Starratt was a despicable human being.

An assessment Judge Chambers heartily agreed with and sent him down for eleven years; apologising to the court, the public gallery and the journalists on the press bench for not being able to incarcerate him longer.

'Unhappily, this is the maximum sentence I can impose,' he said. 'I can only recommend that you are made to serve the full term.'

I watched from the public gallery. Starratt had beaten up and raped a client of mine, and four other women, over a period of seven months. I helped find him and get him arrested. A small victory, in the legal sense – and you have to hang on to those – but Starratt had brutally invaded the lives of five women and changed them forever.

My client and I met downstairs in the lobby. We shook hands.

'Thank you,' she said.

'My pleasure,' I said.

She turned, negotiated the big glass swing door and stepped out into the street.

The chances are, Louise and I will never meet again. She came to me in distress; frustrated and angry that the police were making no progress in finding the man they considered their prime suspect. Upright coppers have to work by the book. I'm liberated from that kind of consideration. Admittedly, I don't have their resources, but I can go places they can't. I found Starratt by breaking in to a flat in Stokes Croft. He swung at me with a cricket bat. I took it from him and hit him with it and delivered him to the police. Louise gave me a cheque, the Inspector heading up the investigation team gave me his thanks and Starratt got his day in court. It was a job satisfactorily done. But I couldn't help to manage the fall-out. There was no sustainable after care I could offer. This is always the bit that bothers me. And the bit that never lets go entirely. My client cases get filed away in my office filing cabinet and each time, I hope there has been something about the case that has added to my learning experience. Something that will short cut the route to a successful conclusion of the next job I take on.

There was an angry bellow from behind me. I swung round and looked back across the lobby. A man in a brown tweed suit was squaring up to a barrister who was taking off his wig. He ripped the wig out of the barrister's hand and threw it across the lobby.

'Call that a fucking defence?' he yelled.

Lloyd Starratt was laying in to his brother's brief.

None of the Starratts could be described as nature's noblemen. The family had lived in the Forest of Dean since Noah was a lad. Earning a living down the years, as woodsmen, charcoal burners, farmers, miners, landowners, petty criminals and local terrorists. The whole tribe of head bangers and hard cases operated, without much correction, like the bad guys in a Kentucky backwoods movie.

This one, Marvin's older brother Lloyd, was the head of the clan. In his mid 50s, odious, obnoxious; at the moment in his default setting and making his presence felt. As hard as nails and a seasoned scrapper, he had a lot of clout in his neck of the woods. A member of the Rotary Club, a big noise in the Severn Valley Hunt and briefly, the local Tory party agent – for a particularly barmy right wing MP who got in at a by election but was, mercifully, ousted at the following general election, when the good people of the constituency returned to their senses. Perhaps more damaging, for a while during the 90s, he contrived, somehow, to get himself on to the JP's bench. An alarming west country re-creation of Elmore Leonard's Maximum Bob.

The barrister took a couple of paces backwards. Lloyd squared up to him again. The barrister looked around for help. A couple of security men sped across the lobby and intervened before Lloyd could do any damage. He elbowed one of them in the chest and attempted to kick the other in the crutch, before they managed to pin his arms to his sides and haul him across the lobby to the swing door. As Lloyd passed me, I was given the benefit of his opinion too.

'As for you, you fucker... Just you fucking wait.'

The security men heaved him into the door and swung him out into the street. He completed a full 360 on the pavement before he regained his balance.

Then he focused on me through the glass and malevolently gave me the finger. I gave him a cheery wave.

The barrister had retrieved his wig. He stepped towards me.

'Mr Shepherd,' he said. 'I'm sorry about that.'

I told him he had no need to apologise.

'If people like Lloyd start inviting me to dinner,' I said, 'it will be time to take a serious look at what I do.'

We shook hands.

'I'm truly glad you lost.'

'In truth, so am I,' he said.

This was all pleasant and it had been a successful morning, but there was something else to do today. I walked the three hundred yards to Charlotte Street Car Park.

I had left the Healey on the top floor. I opened the driver's door and slid in behind the steering wheel. My mobile rang from inside the glove compartment. It was one of those unbelievable 'movie moments'. Like when a character switches on the car radio, immediately to have the music interrupted and a news announcer tell him something the plot badly needs to know.

'Jack Shepherd,' I said, into the phone.

The call was from Trinity Road CID. Detective Sergeant George Hood. I had known him a couple of years. He was the first choice hound dog of an old friend of mine, still on the force – Superintendent Harvey Butler.

'How are you today Jack?'

'I'm alright.'

'That's good,' he said.

What he meant was – at least that bit is; the next bit is likely to be less jolly.

'We want to talk with you about Philip Soames,' Hood said.

Philip Soames... A psychiatrist with a private practise in Clifton. Recently a client of mine. Filed under S in the middle drawer of my office filing cabinet.

'You can confirm that you know him?'

I did my best to sound matter of fact.

'Talk away,' I said.

'No, not right now,' Hood said. 'Are you busy later?'

'I hope to be.'

'Okay... It's not our policy to keep the private sector away from paid work. At the moment, this is no more than routine. But we would be obliged if you could get round here tomorrow. Around noon.'

Hood was being polite. But his request was certain to prove a lot less routine than he was making it sound.

'Okay,' I said.

He thanked me and rang off. Distracted for a moment or two, I listened to the buzz on the line. Then I disconnected the call and put the mobile back in the glove compartment.

As Scarlett said – tomorrow is another day.

The Healey's engine fired up as soon as I turned the ignition key. The straight 6 settled into a rhythm and began to rumble softly. I listened to it for a while, then reached up and unclipped the front of the soft top. I raised the top and pushed it back. A 1966, classic 3 litre, is an indulgence I know. Expensive to run. I can sit in traffic and watch the fuel gauge needle go down. No breeze to service either, but for that, there is Mr Earl – twenty-five percent Jamaican and seventy-five percent south Bristol. A man of few words, laid back and totally unfazed by the complexities of the world around him, he lives above his workshop in a cul-de-sac in Southville. His son Hamilton works for him, his wife Alesha runs the local soul food café. A more well-adjusted bunch you could never hope to meet. Each time he presents me a bill, Mr Earl shakes his head sadly. But I've had the car fifteen years and my conscience remains resolutely untroubled by those who say we should all drive small, fuel efficient machines. Yes, the Healey pumps out more CO2 than my neighbour's wife's Nissan. But he flies to Toulouse twice a month. I don't fly anywhere – I hate airports – so my personal carbon footprint is tiny by comparison.

I drove out of the car park.

Saint Edward's Church is a tiny place, in a quiet part of Redland. Where Emily and I were married and where her memorial stone is placed. Chrissie and I stood side by side, in the corner of the churchyard and looked down at the stone.

In memory of Emily 1969 to 2011.

Chrissie reached out with her right hand, brushed my hip, found the fingers of my left hand and squeezed gently.

'I can't believe twelve months can go by so quickly,' she said.

It was a serene, late August day; with a soft breeze barely stirring the branches of the old yew tree behind us. Summer was stretching on, refusing to let go. So were the memories. Emily had loved, cared for and looked after all of us; mending and healing and resolutely not regretting.

Chrissie let go of my hand and reached into the inside pocket of her jacket. She produced a small photograph, set in a silver frame.

'This is the picture of Mum you always liked.'

Emily smiled at us from inside the frame. A photograph taken eighteen months ago in the Cotswolds, before the cancer took its final unbeatable grip. No sign of pain on her face. A little gaunt perhaps, but still beautiful, and at 42, far too young to die. Twelve months on, the grieving had distilled into remembrance. And Emily's legacy was substantial. Her continued presence in most things I did most days, was positive and welcome. Chrissie and I were closer than we had been in a long time. Her partner Adam and I were good friends. A relationship which had evolved and matured, in spite of my best efforts to strangle it at birth.

Adam is a senior reporter on the *Bristol Evening Post*. Eleven years older than Chrissie. When she met him two years ago, I decided it was a relationship to be discouraged. I'd insisted he was too old for her. She'd said he was the best thing that had happened to her. Adam was alarmed by all of it. Emily tried to keep the peace between us and we should have taken note. What began with an argument, was followed by a series of rows and ended in a big fight. Furious with me, Chrissie left home and moved in with Adam. I raged nonsensically in return. And in all of this, Emily was the loser. Neither Chrissie nor I recognised that. Emily watched over us, counselled us, but couldn't knock any sense into us. Driven by our own concerns, Chrissie and I failed to see who was really hurting the most. Leaving home was a simple disagreement. Emily's cancer which came swiftly afterwards, was a matter of life and death. It took something so deadly to bring us back together. We had time to prepare. Eight months to be a family again. At the eleventh hour we did the best we could, but time ran out. Through all the nonsense and eventually the grief, Adam was at Chrissie's side. He kept her grounded and together.

In silence, we looked at the photograph for some time, then Chrissie put it back into her pocket and we stepped away from the stone.

'I think Adam means to propose,' she said, as we were about to leave the churchyard.

I pulled open one of the big, cast iron gates and stared at her.

'Does he?'

'He's working up to it.'

'And is this a good thing?' I asked.

'I don't know,' she said. 'Maybe.'

'Just maybe?'

She thought for a moment or two, then shook her head. 'No it's better than maybe. It's...'

She wavered into indecision. I tried to help out.

'And do you feel disposed to accept?'

'Somewhere down the line, yes, of course. But I've one more year at uni. Then debts to settle and a job to sort out. Or maybe a post grad year. In which case we're looking at a hell of a long engagement.'

'You'll still only be 23.'

'You married Mum when you were 23.'

'And Auntie Joyce said I was far too young.'

'Was she right?'

Auntie Joyce is right about almost everything. But back then, she took to Emily instantly, loved her to pieces and put aside her misgivings. That was no surprise. Generous, big hearted and open to everyone with a problem to share, she and Uncle Sid – my father's brother – had gathered up a distraught child and given him all the love in the world.

Other memories came crowding in...

The day before I started primary school, my father came home with a new family car. A 1968 Ford Zodiac. I stood at his side, my point of view level with his waist. He, my mother and I, surveyed the gorgeous, two-tone blue, chrome trimmed machine. The image was burned on to the back of my retina and has never been dislodged. Not even, when three days later, my father hit a patch of ice on the top of Mendip and the car side-slipped through a fence and down 100 feet onto the floor of a stone quarry. The Zodiac burst into flames on impact. That day, I walked the few hundred yards from school to Auntie Joyce's for tea. I was still there the next morning; whereupon she said I wasn't going to school that day and she had something to tell me.

I closed the church gate behind us.

'She called me yesterday,' I said. 'Auntie Joyce.'

'Of course she did,' Chrissie said. 'She wouldn't forget.'

We walked the thirty or so yards to Chrissie's car, a ten year old blue Honda Civic. She pointed the key fob at the front wing, waited for it to bleep, then spoke again, as if on cue.

'They do seem to be enjoying retirement in Suffolk.'

'She told me Uncle Sid is making things in his shed.'

'What things?'

'Metal things. She said Uncle Sid wants to move. Needs more space he maintains.'

'Why?'

'To make bigger things I guess.'

Chrissie opened the driver's door.

'Why doesn't he just get a bigger shed?'

She got into the Civic. Closed the door, pressed a button to her right and the driver's window slid down.

'What are you doing now?'

I looked at my watch. A few minutes after four o'clock.

'I think I'll go home, take the rest of the day off,' I said. 'Come and have some tea.'

'I haven't got time,' Chrissie said. 'I have to pick up Sam. Call me.'

She started the engine, let in the clutch, found first gear and the Honda pulled away.

I live in a brick and stone Edwardian semi, with a curved bay window facing the street and three bedrooms upstairs. The only house Emily and I ever bought – just before Chrissie was born. There is a small garden at the front. A more substantial garden at the back, leads to a gate into a lane which runs parallel to the street at the front. The garage sits at the end of the garden and opens directly into the lane.

I stowed the car away, walked across the lawn and let myself into the house through the back door. I made some tea and sat down on the living room sofa to drink it.

Out of work again.

Although that wasn't strictly true. To be more accurate, I was currently not being paid by anyone. The self employed person always has work to do. The question is, whose money is he spending? Right now, and for the foreseeable future, I was spending my own.

The sun was shining and the lawn needed cutting. Seize the day.

I got to my feet, went up to the bedroom and changed into an old pair of jeans and my gardening shirt. I fished my gardening shoes out of the cupboard by the back door. My mobile rang from the hall.

The call was from Adam.

'Where are you?' he asked.

'At home. Just about to cut the lawn.'

'Got anything on this evening?'

'Nothing more exciting than cutting the lawn.'

'I think I can help there,' he said. 'Come for supper.'

'Going to be that good is it?'

'There's something I want to talk to you about. Or rather, someone. You remember Philip Soames?'

I took a moment. Sat down on the chair by the phone table and stretched out my legs. Adam asked if I was still there.

'Yes,' I said. 'What about him?'

'Tell you when you get here. Soon as you like.'

He disconnected. Distracted, I stared across the hall. I hit the call cancel button.

Philip Soames... Again...

Saved from cranking up the lawn mower, I de-dressed and redressed. Decided on a change of shirt and trousers, collected my jacket and car keys and left the house the way I had come in.

I managed to avoid the city centre, crossed the suspension bridge in light traffic, then turned west up the hill through Leigh Woods and on to the Clevedon Road. I drove into the centre of Clevedon a few minutes before 6 o'clock and pulled up outside Adam and Chrissie's house on Dial Hill a couple of minutes later. As I reached for the doorbell, there was an explosion of barking from inside the hall. That could only be the force of nature that is Sam the Bearded Collie.

Indeed so. Chrissie opened the front door and in a whirlwind of noise, swirling hair and thrashing tail, Sam launched himself over the threshold. He reared upright, planted his front paws on my chest and we danced backwards – him Fred Astaire, me Ginger Rogers. I managed to get my hands either side of his neck and slow down the mad fox trot. Sam dropped on to all fours. I bellowed 'Sit!!' And he did, staring up at me, tongue hanging out and panting like an idling steam engine.

Chrissie was hanging on to the door jam, convulsed with laughter. Adam appeared at her side.

'I did tell you I was picking him up,'

Chrissie said.

'Is he on holiday again?' I asked.

Chrissie pulled herself together and stepped on to the drive.

'Likely to become a permanent fixture,' she said. 'Our friends with the Australian connection, may be emigrating. They're out there now, looking for a house. In which case, he'll stay here, with us.'

She addressed the beast directly. 'Isn't that right Sam?'

Sam spun around, looked at Chrissie, threw back his head and barked in agreement.

'Come on,' she said.

Sam dipped his head and looked back over his shoulder towards me, considering his options. I stood up as straight as I could and gave him my best severely disinterested look. He took that on board, reversed his point of view, then loped past Chrissie and back into the house.

'On the button,' she said.

'Sort of,' I said.

I followed Adam into the hall.

Chrissie had cooked linguini carbonara – bacon, peas, red peppers and basil in some kind of cream sauce. We paid serious attention to the meal and conversation was minimal. At one point, Sam padded into the dining room. He looked around, decided there was no mileage in his 'Hey, here I am' routine and lay down in the doorway and dozed off. Adam made the coffee. Chrissie poured a cup for herself and took it into the living room. As she stepped over Sam, he woke up, got to his feet and followed her. Adam passed a cup across the table to me and turned to the subject of Philip Soames. He had a minor bombshell to drop.

'Your ex-client, Philip Soames, is dead.'

I stared at him. He went on.

'Dragged out of the mud in the Severn Estuary, yesterday morning. He was discovered by the man who checks the speed camera on the approach to the second crossing. You remember, it's up on the gantry above the toll barriers.'

'He saw the body from there?'

'Mr Conway is a bird watcher. Takes his binoculars with him every time he goes up to the camera. Apparently he's the West country's foremost expert on migratory wading birds.'

Adam stood up, moved to the sideboard and picked up an envelope folder. He opened it, took out a page of A4 and passed it to me.

'My copy for tomorrow. Best I could do. The police press statement was a little thin.'

I read it... Apparently, Mr Conway had climbed the gantry to collect the camera data at 8 am. Low tide. His binoculars had revealed a man's body, mid channel, partly submerged in the mud. He had been weighted down. The police statement posited that the deceased, identified as Philip Soames, had been transported out into the channel at high tide – around 2 am – and dropped into the water... I looked back at Adam.

'The wrong thing to do,' I said.

He nodded. 'You noticed?'

Presumably those who had accomplished this, never intended that Philip Soames should re-appear. Not with weights strapped to his chest and his pockets full of gravel. That being the case, the enterprise was a huge mistake. The perpetrators had reckoned without the second highest tidal range in the world; something around fourteen and a half metres. Even though there are two miles between the English and the Welsh at that point in the channel, at low tide – presuming you had mega waders and didn't get sucked into the mud – you could walk across.

Out in the hall, Sam sloped past the dining room door on his way to the kitchen. Adam looked at me, raised his arms and turned his palms outward.

'So, our rationalisation of the situation would be?'

'Those who did this deed were, at the very least, extremely foolish.'

'Or extremely ill informed.'

'Which leads to the most obvious assumption. They weren't local. Any west country person in the removals business would know about the estuary tides. No one would dump a body any closer than five miles out at sea.'

'That was my conclusion too.'

'You can't let this theory loose on your readers,' I said.

'Not without getting into trouble,' he said. 'But in the meantime, the piece needs some colour. I was hoping you could provide a little of that.'

I looked at the A4 page again.

'There are no details of how the police managed to identify him.'

'Not released.'

Not surprising. But at least intriguing. Adam seemed to lock into it too. Then a couple of seconds consideration was gate-crashed by the rattle of a choke chain from the hall, followed by extreme barking from the kitchen. Sam sped past the dining room on his way to the front door.

Chrissie yelled out, 'We're going for our evening stroll.'

There was a lot more barking and panting and squeaking from the hall, followed by the sound of the front door opening and closing and then silence.

Adam linked his fingers, put his hands behind his head and leaned back in his chair.

'So why would Philip Soames, eminent Bristol psychiatrist, incur the wrath of a bunch of out of town enforcers?' Then he grinned. 'Surely not because he was once a client of yours.'

'Is there any burgundy left?'

It was half an hour before Chrissie and Sam returned. By which time, we had finished the rest of the burgundy and shared all we knew about Philip Soames. Adam, his press ticket stuck firmly in his hat band, had the bones of a page one story, but it was little more than fiction at that moment. I couldn't see any harm in telling him all I knew.

'Was Soames married?' Adam asked.

'No. He was gay,' I said.

'In a relationship?'

'Not when I knew him.'

'And that was when ... nine months ago?'

'About that.'

'Can you talk about what you did for him? Or is that confidential?'

'I traced his aunt.'

Adam looked at me in amusement. Obviously not the sort of high end criminal activity he was expecting to hear about. I explained.

'Philip's mother died early autumn last year. The only surviving relative – apart from him – was her sister, his aunt. Neither he nor his mother knew where she was. There had been a big family bust up years earlier. Philip was his mother's sole beneficiary, but he wanted his aunt to know she had died. He did some digging himself and got nowhere. So in the end, he hired me to find her.'

'And being the super sleuth you are...'

'She lives in Ambleside, in the Lake District. I went up to see her.'

'How did she take the news?'

'She said "Thank you for telling me" and made me some tea. I reported back to Philip. He smiled and said "So be it" and asked me to send him my invoice. In return, he sent me a cheque. Since then, I've passed him in the street, met him in the foyer of the Colston Hall and had a drink with him on a couple of occasions. The last time, a couple of weeks ago. We were not close by any definition.'

The front door opened and Sam's choke chain rattled again. Seconds later, he was in the dining room, looking for trouble. Chrissie called him into the kitchen. He gave us a resolute 'I'll be back' stare and reversed out into the hall. In the kitchen, he downed his supper biscuits and slurped away in his drinking bowl for ages. Then he re-appeared in the dining room doorway, his soaking wet beard dripping water steadily onto the carpet. Chrissie materialised behind him with a towel.

'Sam,' she said.

The beast turned to face her and she wrapped the towel around his muzzle. This was clearly part of the late night game. Sam waited calmly until Chrissie had finished drying his face, then he stepped back, barked once, shook his head fiercely, circled round three times and sat down in the hall. He dropped his head onto his paws, his ears stretched out flat on the carpet. He let out a contented sigh and lay still.

'Is that it?' I asked.

'Usually,' Chrissie said.

I got up from the table.

'Are you going to stay over?' she asked.

'I'd love to,' I said. 'But not tonight.'

I turned to Adam.

'I'll look into this Philip Soames business. If I find out anything I can tell you, I will.'

He nodded in acknowledgement. 'Thanks.'

I moved to the dining room door.

'Good night,' I said. I looked down at the dog. 'And you Sam.'

He offered a soft rumbled response, a kind of grace note to the evening, and lay quiet as I stepped over him. Chrissie escorted me to the front door.

Chapter Two

Scarlett was absolutely right of course. Tuesday was another day. In all respects. To begin with, summer seemed to be over. I woke to the sound of rain. Hard rain. Stair rods battering down on the roof. I opened the front door into the onslaught of the prevailing wind and got comprehensively soaked collecting the milk. While I dried out, I made coffee, toast and scrambled eggs.

I took my mobile off charge and switched it on. It rewarded me with a message saying I had missed three calls. I finished the eggs and poured my third cup of coffee. The mobile rang.

A woman's voice, low register, asked if I was free to talk. I replied that I would be in my office within the hour and we could talk there. There was a pause. I waited. A car drove past the front window. The voice came back to me and said that would be fine. I asked who I was talking too. The voice said that was the issue at the heart of this. There was another pause. Irresolution seemed to be seeping down the line. So I made a suggestion.

'How about nine o'clock?'

‘Yes. Nine o’clock,’ the voice said.

‘Do you need directions?’ I asked.

‘I know where it is,’ the voice said and the line was disconnected.

I put the mobile into my jacket pocket and finished my coffee. I hadn’t much to consider, other than the mystery woman I was about to meet, so I got on with the day.

At 10 minutes to 8, I sprinted across the back garden lawn to the garage, getting marginally less soaked than I had done half an hour earlier. I drove to the office, the ancient de-mister on full and wipers at maximum speed – still not managing to shovel the water away.

Bristol’s traffic problems border on the irredeemable. And in the rain, the snarl-ups spread like runny tapioca.

The city was built on a swamp by the Avon and across the hillsides surrounding it. John Cabot sailed to the New World and ushered in Bristol’s ‘golden age’. Slavery. Fortunes were made by merchants who built more churches per square mile than anyone before or since, to salve their collective conscience. The slave masters identified the docks as both the hub of commerce and the centre of town. They drove from their enormous mansions on the Downs to their places of evil employ in gilded carriages; before which the traffic made way and members of the underclass stooped and tugged their forelocks. The rest of the populace struggled to get on and get by. The motor car arrived and jammed up the city centre completely. The Luftwaffe did its best to sort out the problem; but the town planners of the 50s and 60s reversed the process, filled the holes with concrete and built one of the most user-unfriendly city centres in Europe. The result ... the city's one way systems are impenetrable, parking is impossible and nothing moves faster than the slave master's tumbrels did two hundred and fifty years ago. And the statue of Sir Edward Colston, builder of schools, endower of almshouses, millionaire plantation and slave owner still stands proudly in the city centre. While barely half a mile east of him is a retail complex the size of a small airport, Cabot Circus; a monument to the enterprise culture, appropriately named after the man who started it all. So we've come full circle. And commerce is, as always, top of the agenda.

It took so long to get to my office, the clouds had rolled away and the rain had stopped by the time I arrived. A bright morning sun was out and the day was warming up.

The office is located in a converted, multi-storey, red brick tobacco warehouse on the north bank of the Avon, west of the city centre. An over optimistic pre-millennium development, now rented out at £7 per square foot because times are hard. It looks out across the river – towards Coronation Road and the Victorian built terraces which crowd the hinterland between Asda's hypermarket in Bedminster and Bristol City's ground at Ashton Gate.

The urban renewers were making another assault on the banks of the river; tearing brambles and nettles out of the ground and hacking away optimistically at wild hedging clogged with plastic bags, empty food cartons, battered drinks cans and materials much more insanitary. A bunch of men with a generator and a brace of heavy duty sand blasters, were bombarding the graffiti on the ancient iron footbridge which links this side of the river with the old badlands of South Bristol.

'They've promised to do our car park before they leave.'

I turned back into the room. Linda was standing in the office doorway. 41 years old, smart and funny and by some miracle, my friend as well as my accountant. And in spite of numerous threats to move, still occupying the office next to mine. Five feet six, dark hair and dark blue eyes, a composure and an instinctive body language that gave her all the confidence in the world. She and Emily had been close. Her mother died of cancer when she was fifteen and her empathy with Emily's condition was instinctive. She supported us, day after day, right down to the wire.

She was dressed for business, in a charcoal grey suit which wasn't remotely off the peg. It would have looked like just another expensive statement on anybody else. But it fitted Linda like Versace had sculpted it on her. She spread her arms wide and stuck out a hip.

'Sexy, yet purposeful is the intention. What do you think?'

'I think you look terrific,' I said.

'Thank you. Drink later?'

'Absolutely,' I said.

'Great. I'm off to Harrison Harrison Wallingford and Battersby.'

'Knock 'em dead.'

'That's the mission.'

She swayed back into the corridor and slipped out of view.

I got to my feet, turned to the window and looked down three floors to the battered tarmac that did duty as an access road to the building, before it disintegrated into the 'car park'; in reality fifty square yards of pounded down hardcore enclosed by corrugated iron sheeting, proudly displaying the efforts of local graffiti artists. I didn't mind the work – I thought it cheered up the place – but Banksy it wasn't. So it was next in line for an assault by the men with the sand blasters.

The wet tarmac was steaming and the warm day had encouraged tenants to throw open their windows. I could hear Patsy

Cline's *I've Got Your Picture* drifting up from the office below, underscored by the distant throb of engineering. Patrick, the web designer, had a library of torch song CDs, which he played to help him through his labours at the pc keyboard. We didn't socialise exactly. We met in corridors, in the lift and in the lobby. I didn't know much about him. But he didn't seem gloomy per se...

I left the window open, stepped to the officer door, swung it round until it was almost closed and looked into the dress mirror hanging on the back of it. It seemed only courtesy to check I was presentable enough. I stared at the face in the glass, nine years older than the face that first moved in here. I was 37 then, still young. 46 is middle aged. I decided my hair was tidy enough. I turned through ninety degrees and looked at the body profile. That was okay. I wasn't carrying any extra weight. Still comfortably straight backed and half an inch short of six feet tall.

I swung the door open again, moved back across the office, sat down in the chair behind my desk and waited. The phone rang. I picked up the receiver. It was Jason, on the security desk.

'Mr Shepherd...'

Jason's politeness is resolute. No one in the building has managed to persuade him to call them by their given names. He is young and the smartest member of the day shift, by a mile. A real bonus at the front desk, for tenants and guests alike. He has a sports management degree from Bath university. An accomplished kayaker, he missed 2012 Olympic qualification by a whisker. So while he figures out what to do next, the building can rest secure.

'There is a Ms Thorne here to see you,' he said.

'Thank you Jason, send her straight up.'

I put the receiver back in its base and waited a bit more. I don't make any attempt to appear busy at moments like these. Doesn't fool anybody.

Two minutes later, I heard the rumble of the lift, followed by a couple of judders and a thump as it came to rest. The door slid open, clanged and then slid closed again. A determined visitor takes twelve seconds to stride purposefully to my office door. A worried guest takes longer. I couldn't hear the sound of footsteps – someone with a light tread obviously – and it was some twenty seconds before my putative client appeared.

The lady made something of an entrance nonetheless. She glided into the office like a ballroom dance champion, stopped and waited for a moment or two. She obviously worked out, but she had all the lightness and grace of a rugby winger on the move. She was wearing a linen jacket over a white tee shirt and washed out blue Wranglers. She had a pink silk scarf around her neck. The noiseless tread was explained by the expensive pink and powder grey Hogan trainers.

'Are you Jack Shepherd?' she asked, in the husky voice I'd heard down the phone line.

I said I was and motioned her to the client chair in front of my desk. She sat down in it.

'Do you find people?'

'It's part of what I do,' I said. 'And sometimes, I'm successful.'

'Only sometimes?'

The relationship was barely seconds old, so I couldn't tell how serious that question was. I decided we should begin by keeping the conversation as light as possible.

'Well, on a scale of one to ten...'

She interrupted me. 'Yes of course. Silly of me. I'm sorry. It's just...'

She stopped talking, sighed, then bit her lower lip. The nervous twenty seconds in the corridor hadn't quite done the trick. The confidence displayed on her entrance seemed to have seeped away; as though she had psyched herself up, only to run out of steam. We looked at each other, neither of us entirely convinced that she was in the right place. So I offered her an abbreviated CV.

'I was a policeman for twelve years. I couldn't work inside the system, but it seemed churlish to throw away all that training and experience. However, the job opportunities for ex-coppers are limited to the same thing only different. It was either this or the security business... So I chase up disappeared wives, spy on errant husbands and yes, I find people. I should say however, those who cross this office threshold, usually do so as a last resort. *Shepherd Investigations* is the "go to" place for those who have run out of options.'

She considered the summary and stood up again. That appeared to give her some resolve. She swallowed, took a deep breath then exhaled slowly.

'I want you to find someone for me,' she said.

'And who would that be?' I asked.

'Me,' she said. 'I want you to find me.'

I stared at her. For what seemed an eternity, she stared obligingly back. And then she conjured up the most extraordinary smile I had ever seen. From nervous to laid back in a moment; the transformation was astonishing. Sparkling white, perfectly even teeth, set like stones in a bracelet. Then suddenly, it was gone, like she had never smiled in her life. I was in turn surprised, transfixed and then distracted. Below us, Patsy Cline had segued into Frank Sinatra and *One For My Baby*.

'You come highly recommended…'

I heard her from miles away. I dragged

myself back to the conversation.

'By whom?'

She shook her head. She was nervous again.

'I won't tell you that,' she said. 'If I do, you'll know where to start.'

'And that's a bad idea?'

'Yes.'

'So, where can we start?'

She sat down again, arranged herself comfortably in the chair, stretched her long legs out in front of her, pressed the palms of her hands together, raised them to her face as if she was about to pray, then tapped her chin several times. It gave me time to pull myself together and take stock. Tallish – about five ten – shoulder length light brown hair, green eyes, carefully applied makeup, a mole just below her left cheek bone. A friendly face, but one, minus the smile, which showed signs of strain. Probably a recent thing. The look in her eyes was resolute enough, there was no fixed expression of worry, no permanent lines of pain. But something was distressing her.

'Here's the thing,' she said. 'I have reasoned that if you can't find me, there's a solid chance that others won't either.'

'Which others?'

She shook her head. 'You mustn't know that. At least, not at this stage. And not from me.'

'Are you in trouble?'

'I won't answer that sort of question. So don't re-work it and ask again.'

Something approaching the truth from a client, or information intriguingly close to the truth, is normally required to kick start any private investigation. Keep information from the police if you must, mislead them, be economical with the truth. But don't lie to your P.I. Defeats the object. In those circumstances, the preferred response is to swiftly show your client the door.

But a job defined by no information at all... Well that was something else.

'Okay,' I said. 'We need a base to start from. If I don't know anything about you, I won't be able to find you.'

'That's what I'm hoping.'

'If that's the result you want, fine,' I said. 'However, if I do manage to find you, starting with no information at all, then the aforementioned "others" will be able to do so too.'

She looked at me in silence.

'And they have a head start. Given that they already know who you are.'

She searched for the line she'd rehearsed should this approach come up. I persisted.

'I need to know all that's in the public domain. There is no advantage in me being less informed than the people you're afraid of. I need to know at least as much as they do. You can concede that proposition surely?'

She nodded. 'Yes. So if you take this on, I will tell you as much as they know about me and my current situation.'

'Why don't you want them to find you?'

'You've just re-phrased the question I told you not to.'

'It's difficult to be so non-specific,' I suggested.

'If that is indeed so,' she said, 'then you're not the man I was led to believe you are.'

It was difficult not to get irritated by all this. But prospective clients have to be indulged to a degree.

'I can only repeat my question,' I said. 'By whom?'

She shook her head, stared across the desk at me, then sat up straight in the chair.

'Mr Shepherd. I have rehearsed this...' she searched for the right word,

'...encounter, for some days now. This is neither a game nor a bargain basement intellectual exercise. I haven't created this scenario so that we may both walk what is left of our wits. There is no room for error here. I am deadly serious.'

The equal emphasis on every word of the last sentence, the body language and the focus of her attention, all combined to reinforce the message. Her eyes locked onto mine, unblinking.

'Believe me,' she said.

It was hard not to do so. My next ploy

would have been to ask her what else she had rehearsed and how much more she was prepared to divulge. She pre-empted that by slipping into business mode.

'What do I have to pay to retain your services for say, a week?'

'I charge 250 a day, plus expenses,' I said. 'Seven days for the price of five.'

'That's fine.'

She dug into the inside pocket of her jacket, produced a money clip, stood up, leaned over my desk, counted out twenty-five £50 notes, placed them on the leather desktop and pushed them towards me. I stared down at the money.

'Do we have a deal?' she asked.

'Do I get to know your name?'

'You get to know the name by which others know me. Not the new name I have just taken.'

Then she offered the smile again. A little less lustrous than before, but it was worth the effort.

'You know, that's a good smile,' I said. 'A little rusty round the edges maybe, but you should let it work for you more.'

'My name is Deborah Thorne. Debbie if you wish.'

I looked down at the money again.

'Are you going to take it?' she asked.

The question of the day so far. It would be easy to do that. Then spend a day or two on a minimum amount of sleuthing; make a couple of phone calls, check the internet, go through something approaching the motions of an investigation and wait for Deborah to call back.

'Have you considered I might take the twelve hundred and fifty pounds,' I said, 'do absolutely nothing at all and when you next contact me, simply say I had failed in all my endeavours to trace you?'

'You won't.'

'I might.'

'No. Not you. I've checked you out remember.'

It was immensely gratifying to learn I was a man of such probity. But no one, however quixotic, can accept such glowing references without some response. Between us, we had to be really clear about all this.

'Okay,' I said. 'We'll leave the money there for the moment. Tell me as much as you can.'

That seemed to do it. She leaned back in the chair and returned to the script.

'Deborah Thorne is my real name. It's not the name I'm using now. I'm 36 years old. I was born in the Midlands. I've moved around a lot. Until five months ago, I worked at a call centre in Reading. For a company called *Home and Domestic Services*. Providing insurance for house contents. Electrical appliances, cookers, fridges, dishwashers, that sort of stuff.'

She paused, to collate the next bit of information. Now the background track was being provided by Roy Orbison and *Cryin'*.

'I came to Bristol in April,' she said. 'A week after Easter. I bought a house in Windmill Hill, near Victoria Park. Number 15. I dealt directly with the owner and paid cash. So there is no mortgage trail to follow. I am assuming that the people who may be looking for me don't know where I live. I think if they did, they would have found me by this time. But to make sure, I've moved.'

There was no point asking her where to. So I contented myself with asking her how long ago.

'Six days,' she said.

I decided to move back a few paragraphs, see if I could catch her off guard.

'Why did you leave Reading?' I asked.

The change in narrative line didn't faze her a bit.

'Do you mean why did I leave my job? Or do you actually want to know why I moved from London?'

I responded as deftly as I could.

'Okay... Was your move to the west country job related, or was it a personal thing?'

'It was a personal thing. There was no problem with my job – other than it was unrewarding, boring, and frustrating.'

'Did you tell anyone at *Home and Domestic*

Services where you were moving to?'

She shook her head. 'No.'

'Are you working now?'

'No. I don't need to.'

I looked down at the money on the desk.

'Because you can afford not to?'

'Yes.'

'So where does this money come from?'

There was a beat, only just discernible, before she replied.

'That's not relevant. Savings, if you must know.'

That was another of the moments she had anticipated and rehearsed. Savings maybe. Whatever, money wasn't an issue and she had recently bought a house for cash.

'How much do the "others" know about West London and Reading?'

'As much as I've told you.'

'So if I, or they, pitch up at *Home and Domestic Services?...*'

'It will be a waste of time.'

We were silent for a while. I looked at her and she looked at me and we stared as if we had forever. Down in Patrick's office, Abba took over with *The Winner Takes It All.* In the torch song hall of fame, Benny and Bjorn's lament for a broken relationship has to be the most revered. Deborah motioned to the desk.

'So will you take the money now?' she asked.

'Maybe,' I said and switched topics again. 'Do you have friends in Bristol?'

She took time to go back over the response she'd rehearsed to this question.

'A couple of friends. And half a dozen acquaintances. One person in particular, has been to my house on a number of occasions.'

'Someone close?' I asked.

'Close enough,' she said. 'I won't tell you who the person is.'

'Because I would find a way to talk to him...'

'Or her.' She smiled again; just enough to acknowledge the ploy. 'Please don't assume anything in this matter.'

'Can you tell me who the acquaintances are?'

'No.'

'Deborah...'

'As I said, I am assuming that the significant others don't know where I am. If that is the case, they won't know my friend and acquaintances.'

'However, since you moved, the "friend and acquaintances" no longer know where you are,' I suggested.

She stared at me and then shifted in the chair. I had finally taken her by surprise. She nodded.

'That's right.'

'Which means you're out of the loop.'

She nodded again. 'So?...'

Suddenly on a roll and ignoring the risk of complicating the dialectic, I ploughed on.

'The reverse may not apply. There is no way you can be sure that the "others" have not traced the "friend and acquaintances" in the meantime. Because since you disappeared from their radar, you currently have no idea what's going on. At all. The "others" may have made progress. Six days is a substantial time, it could be that–'

This was working. Irritating the hell out of her. She held up her hands, got to her feet and shouted at me.

'All right all right!...'

I mustered my best injured innocence look and pasted it on to my face. She shook her arms, took a couple of deep breaths and calmed down again.

'That was very clever. And the point is well made,' she said. 'However, it only serves to show that my position really may be as...' Again she searched for the appropriate word. '...compromised, as I believe it is.'

She was absolutely right. But we had made progress. And I reasoned that I'd done as much due diligence as possible under the circumstances. I picked up the £50 notes. She blew out her cheeks and sat back down in the client chair.

'Thank you,' she said.

'This may be a very bad investment. I can't guarantee anything.'

'I appreciate that.'

I put the money in the top drawer of the right hand pedestal of my desk and looked back at her, dead centre. She didn't flinch.

'Okay,' I said. 'A couple more questions. Parents?'

'Yes. Both alive. I won't tell you where.'

'Relatives?'

'I have an aunt and uncle in Australia. A sister in Dublin. Her name is Helena. Others know this, but nothing else She's married.'

'So not called Thorne?'

'No.'

'Good.'

She suddenly remembered something. Took an A5 size envelope out of a jacket pocket and passed it across the desk. I opened it and shook out a photograph. Deborah smiling straight down the lens, apparently happy and relaxed.

'It's a good likeness,' I said.

'Others have that photograph, so you qualify also.'

I found myself admiring her and her attention to detail. She had gone about this in a highly organised fashion. Presumably spent days covering all the bases. Apart from one moment of confusion, she had stayed on script and in control throughout our conversation. There was just one item that still bothered me.

'I take it you have a passport.'

'Yes.'

'So you could leave the country.'

'I don't want to leave,' she said. 'This is where I live. And I have decided to hide in plain sight. Not in some cottage on a remote hillside, or some village in the country where people will ask questions about the solitary stranger. I need a place where I can get lost in a crowd. And where, if push comes to shove, I can get help.'

Deborah looked purposefully at me. I nodded, in acknowledgment of the responsibility. She remembered one more thing. She hitched at the waistband of her jeans, dug into the right front pocket, produced a set of house keys and held them out to me. She told me the address again.

'Number 15, Windmill Hill,' she said. 'I would prefer you didn't break in. Keep these until this is...'

I could understand why she was reluctant to finish the sentence with 'all over'. I held out my left hand, palm upwards. She dropped the keys into it. Then she went into overdrive.

'There is no point in lifting my finger prints from the keys. I know you have a good police connection, but don't waste his time and yours. My prints are not on file anywhere. The money you have in the drawer is in used notes. Three weeks ago, I sold the car I brought down from London. The one I currently drive is registered with the DVLA at that old address – which is of course, the address on my driver's licence. I haven't changed it. Today, I came here in a cab. I shall call another from the lobby downstairs when we have finished. I assume you will make a note of the number, but I'll take several more cabs. I might take some buses. Cross and re-cross the city until I'm sure you're not following me... I don't want your job to be difficult Mr Shepherd, I want it to be impossible.'

So, in a nutshell, my client had handed over twelve hundred and fifty pounds, in the fervent hope I would fail to do what I do.

She stood up.

'Would you like a drink?' I asked. 'Coffee, tea?'

She smiled the smile again.

'No thank you. But that's genuinely because I don't want one.' She nodded at the mugs on the shelf above the sink. 'Please don't be disappointed. I'm not on any DNA database either, so I wouldn't leave a trace. You get my admiration for trying however. Goes to show, the right man is on the case.'

I stood up too and thanked her for the compliment.

'So I'll leave now,' she said, turned and walked out the office door.

I watched her go. There was something in the way she moved...

Shepherd Investigations may be a one person operation, but I like to believe that the owner-operator is an honourable and diligent sleuth. I had work to do, but there was no point following Deborah out of the building. Like she said, I would simply lose her somewhere in the city centre. However, I should do the basic stuff.

I called Jason.

'Mr Shepherd...'

'Ms Thorne is on the way out again. She'll call for a taxi. Will you make a note of the operator?'

'I assume it will be City Cabs. That's who she came with.'

Jason didn't miss much either.

'And get the cab number if you can?'

'Of course.'

'Thanks Jason.'

The taxi driver would be an unlikely source of information – *I picked her up outside your office and dropped her in the centre* – but following a lead, if no more than half a mile, is a text book requirement. I could find the taxi driver and talk to him later.

I swung my desk chair round to face the window, leant back and started thinking. And suddenly, up from Patrick's office, came Rainbow and *All Night Long*. A quantum leap by any definition...

I listened to Graham Bonnet's soaring

vocal for a line or two, then stood up and closed the window. I crossed to the sink, filled the kettle, plugged it into the wall socket, switched it on, spooned some coffee into the cafetière, went back to my desk and sat down again. I took the fifty pound notes out of the desk drawer and stared at them.

A fistful of money and no leads.

On reflection that wasn't true. Actually, I had two leads. *You come highly recommended,* Deborah had said. And *I know you have a good police connection*. The latter had to be Detective Superintendent Harvey Butler. The straightest of straight arrow coppers, the best that Avon and Somerset Constabulary could boast about. Tough and clever, with an amiability that disguised his thoroughness and his determination. He was a Detective Sergeant when I first met him – the day after I joined CID some twenty-five years ago. Destined to be the career copper I never could be, he took me under his wing and taught me the ropes. And he supported me through the weeks following the shooting which changed my life. A seventeen year old, out of his mind on angel dust, came at me in an alleyway with a meat cleaver. I had seconds to make a decision – time enough – and the one I made, drove me out of the job. The pictures still come back to me in dreams and dark moments and on less successful days.

And suddenly, Harvey wanted to talk to

me about Philip Soames.

I locked the money back in the desk drawer. The kettle boiled. I switched it off, filled the cafetière and depressed the plunger.

Deborah's recommendation could only have come from someone I had worked for. Or someone, who knew someone I had worked for. She had been in Bristol five months. Enough time in which to meet someone she could trust. Someone she was now protecting.

My client list isn't extensive and certainly not blue chip, but the files do fill all three drawers of the filing cabinet. I poured a mug of coffee, opened the top drawer of the filing cabinet and started with A.

I was into the Ds and my second mug of coffee – my fifth of the day – when the phone rang. I picked up the receiver.

'It was City Cabs,' Jason said. 'They're not far from here. Across the river at the bottom of Bedminster Parade. Mrs Thorne was picked up by cab number 643.'

'Thank you.'

'I rang them. The driver's name is Gerry Simpson.'

I picked up a pen and wrote the name on a post-it note. Jason appeared to take the momentary silence as some kind of reprimand.

'I'm sorry Mr Shepherd,' he said. 'I didn't

mean to er... I just thought that I could help out.'

'No that's fine Jason. Saved me a phone call. Thanks.'

I made a mental note to invite Jason to do more legwork for me. I got to my feet, filled my coffee mug once again, then went back to the Ds.

Chapter Three

It was noon by the time I'd read all the files. I concentrated on names going back five years – I reasoned that was far enough – and ended up with a list of twenty-eight. Two, at least, I knew were dead. Ronnie Lister, a one-time short con artist, whose funeral I had been to seven months ago and the recently deceased Philip Soames. Two of them were in prison. More evidence of my lack of top echelon work.

Twenty-eight souls. Most of them had come to me because they were frightened, lonely, desperate, bereaved, sad, angry, or just plain lost. Some of them had gone away feeling better. Like Philip Soames, on reflection perhaps the most well adjusted person on the list. A few, like Louise earlier in the day, with the result they had fervently sought. But some had found they had lost more than they bargained for. To them I could only apologise. Words that always fell too short of the mark. Some investigations have happy endings. Some don't. I am the keeper of the *Last Chance* saloon.

So, what to do? Call all twenty-four still alive or at liberty? Or concentrate on the person whose name I'd heard several times today?

Linda saved me from further contemplation. She arrived in the office posed in the doorway again and beamed at me.

'I got the gig,' she announced. 'Congratulate me.'

'You were a shoe-in,' I said.

She stepped into the room.

'It's hot in here,' she said. 'Mind if I open the window?'

'Help yourself.'

Linda crossed the office. Behind me I heard the window catch snap and Guns 'n Roses *Live and Let Die* blasted up from downstairs.

'It's a new development,' I said.

Linda moved around the desk back into my line of sight and sat down in my client chair.

'An improvement on *Achy Breaky Heart,* don't you think?'

'I don't suppose the two songs are mutually exclusive,' I said.

'Everybody's just a little bit country,' she said.

I stared at her. She beamed at me again.

'And how was your morning?'

We sat at a table outside the Nova Scotia pub; on the dockside, in a well of quiet, ringed by the noise of distant traffic. Hotwell

Road was a couple of hundred yards away, across the other side of the floating harbour. To our left, the water in the Cumberland Basin was perfectly still. Beyond it, traffic leaving the city eased up the ramp to the swing bridge and met the stream coming into the city from the west, along the Portway. To our right looking east, the floating harbour stretched almost a mile towards the city centre; past the SS *Great Britain*, the marina the workshops and the ships chandlers; past the veteran steamship *Balmoral*, midway through a refit, tied up outside the former industrial museum, now re-born as the hi-tech, hands-on, interactive M Shed; and on to where the waterfront bars and bistros met the dead end of buildings and the business of the city.

We had eaten the toasted sandwiches and Linda was drinking a glass of the Nova Scotia house white. I was risking half a pint of Old Ferret – brewed in a back yard a few streets away from the pub. Many people still believe that Bristol is Real Ale Central.

'So?...' Linda broke the silence.

'What?'

'I repeat. How was your morning?'

'Lucrative.'

'Really?'

'A little less scorn if you please.'

She looked hurt. I swallowed another mouthful of Old Ferret. She waited. I gave up and spilled the beans.

'I have a new client. Deborah Thorne.'

'Who is she?'

'I don't know.'

I stared at Linda. There was obviously no chance of her bursting into something like *'My God, Debbie. I've known her for years...'*

'Sorry,' she said. 'I shouldn't ask. Client confidentiality and all that.'

She took another sip of the house white.

'No, ask away,' I said. 'That's what I've got to do. Client confidentiality only matters if there's a bunch of secrets to keep. So far in this case, I don't know any. I know my client's name. She gave me twelve hundred and fifty pounds to find her.'

Linda swallowed the house white. 'Find her?'

'Yes. That's the job.'

'Why? Is she going to get lost?'

'She already is, kind of.'

'I don't understand.'

I pointed to her wine glass.

'Finish that. I'll get another round and I'll explain.'

I drained my glass, got to my feet and went into the pub. The Old Ferret had gone down quite well, so I stayed with it. I had my glass re-filled, bought another house white and went back outside. Linda said thank you and I gave her a précis of the morning's encounter. She took another drink and looked out across the water.

'No address, place of work, phone number, car registration...'

'I have a photograph,' I said.

I fished the picture out of the inside pocket of my jacket. Linda studied it.

'Very attractive,' she said. 'In a broad shouldered sort of a way.'

She handed the photograph back to me.

'So... Where are you going to start?'

'Check with the taxi driver for form's sake. Then put on my best smile and go see Harvey Butler.'

We walked back to the office building. Linda had emails to check. I picked up my car keys.

I drove out of the car park, around the office building, onto the ramp up to the swing bridge across the Cumberland Basin and immediately came to a standstill.

It took the best part of fifteen minutes to navigate the mile and a half to City Cabs office – a double aspect, ground floor room in Bedminster that had once been the local corner shop. Gerry Simpson, in his mid 20s, with a retro mullet of brown hair and a Zapata moustache, was sitting on a battered sofa waiting for the dispatcher to send him out again. He told me exactly what I had expected to hear.

'I left her in the centre. On the north side. She joined a bus queue. I drove back here.'

'Which bus queue?'

'Hell I don't know.' He pondered for a moment or two. 'Okay... If you stand in the middle of the pedestrian area, with the fountains on your left and look towards the Hippodrome, there are what ... er ... three bus stops? She joined the queue on the right, the first one you come to when you're moving anti-clockwise round the centre. I don't know which buses stop there. You'll have to check.'

I got back into the Healey and set off to do that. It was 1.45. I was going against the traffic flow now. I left the car in Baldwin Street and walked the couple of hundred yards to the centre. The sun disappeared. I looked up at the sky. A ridge of dark cloud was sprinting up from the south west.

Bus numbers 71, 72, 105 and 106 picked up from the queue Deborah had joined. The routes covered huge chunks of the west side of the city. Buses, taxis, whatever... Deborah could be anywhere. I walked back to the Healey.

Just as the rain began again.

Sitting in the car, I weighed up the options. I had two people to see...

Philip Soames ran his practise exclusively. No partners, no associates. His secretary was a lady called Sarah; late 30s, extremely efficient and user friendly. It would be difficult talking to her, but I had no choice. The difficulty quotient racked up considerably with my second appointment however. He had given me a noon deadline, but I decided to take on Harvey Butler after I'd seen Sarah.

I drove round the city centre and up Park Street into Clifton, the rain thudding down on the soft top. Philip Soames' office suite was housed on the second floor of a three storey regency building in Victoria Square; once the town house of some rich merchant, re-developed, as were many other houses in the square, into serviced offices during the 80s. I managed to find a parking place about fifteen yards from the front door and got into the building relatively dry.

The door to suite 2A was ajar. I knocked on it. I heard Sarah say 'Come in'. I pushed the door. It opened into her office, which overlooked the square. It was part waiting room and part reception space. A door in the far right hand corner led to the rest of the suite – a kitchen, a small bathroom and Philip Soames' consulting room. There were two large sofas set in a L shape to the right of the door, a low coffee table in front of them. Sarah's space occupied the rest of the room. Her big mahogany desk sat in front of matching mahogany storage systems and filing cabinets which ran the length of the wall behind her chair. She was sitting at her desk, smartly dressed in an expensively cut navy suit, designed to be attractive, but business like. Not so today however. Today she looked lost and disorientated.

She stood up to greet me. I said hello.

'I have cancelled all Philip's appointments,' she said. 'For this week, that is. I will have to go through the whole of his diary and ... well…'

She faltered into silence.

'Sarah…'

She looked down at the desk. 'I don't make appointments on Friday afternoons. We use that time for business review. But not last Friday. Philip came back from lunch and said he had something important to do. He picked up his laptop and left. Later in the afternoon, I called his mobile and his home number. There was no answer from either.'

'He didn't come back to the office at all?'

Sarah looked up at me and shook her head.

'When he did not arrive yesterday, I called the police. I spoke to a very polite constable who took a statement and told me not to be concerned. He said there was probably a very simple explanation. I called all the clients with appointments and ... sat here ... waiting for something to happen. Mid morning, about 11 o'clock, a Detective Sergeant arrived. He took me to a mortuary in Avonmouth. He asked me to look at three bodies. One of them was Philip.'

She sat down again, lowered her head and closed her eyes. There was a long silence, underscored by the sound of rain beating on the window. I waited. Then Sarah raised her head and placed her palms flat on the desk top. She needed to know something.

'What is this about Mr Shepherd? What did Philip do to deserve this? What sort of people?...' She left another sentence hanging in the air.

'Can I look at his diary Sarah?'

Her pupils seemed to enlarge, but she didn't look away.

'I'm sorry, the police have it.'

Which explained how they knew of my connection to her boss. Presumably he listed his lunchtime appointments as well as his consultations. 'Why do you want to see Philip's diary?'

'I've been retained by a lady who was recommended to me by a client. That client may have been Philip. If that was the case, then she would have been a client of his. I need to confirm that.'

'Do you believe this person may have something to do with his murder?'

'I don't know, but I would like to find out.'

Sarah processed that information, then responded.

'And the lady's name?'

'Deborah Thorne.'

She didn't look away. I carried on.

'Perhaps you could check Philip's case notes.'

There was another moment of silence. Then she stood up, moved around her desk and gestured towards the sofas. We sat down, two of us on two sofas, alone in each leg of the L. She looked at me, dead centre.

'I will not give you access to Philip's case notes under any circumstances, but I don't need to check. I can tell you that Deborah Thorne is a client of his.'

'Can you tell me what she is, was, seeing him about?'

'No Mr Shepherd, I can't. I'm sorry.'

'Is that what you've been saying to the police?'

'Yes,' she said. 'I told them I would respect the confidentiality of Philip's clients as long as I could. They are coming back with a court order and a search warrant. Within the hour, I expect.'

I looked at the clock on the wall behind Sarah's desk. 2.55. Sarah was displaying extraordinary control, considering the circumstances. She was hurt and devastated, the world was going to hell around her, but she was not going to compromise on ethics or procedure. I changed tack.

'Can you tell me when Deborah last saw Philip?'

'Why not ask her yourself? She is your client.'

'I can't,' I said. 'I don't know where she is. That's the problem. I need to find her. And any reference may help.'

Sarah got to her feet, moved back to her desk and sat in front of her pc. She tapped a key or two, clicked and double clicked the mouse, waited a couple of moments, clicked the mouse again, then looked up at me.

'10 o'clock,' she said. 'Three weeks to the day.'

'Was that a routine appointment?' I asked.

Sarah considered the implications before deciding to reply.

'No. She had a series of appointments over four years. The consultations finished some time ago. But then she rang up out of the blue and asked to see Philip again.'

'About what?'

She looked at me with some indulgence. I lifted a hand in apology. She nodded in acknowledgement and came back to the sofa. Silence descended again, as we both worked out what to say next. The sound of the rain on the window was quieter. Sarah spoke first.

'Will these kind of questions help to find the people who killed Philip?'

'I don't know. But my investigation has to start somewhere,' I said. 'As for the police, I don't know where they'll start. But they will dig around until they find something.'

'I'm sure there will be nothing to find,' Sarah said.

I thought for a moment or two. Resolved

what it was I wanted to say.

'Sarah... Just like this practice, I have a confidential relationship with my clients. I understand the imperative not to divulge privileged information. But I believe Deborah came to see me on a recommendation from Philip. She was looking for a private investigator and he gave her my name and address. Deborah has disappeared, Philip is dead.'

I thought that last sentence was weighty enough and I paused for a reaction. Sarah gave me her dead centre look again.

'And, you think that the two events are related?'

'Yes.'

This was the tipping point in the conversation. I pushed a bit harder.

'Sarah, I don't believe in coincidences. Philip's death has something to do with the reason Deborah came to see me. I need to find her.'

'Yes,' she said. 'I can see that.'

The decision was made. Sarah gestured to the table at the side of the left hand desk pedestal. There was a printer sitting on top of it, a hard drive on the shelf underneath.

'All client information and case histories are stored on that hard drive. They are backed up on data sticks. And on hard copy in the filing cabinet. Philip's laptop has his personal correspondence on it and the information he needs to stay current. That's all.'

'And that's not in his office.'

'As I said...'

She offered no more. Waited for me to go on. We both knew that I had to propose something. I began with the straight forward bit.

'When CID get back here, co-operate with them right down the line. It will be a serious mistake not to. All the practise paperwork will be seized anyway. They will get phone records and bank statements. They'll turn Philip's office upside down. They'll find his laptop, wherever it is. So give them all the help they ask for.'

She nodded. 'Very well,' she said softly.

That agreed, I proposed the minor conspiracy.

'But don't volunteer any information. Just answer the questions they ask. They shouldn't ask anything specific, they don't know anything.'

'So far,' she said. 'What if they extemporise?'

'They're not known for it.'

'Supposing they ask if I have had any visitors.'

'Then you will have to tell them I called.'

'And what do I say when they ask why?'

This was the tricky bit.

'Tell them that Philip was a client of mine,'

I said. 'That much is true. Their knee-jerk reaction will be to ask what I was doing for him. Your reply will be that you do not know. That much is true also.'

'And if they ask why you have turned up at such an inappropriate time?'

I took a deep breath.

'Tell them I came to see how you were.'

'Which will be a lie,' she said.

'Just a small one,' I said.

'Hardly,' she said.

'They won't pursue the matter. At least not with you. Simply say I called and they'll take the matter up with me.'

Once again, she took time to consider her decision.

'Very well. I can do that. But that is not all is it?'

I conceded it wasn't.

'I need you to copy Deborah Thorne's files onto a data stick for me,' I said. 'I don't want you to tell the police you have done this. You won't be deceiving them. At least not in any pro-active sense. You certainly won't be lying to them. Just not telling them something they don't know.'

'Something they don't know they would like to know, however,' Sarah said.

'Yes, but if they don't know they'd like to know, you can't be blamed for not telling them,' I said.

A somewhat insubstantial piece of linguistic hocus-pocus, but we had debated enough. Sarah went back to her pc, called up Deborah Thorne's files and copied them onto a data stick.

The carefully constructed subterfuge went to rats out in the street.

The rain had stopped. Detective Sergeant George Hood – a couple of inches shorter than me but wider and tougher – was standing on the wet pavement, staring at the Healey.

'This doesn't have to be my car,' I suggested.

'It is nonetheless,' he said. 'And parked outside the office of a man brutally done away with forty-eight hours ago. I take it you have been in there.'

I fished the Healey keys out of my pocket.

'It would be helpful if you could drive straight round to Trinity Road,' Hood said. He waved his mobile at me. 'I've just been on to Superintendent Butler.'

'I don't suppose there's any element of choice here,' I said.

Hood nodded to a uniformed constable, standing by a patrol car, double-parked alongside the Healey.

'I can always get PC Stratton to take you personally. He does need to move that vehicle.'

I bowed to the inevitable, climbed into the

Healey and fired it up. PC Stratton reversed the patrol car five yards. I turned into the road in front of it and set off for my meeting with Harvey.

Not all coppers are sexist, racist and homophobic. Mostly they're just not very bright. Harvey Butler is an exception. A perspicacious detective, tough and clever and so straight it hurts. A man with more than his share of insight into the nature of the human condition. And something close to an unshakeable faith in the eventual triumph of good over evil. Twenty-five years as a detective has not diminished one iota his capacity for seeing through to the heart of a situation and knowing exactly what to do about it. Nor have the years made him cynical. He never takes a short cut, never pursues the line of least resistance, never contrives to make his job easy for himself. The best young coppers in town grew up under Harvey's wing.

His problem however – even though he's not above improvising a bit – is that he believes in the system. I don't. Harvey and I are friends, but he regards me at best, as unhelpful. I look at it from a slightly different angle. I am a private investigator, with the emphasis on the first word of the job description.

All of which meant that neither of us brought any baggage to the moment. Harvey granted me the courtesy of saying hello and then waded in without getting up out of his chair.

'How well did you know Philip Soames?' he asked.

'He was a client of mine,' I said.

'Is or was?'

If Harvey could be succinct, so could I. He stared at me. Then expanded the premise a little.

'Was, in the sense that he's now dead?'

'Also in the sense that it was some time ago.'

'What did you do for him?'

'I found his long lost aunt in Ambleside.'

Harvey decided I was trying to be funny. Disbelief morphed into impatience. I ploughed innocently on.

'That's in the Lake District,' I said.

'I know where it is,' he said. Then, after a beat, 'Long lost aunt?...'

'I can give you name, address and telephone number.'

'And when did you accomplish this essential piece of detective work?'

I ignored the disdain.

'November last year.'

'Have you seen Philip Soames since?'

'Three or four times.'

'Socially, or by way of business?'

'The former,' I said.

Harvey didn't blink.

'And you went to his office today because?...'

'It seemed the thing to do.'

This conversation was developing a life of its own. It had the propensity to go on for the rest of the morning. Harvey decided enough was enough.

'Here's what we'll do,' he said, with all the patience in the world. 'I'll start drilling. And you can tell me when it starts to hurt.'

He'd made his point. The longer we went on sparring, the more irritated he would become. So I detailed the number of times Philip Soames' name had come up in conversations over the last twenty-four hours. And I concluded by saying that I went to his office to share a few minutes with Sarah. I omitted the Deborah Thorne stuff.

Harvey sat and listened without interrupting. When I finished, he cleared his throat, swallowed and sucked at his teeth. There were two phones on his desk. He chose the silver one and picked up the receiver. He dialled a number and waited. Then he spoke.

'George, where are you?' He listened for a moment, then spoke again. 'Did you ask her why our favourite PI was visiting today?' He listened again. 'Is that all?' He listened again. 'No, if she's upset, don't do that.'

He put the receiver back in its cradle, sat back in his chair, folded his arms across his chest and blew out his cheeks.

'In essence, she says what you say.'

'QED.'

'So why can't I shake off the notion that it's all bollocks?'

I assumed Harvey wasn't actually expecting a reply, so I said nothing. He unfolded his arms and leaned forward across the desk top.

'I have to tell you that Philip Soames wasn't just sent on the big downer. He was tortured. There are two fingers missing from his left hand. We both know he wasn't supposed to re-surface and I presume we both have theories about that.'

He paused. This time he was waiting for me to say something.

'I presume we do,' I said. 'But I've decided not to dwell on anything.'

'Which is the best thing, all in all,' he said. 'This is an open case Jack. And if I find that you're poking around in it...' He left the sentence unfinished.

'I'm not,' I said. Which was true in a way, because I had no idea what I was poking around in.

Harvey got to his feet. I noticed he had lost some weight. He was still carrying a pound or two more than he should, but he looked fitter than when I last saw him.

'So,' he said. 'Go now.'

I went straight home.

I switched on the pc and plugged in the

data stick. And read the story of Deborah Thornton in forensic detail. Two hours later, I was still staring at the monitor screen. Mesmerised.

Deborah Thorne had only been Deborah Thorne for a little over six years. Until then, she had been Daniel Thornton.

I switched off the pc, locked the data stick in a desk drawer and went for a walk in Canford Park.

I knew nothing at all about trans-gender surgery. Only that, despite the now relatively safe surgical procedures, it was a brave, no going back, psychologically dangerous, thing to submit to. Deborah's appointments with Philip Soames covered a three and a half year period, during which she had begun and completed the whole trans-sexual process. Hormone drug treatments, facial hair electrolysis, facial surgery, genital electrolysis followed by genital surgery, breast augmentation, vaginaplasty and finally labiaplasty. Each stage monitored psychologically by counselling sessions with Philip Soames, working in partnership with surgeons in a clinic in Oxfordshire.

One hell of a life changing experience, by anybody's standards.

I came back to reality at the east gate of the park. The front door of the Canford Vaults beckoned from across the road. It was happy hour, the sun was out again and the alfresco drinkers had spilled out of the pub and filled the terrace. Perhaps there was room inside the inn.

I sat in a corner of the lounge with a pint of Butcombe Gold and drank it slowly.

Half an hour later, I was once again, the cool, rational investigator my client was paying for. On reflection, I had made progress in twenty-four hours. The Philip Soames connection to Deborah was clear. The question was, why had he died? *Brutally done away with* George Hood had said. And tortured. For information about Deborah's whereabouts? And did that mean, whoever she was running away from knew her intimately? Knew that she had once been Daniel Thornton? If so, he, she, or they, still knew gigabytes more than I did.

I walked home via the Redland Chip Shop and collected cod and chips and mushy peas. At home, I added a bottle of Alsace beer to the feast, sat in the dining room and ate it.

Substantially refreshed, I spent an hour at the pc, writing up my notes on the case so far. I have a safe under the floorboards in the cupboard under the stairs. I locked Sarah's usb stick in it.

Then I switched on the TV, in search of some post watershed entertainment. It was pretty dismal fare. On BBC1, an over-excited presenter was standing in a bog in Wales, amazed by the knowledge that, millions of years ago, dinosaurs had stood in the same spot. BBC2 was ten minutes into a documentary on 'nuclear power reality'. ITV1 was offering a drama series, proudly proclaimed as high concept, about a surgeon who specialised in body part surgery and was an amateur sleuth in his down time. Kirstie Allsop was berating a gloomy Phil Spencer on Channel 4. On Five, there was a Uefa Cup match between two second string European sides. I followed this for a few minutes, but it was difficult to concentrate on the action. The commentator was coping well with the names of twenty-two foreigners, but he was in hyper-drive and constantly in flow. I searched through the rest of the multichannel stuff, with little reward. Re-runs of re-runs mostly. I settled on Film 4 and *The Day of the Jackal*. Never disappointing, even though we know he's never going to get the job done. But with commercials between every reel, it ran at almost three hours. And despite Fred Zinnemann's brilliant storytelling I couldn't stay awake.

I opted for bed as Edward Fox was going in to the Turkish Bath.

Chapter Four

I woke up from a dream at 6.30 the next morning – Wednesday – and instantly forgot what I had been dreaming about. An hour later, despite my best efforts to relax, I was still awake. I got up and took a shower.

The front doorbell rang as I was contemplating breakfast.

The post person, a soft spoken lady in her 50s, proffered a large brown cardboard box.

'For me?'

'No, sorry,' she said. 'For next door. There's nobody in.'

'They're on holiday. In Tipperary.'

'That's a long way to go,' she said.

We both enjoyed the joke.

'Will you take it then?' she asked.

'Yes, of course.'

She handed it to me.

'Wait a moment,' she said.

From her shoulder bag she fished half a dozen envelopes of assorted sizes and colours wrapped in an elastic band and dropped them onto the box.

'Your mail. Looks like a bill or two there. Sorry. Cheerio.'

She turned and set off down the path to the

gate. I reversed a couple of paces, reached out with my right foot, collected the door and swung it shut. I put the box down at the foot of the stairs and walked back into the kitchen to open my mail.

I support a number of charities on a regular basis, but all of the appeals in the bundle were unsolicited. One of them tugged substantially at my conscience. I kept that and dropped the rest into the bin, then took them out again, looked through them once more and kept another one. Sometimes it's difficult to separate feelings of guilt from notions of responsibility.

The phone bill was enormous. What the hell was I doing? Ringing Australia twice a week? BT were not to be gainsaid however. It was all there. Cheerfully itemised calls, plus landline, plus broadband, plus preference service. I decided to have my calls screened by BT, after I finally got sick of people with foreign accents calling me at all hours of the day and night, offering to assist me in claiming money back on payment protection insurance sold to me without my knowledge. I haven't taken out a loan in twenty years. A recipe for disaster for the self-employed – there are no guarantees you'll ever pay it back. Unless you take out payment protection insurance...

From such ramblings do certain basic questions evolve. Like the wisdom of paying two sets of bills. Here and in the office. Spaces I occupy, at least for most of the time, by myself. Maybe I should relocate my business here at home. There was more than enough room to do it.

In the beginning, *Shepherd Investigations* was based in the study; the intention being to cut down overheads and for me to work more user-friendly hours than I had done when I was on the force. The practise proved to be flawed however. There was tension in the house throughout every case I worked on and disharmony when I wasn't working at all. *Shepherd Investigations* moved out of the study after I finally accepted that personal and business affairs needed to be separated, preferably by some distance. Truthfully, Emily ran out of patience. She decided that separate home and work places, while unlikely to improve relationships or business opportunities, would at least provide definition. Linda announced that the office next door to her was empty. The landlord offered me the first two months rent free and so I moved in. Now I could revise all that. There was nobody at home but me. And consequently, nobody else to inconvenience or stress out.

I set out for the office at 8.30. For once, the traffic was light and I got there in twenty minutes. I parked my car, walked into the building, said 'hello' to Jason, collected my mail and took the stairs to the third floor.

It was like Yogi Bear said – 'Déjà vu all over again'. Same A5 envelopes, some with windows and one of them, a cheerful note from the landlord, proposing a rent increase.

Time to do something constructive.

Windmill Hill is in the heart of old town, south Bristol. Streets of Victorian and Edwardian semis and terraced houses, clustered around Victoria Park. Popular with first time buyers, but still the home of long established working class families. A part of the city that keeps a low profile. By no stretch of the imagination the centre of the crime universe. Nonetheless, if I was looking for Deborah, I would have somebody watching the place. Though maybe not after ten days...

Still, best to be sure.

Linda found me sitting in the lobby.

'What are you doing?' she asked.

'Waiting for a taxi,' I said.

'Something wrong with the Healey?'

'I have to go and look round my client's house. Others may have the same idea. I don't want to announce my arrival.'

'I'm on my way out, I'll drive you,' she said. 'You may need a wing man.'

'A what?'

'Someone to watch your back.'

'Where do you get this stuff from?'

She shrugged. 'Just trying to stay hip.'

'If such is the case,' I said, 'then I don't want anyone else involved. Not you. Not anyone.'

That must have sounded harsher than I intended, because Linda looked surprised. I apologised.

'Sorry, I didn't mean to be ungrateful. Thanks for the offer.'

A horn sounded outside the door. A taxi u-turned on the tarmac.

'Be careful,' Linda said.

It was just after nine and the traffic was still clearing. But the cab driver knew his business and the back streets were empty. Fifteen minutes later we were coasting around the southern boundary of Victoria Park. Windmill Hill was a few streets to the east. I stopped the cab, paid off the driver and walked the last two hundred and fifty yards.

There were cars parked, sparsely, on both sides of Windmill Hill. Maybe a couple of dozen. Presumably, most of the residents were at work. Number 15 was two thirds of the way along on the left. There was space in the road in front of the house and space opposite. I chose the right hand pavement and walked the length of the street. All the cars were empty. No one I could make out lurking in a doorway. I took a deep breath, backtracked, crossed the road to number 15, unlocked the front door and stepped inside.

I stood silently in the hall and waited.

Rooted to the spot for several minutes. No one materialised from anywhere. Onwards then...

The house didn't give much away. It had been searched by experts. Not tossed and ripped up, but carefully and methodically gone over, as though by a scenes of crime team. Stuff had been moved, inspected and put back in place. There were trails in the dust and shapes on shelves and work surfaces with streaks of polish exposed. The visitors had got in via the back door – a window pane was smashed and the mortice lock levered off the door frame.

The house was built originally as a two up two down, with a wash house at the back. The kitchen dining room and what would once have been the front parlour, were now one living room, stretching front to back. Upstairs, a second storey had been added to the wash house, creating a small neat bathroom, leaving the two bedrooms intact. The whole house was light, bright and simply furnished. Not exactly Heals, but with more ambition than Ikea. Seemed like all it was doing, was waiting for its owner to come home from work.

This inspection exercise was a bit like my taxi driver encounter – a detective going through the motions. I couldn't tell if anything was missing. I didn't know what I was looking for, so I was unlikely to find whatever it was. Deborah's desk was tucked away in a corner of the living room. A single pedestal with three drawers, none of them locked. Two were empty, the third contained half a dozen envelopes and a few sheets of A4 copy paper. There was a broadband hub on the desk, still plugged into the wall socket but not switched on. No sign of a hard drive or laptop.

If a coffee pot had been percolating away in the kitchen, the place could have been the *Marie Celeste*.

So, two questions... Where to look and what to look for?

I went looking in the cupboard under the stairs. My own version at home is just big enough to step into, as long as you don't straighten up. It's full of stuff, piled in and squared away, stored for the duration because it used to be important, although now difficult to recall exactly why. The only thing I take out of the space each week is the vacuum cleaner.

Deborah's cleaner was in her cupboard too. The hose was still attached. It sprang out of the door as I opened it and hit me on the chin. I wrestled with it for a moment or two, then reached into the cupboard, dragged Henry and all his bits out into the hall and stuck my head into the space. There was less room in this stacked hideaway than in mine. Absolutely no incentive to pull stuff out and search through it all. And maybe that was the choice. Maybe the visitors had decided not to do so. And you have to be in it, to win it...

The space under the stairs was no more than eight feet wide, sloping upwards from left to right as I looked at it. Three feet deep and around five feet six or seven at its maximum height. With Henry out in the hall, keeping low I could step in, turn around and step out again, but that was it. There was a pile of boxes directly in front of me, heavy and apparently filled with books. I lifted them out, one at time. Behind them was an old pine chest of drawers. The top drawer was packed with dusters. The middle one housed a collection of 13 amp plugs, plastic wall sockets, light bulbs, curtain rings, a couple of torches and some batteries. The bottom drawer was full of tools. To the left, wedged across the space, were more boxes and a pile of rugs stacked on top of a wooden, ribbed steamer trunk. I got the rugs and the boxes out of the cupboard, but couldn't shift the trunk at all. I stood up and banged my head on a stair beam.

I reversed back into the hall and stared into the space. There was carpet on the floor. An off-cut from the living room, neatly edged and positioned. I had done that as well, at home. I knelt down, reached forward with both hands and lifted the front edge of the chest of drawers. It tilted back enough for the front feet to leave the floor. I shuffled forwards, leaned all my weight against it and pulled the carpet out from under. I shuffled back into the hall and dragged the carpet with me. The exposed floorboards were securely nailed down. But there were two short sections side by side. Like the boards in my cupboard. I raked around in the bottom drawer of the pine chest, found a screwdriver, a hammer and a small cold chisel. It took a less than a minute to prise the boards up.

Wedged in the space between two underfloor beams was a small safe. A little smaller than the one I had installed at home.

All we needed was a safe cracker.

Over fifteen years as a private investigator, I have encountered a Pandora's box of entrepreneurs. Forgers, fraudsters, con artists and second-storey men; wheeler dealers, blackmailers and bent coppers; a bunch of people implacably more evil; and more personable than all of those put together, a retired safe breaker, appropriately named Joseph Locke – after the Irish tenor his mother adored. Joe is now in his 60s, though you wouldn't know it. Tall, slim and a bit short sighted for a man who does close work, he still referees kids football matches on the Downs on Sunday mornings. The skills he has honed over three decades, he now uses as a locksmith, semi-retired.

He was in his workshop when I called.

‘I am authorised to hire you to do this,’ I said.

‘On behalf of good people or bad people?’ he asked.

‘Good people. Scouts honour Joe.’

‘Your word is good enough.’

‘Come in the back way, through the garden. There’s an alleyway behind the house.’

‘Give me half an hour,’ he said and hung up.

I went through the kitchen into the old wash house, now tidied up and re-plastered. A washing machine and a chest freezer shared the space with a small table, a couple of fold away garden chairs, a spade, a fork, a trowel and two pairs of gardening gloves. A tea chest in one corner was stuffed with bits of wood – pieces of battening, odd shaped shelf cut-offs, short lengths of planed two by one and some squares of three-ply. I collected one of them.

I found a power drill under the stairs with enough battery life to drill four holes. In the chest of drawers I found an old coffee tin of assorted screws. Back in the kitchen, I screwed the three-ply on to the frame around the broken window. A raw piece of DIY, but probably solid enough.

Five minutes later, Joe came in through the back door. In another ten minutes, the safe was open.

‘Worse than useless this model,’ Joe said.

'Anybody could open it.'

It seemed superfluous to assure him that I couldn't.

'Do you want me to disable the lock?' he asked. 'Will you need to get into the safe again?'

'I might do.'

Joe took the lock apart, removed the lever mechanism then put the rest of it back together.

'The handle still works,' he said.

He packed his tools. I offered him three of Deborah's fifty pound notes. He waved the money away.

'Not if it's for good people,' he said.

He left the hall, went through the kitchen and back out the way he had come in.

There wasn't much inside the safe. Another bundle of fifty pound notes. A small pendant on a silver chain, a garnet set in a ring of diamonds. A building society account book – Deborah had £16,500 in an ISA. Two A5 size envelopes, a brown one and a white one with a window in it. And two birth certificates. Daniel Charles Thornton was born on July 8th 1976, in Northampton. His mother Elizabeth Jane Bassett was a court stenographer, his father William Frederick Thornton was a solicitor. Resolutely white collar. I wondered where they were now. What they thought of Daniel becoming Deborah.

The copy of her birth certificate, with her

name registered as Deborah Charlotte Thorne, had been issued on July 25th 2006.

There were two postcard size photographs in the brown envelope. I studied the first one I pulled out, taken on a beach somewhere. A young woman in a red, one piece swimsuit smiled at me. Streaked blonde hair, green eyes and what looked like a carefully nurtured sun tan. I guessed her age at early 30s. The other picture, taken somewhere else, was of a child. A little boy, maybe four or five years old, with dark wavy hair, brown eyes and freckles. Both pictures had the same hand written notation on the back – 'Devon summer 2006'

There was a bank statement inside the window envelope, dated nine days earlier. Deborah had a special reserve account at the NatWest in Clare Street. In the account, £65,000 plus some small change.

I sat down on the floor in the hall and stared into the cupboard. I took the bundle of fifties out of the safe and counted them. Thirty. Another fifteen hundred pounds. I got to my feet again and went into the kitchen, found a wall cupboard with drinks in it and helped myself to a glass of Bowmore. I moved into the living room, sat down on Deborah's large sofa, lay back into the cushions and for two or three minutes enjoyed the malt exclusively.

I took the empty glass back into the

kitchen, put it in the sink, ran it under the tap, tipped it upside down on the draining board and returned to the hall. I folded Daniel's birth certificate and put it into the brown envelope, put the envelope into the inside pocket of my jacket and the rest of the stuff back into the safe. I replaced the floor boards and the carpet and put the boxes and rugs and Henry back into the cupboard space. Then I locked up and left.

I walked back to the office. Across the river, past the old General Hospital and along Cumberland Road. Two miles, plus a few hundred yards. It took me forty-five minutes and I talked to myself all the way. I had discovered a lot about Deborah Thorne in a bit less than thirty-six hours, but I still didn't know where she was and had no means of contacting her. Philip Soames, the person who knew more about her than anybody else, was dead and the odds on being able to find the secrets he and Deborah had shared were lengthening all the time. And somewhere, there was a swim-suited blonde and a small boy who had something to do with whatever was going on.

I should have concentrated on enjoying the walk.

In the car park behind my office, I caught up with the efforts of the sand blasters. The job was half done. Fifty percent of the wall was now a deeply unattractive sludge brown colour. Hardly an improvement.

Behind me, I heard the man who had been following me say, 'It's a bit of a mess.'

I turned round to face him. He was taller than me, probably six three or four. He stood upright and straight, but relaxed. Feet slightly apart, his body weight evenly distributed, everything in balance. He was wearing a long grey city coat. Unbuttoned. It looked expensive. He obviously didn't shop in high street chain stores. At least not for his clothes.

I had to agree with his assessment regarding the wall.

'Yes,' I said. 'They should have left it as it was.'

'Sorry to intrude,' the man said. 'My name is Grant. I would like to talk to you.'

The best received pronunciation I had heard, outside of re-runs of Pathé News. No accent. Measured vowels, separation of adjoining consonants – *I would like to talk to you...* His words as tailored as his overcoat. He was very impressive. I nodded graciously.

'Talk away,' I said.

'What were you doing in Ms Thorne's house?'

I must have looked disappointed, because he went on to explain.

'I wasn't there to see you go in. A colleague of mine failed to do that. But I did get to Windmill Hill in time to see you leave.'

That was some consolation. If he was at the front of the house, then he couldn't have seen Joe leave at the back.

'Well,' he said. 'Must I repeat the question?'

That would be a tad unnecessary. The real question was, what was he going to do when I didn't answer him? He provided a little emphasis. He took hold of the left hand collar of his coat and eased it slightly away from his body. No jacket under the coat, just a five button velvet waistcoat and a compact automatic, sitting snugly in a holster against the left side of his rib cage.

My heart rate went up and my chest started thumping.

'This is a Glock 357. It fires thirteen rounds,' he said.

A very professional piece. Mr Grant was no two bob hard case.

'I will give you a moment or two,' he said.

He dipped his right hand into an interior coat pocket and took out a mobile, thumbed three buttons and put the phone to his ear.

'We are behind the building,' he said. 'In the car park.'

He disconnected the line and put the phone back into his pocket.

'You have two choices. You can answer my questions, here, in this place. Or you can come with me to another place and answer them there. I feel obliged to tell you, that option one will be far less painful.'

He waited for my response. We stood in silence for a while, the ambient sound provided by traffic circumnavigating the lock basin two hundred yards away. Then the noise of a single car engine seeped through the background. A dark blue Lexus nosed round the side of the office building, into the car park and stopped. The driver kept the engine running and stayed inside the car. Grant spoke again.

'The vehicle is for us, should you choose the latter.'

The rear access door to the warehouse opened and Jason emerged, out of uniform. He always took his lunch early. Around noon. He stopped and looked round at the car park tableau, then back at me.

'Enjoy your afternoon Ben,' I said.

Grant was looking directly at me. He didn't see the momentary confusion on Jason's face.

'Don't forget our 10.30 tomorrow morning,' I added.

Jason knew deranged from deliberate and quickly realized what was going on. A tall man in a long dark coat, was frozen in position, eyes locked on one of his tenants; and behind him, a Lexus sat with its engine idling. Jason looked back at me.

'Of course not,' he said. He fished an ignition key out of a trouser pocket and moved to the door of his Land Rover – a twenty year old Defender he off-roads at the weekends.

He climbed in and the engine fired first time. In front of me, Grant rotated his shoulders and took a couple of steps towards me. Rear tyres smoking and squealing, the Defender roared backwards and swung right as Jason spun the driving wheel. The reinforced rear bumper cage hit Grant on the back of his thighs just above his knees. His torso arched up and backwards, his head slammed against the Defender rear window, then bounced forwards again. His body crescent mooned downwards and his face hit the hardcore in front of my feet.

For a second or two, the Lexus driver contemplated getting out of his car to help. Until Jason selected first gear, floored the accelerator pedal and surged towards him. The driver found reverse and tore backwards along the side of the building, bouncing across the potholes. Jason side-slipped to a halt and let him go. He climbed out of the Defender and walked back towards me.

I knelt down to take a look at Grant and rolled him gently on to his back. Not surprisingly, he was unconscious. His face was a mess; his nose flattened beyond all recognisable shape, bleeding profusely from a hole where the bridge cartilage used to be. There was a deep jagged cut across his forehead, a length of skin ripped off the bone. Tiny bits of loose gravel, embedded in his face, pocked the skin of his cheeks. I dug the mobile out of my jacket pocket and dialled 999.

I heard Jason say, 'AX95 7BT.' I looked up at him. 'The registration number of the Lexus.'

The emergency operator asked me to describe the injuries, asked for my name and number, then said that both ambulance and police were on the way. She asked if anyone else was hurt. I said no. She said 'thank you' and disconnected the line.

I was still kneeling on the ground next to Grant. Jason helped me to my feet. He seemed remarkably together, considering the violence of the last few moments. Then the colour drained from his face. He swayed on his feet. I asked him if he was all right. He nodded.

He looked anything but.

There was a bottle of water in the driver's door pocket of the Healey. I found it and sat Jason on the front seat, legs outside of the car. He took a drink, then put his head down between his knees.

The police arrived first. Two young constables in a traffic patrol car who had sped the mile or so from Winterstoke Road and seemed to be under the impression they were attending a road accident. I tried to keep the story simple, but as it unravelled, PCs Bullock and Worthington began to view Jason and me with ever increasing suspicion. Hard to blame them really. They weren't sure what kind of felons they had on their hands. They did have time, before the ambulance arrived, to relieve Grant of his holster and gun and search his pockets. Which were empty. No wallet, driving licence, keys or small change. Nothing to identify him.

Grant was still unconscious when the ambulance took him away. By which time, PC Bullock had talked to CID at Trinity Road and was under orders to hold on to the miscreants and seal off the area. Jason and I sat in the Defender and waited.

'What happens now?' Jason asked.

'Our interrogators will believe everything you say and let you go home,' I said. 'They won't believe a word I tell them and, in all probability, will invite me to spend the night in a police cell.'

'What have you been doing Mr Shepherd?'

I was considering whether to tell him, when a black Mondeo swung into the car park. I twisted the Defender rear-view mirror and watched Harvey Butler climb out of the back of the Mondeo. He asked one question of PC Bullock, who stretched out his arm and pointed at the Defender. Harvey strode purposefully across the hardcore.

As I expected, Jason was dismissed swiftly, told to leave his vehicle in the car park and handed over to PCs Bullock and Worthington, who asked him a couple more questions and let him go. By which time, another patrol car had arrived. Harvey ordered the area round the Defender and the Healey to be taped off and turned his attention to me.

'It's 12.25. I have a lunch appointment with the ACC. So I won't keep you long. Let's take a walk.'

We crossed the old cast iron footbridge, now graffiti free and all spruced up in battleship grey.

'I liked it as it was,' Harvey said.

We strolled into the park on the south side of the river.

'Who is he, this Mr Grant?' Harvey asked.

'I don't know,' I said.

'Why did he introduce himself to you in the car park?'

'He said he wanted to ask me some questions.'

'About what?'

'We didn't get that far.'

Harvey persisted. 'About what?'

He motioned to an old wood slatted cast iron bench the urban renewers had repaired and re-painted. We sat down.

There are moments when a private investigator has to bend with the breeze. This was one of them. It would take Harvey no time at all to trace the owner of the Lexus. Which would, in all probability, lead him to the Lexus owner's boss – the person who was looking for Deborah Thorne and who had hired the aforesaid Mr Grant. That done, Harvey would be measurably better informed than I was. He would know who was looking for me. Which was what I needed to know. We had to make a deal. And as long as I managed to protect my client...

'Yesterday,' I said, 'I was hired to find someone. It now appears that Mr Grant and the Lexus driver are looking for the same person.'

'Why?' Harvey asked.

'I don't know.'

He looked at me, suspicion edged deep on his face.

'Slit my throat and hope to die,' I said.

'What's the name of the person you're looking for?'

'Deborah Thorne.'

'Who hired you to find her?'

'Deborah Thorne.'

Amazingly, Harvey didn't flinch. He simply stretched out his legs, put his hands into his trouser pockets and stared across the river.

'I should know better,' he said after a moment or two.

'Bear with me,' I said.

I gave him a précis of Deborah's visit to my office. He listened without interrupting once. When I finished, he picked out the piece of core business.

'So it would help your investigation if you were to learn the identity of the people who menaced you today?'

'Yes.'

'And you want them, or at least the man in the Lexus, to be free to approach you again?'

'All I'm saying is, that a police investigation, at this point, will only serve to endanger my client more.'

There was long pause. One of us had to go on. I did.

'Look Harvey, I have absolutely no desire to go up against contractors with automatics. What I want to do, is find my client. And find out why she is so frightened. Get her into police protection. Then leave the rest to you. What I don't want, is to have any of this compromised by a police investigation into what happened half an hour ago. This all needs to stay private, until Deborah is safe.'

Harvey batted the proposition back to me.

'That could be considered acceptable, were I reasonably confident that the death of Philip Soames, which is somehow glued to you, was not a significant element in all this.'

There was another long pause. Lunch appointment notwithstanding.

Harvey sat on the bench like he had all the time in the world. Yesterday I was ahead. I could reasonably keep what I knew about Deborah and Philip confidential. But the arrival of Grant had stirred everything up. We were playing to a new set of rules now.

‘Deborah was a client of Philip Soames,’ I said. ‘Read her case notes.’

‘Which are full of confidential information, potentially helpful to those who killed him.’

‘My assumption also.’

‘So how did these villains get from Soames to you?’

I told him about my trip to Deborah’s house, omitting the stuff about the cupboard under the stairs.

Harvey got to his feet.

‘Okay. I’ll find out who owns the Lexus and let you know. I won’t pursue it any further. Yet. I can’t stop you working in the best interests of your client. However, the moment your private endeavours collide with those of the public sector...’

I opened my mouth to protest. He waved his hands at me.

‘And they will ... I will nick you and drop you deep in the clarts.’ He looked straight into my eyes. ‘Are we clear?’

‘As crystal,’ I said.

‘Then I’m going to lunch.’

He led the way back across the bridge.

‘It looks like you won’t be able to move your car until the SOCO does the necessary. I’ll get the team out of the car park as quickly as I can.’

Chapter Five

Jason was back at his post. And apparently no worse for wear. Linda was out of her office, so lunch with her was a bust. I walked round to the Nova Scotia, bought a beer and a chicken pesto sandwich and sat on the dockside for a while. I watched the ferry arrive and disgorge a bunch of tourists and floating harbour trippers, then sauntered back to my desk.

I looked again in the envelopes I had taken from Deborah's safe. I studied the two photographs, but I couldn't see anything other than a woman and a child on a day out. Holiday snaps, like hundreds of thousands of others. The location was a sandy beach. The woman was sitting on a towel, smiling at something beyond the camera. The background to the shot of the child was a distant wall of rock, out of focus. With a gap sliced out of it on the left hand side of the picture. A slipway possibly. There was nothing else in the pictures to interpret. I put them back into the envelope. It wouldn't take long for Harvey to come back to me about the Lexus driver, but in the meantime, I had to improve the shining hour somehow.

The Northampton Thorntons had to be first up. I called 118 118. The voice down the line told me there was no telephone listing for Thornton at the address on the birth certificate. A long shot anyway.

I switched on the pc and googled *UK Census*. Only to be denied access.

I called Chrissie. I swear Sam answered the phone. Whatever, there was a joyous round of barking when the receiver was picked up and some time before Chrissie was able to speak.

'I'd like you to do something for me,' I said. 'Have you had cause to log on to the *UK Census* website?'

'Not much call for that with Russian and French studies.'

'Well here's the thing,' I said. 'The latest census data is only available to registered users – academic institutions, government departments, selected research centres. Not to individuals and certainly not to self employed private investigators. You can register through the university.'

'Yes I know. All you need is a username and a password,' she said. Then a huge dollop of suspicion coated her voice. 'What are you up to Dad?'

'Simply working for my client. I have a 1976 birth certificate. The family no longer live at the address on it. I want to find out where they are now. That's all.'

Chrissie thought for a moment.

'You can do this legitimately,' I persisted.

'Do you want it done today?'

'Please.'

'Summer break, Dad. I'll need to find someone who's registered and check if there's anything specific about the username or the password. Give me the details.'

I did.

'Later,' Chrissie said and rang off.

I made some coffee to kill a few minutes. The phone rang as I sat back down at my desk.

'No luck with the Lexus,' Harvey said. 'The registration number isn't on the DVLA computer.'

'Stolen then, and the plates changed.'

'No, it's unlikely to be stolen. Probably bought with cash, then registered and insured before the plates were changed. Unless we get hold of the car we'll never know. And after yesterday's unpleasantness, it's a safe bet that the plates have been changed again. Or the car's on its way to a scrap yard. We're doing routine checks with car breakers, but don't hold your breath.'

'Thanks Harvey.'

'Oh... The boffins reckon they'll be out of your car park within the hour.'

He disconnected the line. I put the receiver back in its cradle.

I tried to do some thinking... It was reasonable to assume that Mr Grant and his associate had tortured and killed Philip Soames. And in the process, Soames had given away my client's whereabouts. Whereupon, they had laid siege to 15 Windmill Hill in the hope that Deborah would, at some point, show up. Instead, it was me who had done that. With a front door key. Giving Mr Grant and his associate, reason to believe I might know where Deborah was.

So... Considering what had happened to Soames, what was the prognosis for Deborah?

That question frightened the hell out of me. If Deborah was part of this somehow, then the 'significant others' were truly that. And truly dangerous. And if what I was rationalising here was remotely feasible, my client was surely in real and present danger.

The trouble was, I was making this up on the hoof. I didn't have a plan.

The phone rang again. This time it was Chrissie.

'Mr and Mrs Thornton...' she said. 'According to the 2011 census, they now live in Ringsmere, in Suffolk. She is retired, he still works as a solicitor. Do you want the address?'

'Please.'

'Easy to remember. Lime Tree House, The Close.'

'Where is Ringsmere?'

'Well here's the bonus. About fifteen miles northeast of Auntie Joyce and Uncle Sid. Get your road atlas out of the car and take a look. Later...'

I found an old road atlas in the bottom drawer of the filing cabinet. Auntie Joyce and Uncle Sid live in Broadmarsh, in the Blyth Valley. A few miles inland from the jewel of the Suffolk coast, the village of Walberswick. To the north, across the river, is another gem, the stunning little town of Southwold. And some dozen or so miles further on, east of the A12, among a cluster of tiny places named after saints, lies the hamlet of Ringsmere.

The Suffolk coast in late August... No contest.

Suddenly I had a plan. Go home and pack a bag, come back to the office and, as soon as my car was released, motor east. If the car park was cleared as Harvey had promised, I could be at Auntie Joyce and Uncle Sid's in time for supper. I picked up the phone.

Auntie Joyce was delighted at the plan. She promised to bake a cake.

Jason was, temporarily, away from reception. I left him a note saying I'd be back later and took a taxi home.

Washed and clothes changed, I was staring into the bedroom wardrobe, considering what to pack, when the telephone rang. I picked up the receiver.

'Jack Shepherd...'

No one responded. There were two or three seconds of line atmos, then a click, followed by the dial buzz. I replaced the receiver and called 1471. There was no number available. Unlisted. Or maybe the call was from a mobile, or a public phone box. Or maybe it was simpler than that. Maybe I had been followed home and the caller was just checking I was still there. Whoever he was, he was now assured of my whereabouts. Given that Mr Grant was in hospital, the only man who might be looking for me – assuming he was still on the case – was Mr Grant's associate, the Lexus driver. Who, depending on how far away he was when he called, could be outside within minutes.

To shake him off, it was best to get out quickly. I grabbed my jacket, put the envelope with the beach photographs into the inside pocket, picked up my wallet and house keys and left by the back door. I closed the garden gate, turned right and headed for the bus stop on the road opposite the lane end.

I attached myself to the back of the bus queue, behind a mother and toddler, an elderly man and his terrier, two teenagers in tee shirts and baseball caps and an overweight lady with a shopping trolley. The number 128 arrived three minutes later, just as a man in a navy blue suit, with dark, short cropped hair, joined the queue behind me. I climbed on to the bus, paid the driver £3.65p and sat down in the first seat after the staircase. From here, I could just about use the driver's interior view mirror to look down the length of the bus behind me. The late arrival moved past me along the aisle and sat down three seats further back.

The mirror theory didn't work in practice, the angle wasn't right. The man was sitting on the edge of vision. I couldn't see enough of him to improve on what I had noted so far. He might be the Lexus driver. He could have stationed himself near the lane end, waiting for an escape plan to develop. On the other hand, he could be anybody's bona fide next door neighbour. The best I could do, was use the journey time to work out how to lose him, should it become necessary.

The bus destination was the city centre shopping jungle. In theory, the ideal place to disappear into a crowd. Working on the assumption that I'd get off the bus into a heaving mass of shoppers, I could take a right and then a left, slip into Harvey Nichols through one door and out through another; then double back through Quakers Friars, cross Broad Weir and walk through Castle Park back to the city centre. If the man sitting behind me was an out of town contractor, he would simply get lost.

It was a plan, as best laid as I could contrive. It began to go wrong as the 128 nosed into The Horsefair on the edge of Broad-mead. There was a sudden hailstorm. By the time the bus stopped at the southern end of Penn Street, the hail had morphed into persistent rain. I got off the bus and walked into the heart of Cabot Circus. The Lexus driver – odds on now – followed me.

In truth, there is nothing special about the retail experience of this monstrous arcade. It's just another shopping complex, with a long central walkway down the middle, leading towards a huge glass covered atrium which rises up three floors to a multiplex cinema. The place has pretention and ambition, but depends for its existence on all the familiar high street names which pack the ground floor. The middle floor has slightly more interest, with half a dozen local retailers, striving to co-exist alongside smaller national chain shops, alternative therapy outlets and opticians. Cafés, take-aways, sandwich bars and fast food restaurants are packed into the food ghetto on the top floor. The signage isn't great and it's easy for first time visitors to get disorientated. The success of my swiftly conjured scheme, depended on the Lexus driver doing just that. But we hit a snag straight away.

I don't know if business is always slow mid afternoon on a Wednesday, but there was no great crowd of shoppers to hide in. Instead of the heaving mass I was anticipating, I could count the punters individually. And the sullen, soaking rain wasn't helping. The less hardy, had obviously sought shelter.

But I was stuck with the modus operandi. And as they say, when plan A fails to work, revert to plan A.

I was saved by a soap star.

Tony Grainger had recently made a sensational exit from his returning drama series after twelve years as the senior villain, when he was shot by a trainee dental nurse he had impregnated one night in the back of his Jaguar. Six months on, times were tougher. Tony was currently the comedy lead in a series of wallpaper commercials and riding the personal appearances wave to keep his profile up. And here he was, an eight feet cardboard cut-out, in the window of Hansons, the city's only native department store. The banner above his head said that his wallpaper road show was in full swing in the 'House and Home' department on the lower ground floor.

There were more people at this shindig than outside in the rain, gathered three deep in a semi-circle in front of a display area. In effect a three wall set, with an entrance to the right at the back, built in front of the escalator riding down to the lower ground floor. I squeezed myself into the audience. The Lexus driver stationed himself about a dozen yards behind me, next to a display stand full of food mixers.

Tony was working his celebrity to the max. He was supported by another actor and between them, they were doing a version of the fifty year old Bruce Forsyth and Norman Wisdom *Sunday Night at the London Palladium* slapstick turn currently going viral on YouTube – the legendary wallpaper hanging routine.

Not exactly in the same league as Brucie and Norman, but the business did what it was supposed to do. Grabbed the crowd's attention and garnered a hefty round of applause. At which point, Tony the consummate pro, segued into the real work and did his one to one with his audience. No need for paste and mess and mistakes with this revolutionary new wallpaper. Measure, cut, soak the wall and slide into place. His assistant demonstrated briskly and efficiently and everybody applauded again. Whereupon Tony issued an invitation to those who wanted to try this new wallpaper hanging experience themselves. Any volunteers?

I stuck my hand up.

'Yes sir, thank you,' Tony crooned. 'Step up here sir.'

I did. Joined him on the dais and shook his outstretched hand.

'And your name sir?'

I told him and took a step backwards. Tony's assistant grinned at me and began re-arranging the props. Tony stepped to the front of the dais and launched into an explanation of what was to happen next. I took another couple of steps backwards. Over by the food mixers, the Lexus driver took a couple of steps forwards. I turned to my left and dived through the entrance to the set.

It was two strides to the escalator handrail, levelling out at the base of the slope. I vaulted over it, landed flat on the floor facing uphill, only to find myself travelling backwards. I looked behind me and began to move forwards, inches before the escalator ran out of track.

Running up a down escalator is a bit tricky. I discovered the principle immediately. You have to hit the steps firmly and accurately. And stay upright. If you don't, your feet will slip back underneath you and you'll be pitched forward, face down onto the steel. I began one step at a time. I kept upright, but succeeded only in walking on the spot. I tried two steps and began to make progress, then three and moved quickly. Luckily, there was no one on the way down towards me. At the top I turned and looked round. The Lexus driver was at the bottom. He ran at the escalator, got it wrong, tripped before he reached the first step, swayed backwards, shifted his weight forwards and fell to his knees. He drifted backwards in a praying position, ran out of track and was pitched on to the lower ground floor carpet.

The nearest store exit was about fifteen yards to my left. It wasn't the way I would have chosen to leave the building, but it was the quickest. I was though the door, outside in seconds and into a narrow access street. And faced with two choices. Turn right and go back into the main shopping avenue; or go straight ahead, down an alleyway to an access door into the multi-storey car park. A maintenance crew had obviously been at work in the alley. There was a red and yellow barrier stretching part way across it. Further back, a ride-on pavement cleaner was parked alongside the left hand wall and behind it a grey circular steel rubbish bin on castors. Between them, they managed to hide the car park entrance from view. Way to go...

I should have thought more about the barrier.

The door to the car park was locked. Sprayed across the door and most of the walls either side, was the proclamation – THE WELSH ARE ALL CUNTS.

The maintenance crew had made some progress in trying to get rid of it, but it was still clear for all to read. They had obviously abandoned the work temporarily and gone off to find a stronger cleaning agent. Whether it was the four letter word or the racism which was considered most offensive, I couldn't imagine. I wasn't sure if I was prepared to give the sentiment a ringing endorsement, especially under the circumstances, but I was suddenly angry with myself for getting sucked in to a cul de sac.

I turned back into the centre of the alley. The Lexus driver stepped out of Hansons. He looked left and right and then ahead, straight at me. Then at the sign telling him there was a car park entrance at the end of the alley. He set off towards me.

I moved behind the steel rubbish bin, out of his line of sight. Hoping he'd think I was on my way into the car park. There was a space between the bin and the wall. I squeezed into it and the bin moved an inch or two – it was empty. I stood stock still, listening to his footsteps on the concrete, the sound growing in volume as he got closer. I had one chance at this.

When I judged he was level, I leaned against the bin and pushed. Then followed on, like a second row forward in a rolling maul. The bin hit the Lexus driver hard enough to knock him sideways. The momentum generated carried the bin across the alley way and bounced him into the opposite wall.

Everything seemed to stop. Complete silence descended. As if the mute button had been pressed. No hiss of rain, no sound of people, no rumble from distant traffic.

Then I remembered the last encounter in an alleyway, eighteen years ago... A teenager loaded with PCP, gone ballistic with a meat cleaver and a detective sergeant with a .38 Smith and Wesson. The subsequent investigation decided I had no other recourse but to shoot and the killing was declared justified. I know how to use hand guns, but I don't like them and I didn't join the police force to shoot anybody.

And now I had to look at what I had done to another total stranger.

I took several deep breaths, leaned against the bin and rolled it away from the wall. The Lexus driver, until that moment propped upright against the brickwork, dropped to his knees and slumped sideways; another version of the praying position I'd left him in at the foot of the escalator. What I could see of the right hand side of his face was skinned almost to the bone. Blood was running from his temple and oozing out of his right ear. He was unconscious.

My stomach heaved. I turned away, crossed the alley and sat down against the opposite wall.

I make no secret of the fact that such equilibrium as I possess is severely tested on occasions like this. Something of a handicap you may think, for a person in my line of work. Not so. I regard my affliction as a kind of tolerance indicator; a measuring point beyond which my brain and my guts begin to revolt. I take some satisfaction from this.

After twenty years working amid foolishness, desperation, cynicism, violence and evil, I still find the propensity to throw up comforting.

Yesterday Grant, today the Lexus driver. One to Jason, one to me. Another broken face. Our signature event it seemed.

Still, opportunity was knocking. The man might have some ID on him. I hauled myself to my feet and stepped back towards him. He was wearing a three button jacket. The middle button was fastened. I crouched down beside him and reached out with my left hand. I twisted the button with my thumb, hooked two fingers under the jacket seam, and pulled. The jacket unfastened, but disturbed the Lexus driver in the process. He slid forward on to his face. I jerked my hand away like he was red hot, lost my balance and fell over. I sat up again and looked at him. Still on his knees, but with his forehead now touching the floor, the genuflection seemed to be complete. I'd started this, so I had to finish. I reached out to the Lexus driver and pulled him towards me. He sagged sideways and rolled over on to his back. There was a hissing noise from what was left of his nose and blood bubbled from his mouth. I dug into his inside jacket pocket, found his wallet and mobile phone, and stumbled back across the alley. My stomach heaved again. Burke and Hare may have been experienced at this kind of thing, but I wasn't. In all my years as an investigator, public and private, I'd never taken to robbing bodies. Until now.

But desperation is a miserable bedfellow. I shook my head, took a couple of deep breaths, swapped the Lexus driver's mobile for my own, dialled 999 and asked for an ambulance. I told the operator where I was and the nature of the injuries to the man I had found in the alley, then disconnected the call.

Two minutes later I was sitting in *Costa Coffee* on Broadmead, drinking a large white and letting my heart rate slow down. I called Jason. He answered after the second ring. He asked me how I was. I told him that, given the circumstances, I was in good shape.

'What circumstances?' he asked.

Car-less and on the run was the best way of describing the circumstances, but I managed to deflect his interest and get to the point.

'I need my car,' I said.

'It's in the car park,' he said. 'And the police team has gone.'

'That's good.'

Jason was confused for a moment.

'Have you lost your keys?' he asked.

'No. I have them with me.'

'I don't understand.'

'I can't come and get the Healey.'

'Why not? Where are you?'

'Jason listen!'

There was a beat.

'Sorry,' he said.

'No no, it's me who should apologise,' I said. 'Suffice it to say, I need you to drive the Healey to me. Can you get away from the desk?'

'In about five minutes. As soon as Alex gets back. He's collecting parcels from the top floor. However, you have the keys.'

'There is a spare set, locked in the top right hand drawer of my desk.'

'And the key to the desk?...'

'I have that as well.'

'So how do I?–'

'Just break into it. Find a screwdriver and jemmy the lock open.'

'Okay. If you say so.'

'You will also find a bundle of fifty pound notes in the drawer. Put them into an envelope and put the envelope into the glove compartment of the Healey.'

I looked at my watch. 3.45.

'Right. In fifteen minutes' time, take the Healey to the car park at Ashton Court. Drive around it a couple of times. As if you're looking for the most desirable place to park. Don't look for me. If you see me, don't acknowledge me. Leave the key in the ignition and walk away. Go straight back to the office. Okay?'

'Yes, of course.'

That was it. No more questions asked. I

finished my coffee and went out to the Broadmead taxi rank.

I could see most of the Ashton Court car park from the Stable Restaurant courtyard. The Healey arrived dead on time. There was no car following behind. Jason did as instructed. He made a couple of tours of the car park, found a parking space, switched off the ignition, got out of the Healey and walked away. I waited for a while. A silver Audi Estate drove into the car park. A man wearing a flat cap and a tweed jacket got out of the car, walked around to the tail gate and opened it. A Staffordshire Bull Terrier bounced onto the ground, spun round and sat down waiting for instructions. The man locked the Audi and pointed to a gate in the car park fence.

'Go on,' he said.

The dog was at the gate in seconds. The man arrived, opened the gate and the dog hared off across the hillside towards the woods. The man closed the gate and began to follow him. I watched them go and waited another couple of minutes. No more arrivals or departures. I walked to the Healey and climbed in.

I called Chrissie at home. Rewarded with the answer mode, I left a message saying I was off to Suffolk for a couple of days. I called Linda and did the same. I found the fifty pound notes in the glove compartment, put the Lexus driver's wallet and mobile in there too and turned on the ignition. I drove to Sainsburys on Winterstoke Road, filled the car with petrol, then got on to the ring road ahead of the late afternoon traffic and headed for the M4.

Forty minutes later, I called Jason from the Leigh Delamere services area and thanked him for his efforts. Then I opened the stolen wallet. I found three fifty pound notes, four twenties and two fives – on this case I was collecting cash like nobody's business. Two petrol bills and a receipt for some pain killers from a chemist in Broadmead. And five pieces of plastic – a London Transport Oyster Card, a membership card for a drinking club in Soho, a Master Card and a NatWest debit card, both valid until well in to 2014, and a driving licence. All the property of one, Francis Copley.

At least the theory Adam and I had come up with, was on the mark. Mr Copley was definitely out of town muscle.

I switched on his mobile. It buzzed, the screen turned grey and asked for a pin code. Locked... I decided to consider this problem later.

There was a predictable range of eateries. Burger King, KFC, a Carvery offering three different roasts, a sandwich bar and a bunch of coffee franchises. But wonder of wonders, a genuine Harry Ramsdens. I ordered fish and chips and mushy peas, tea and bread and butter and paid the bill with one of Copley's twenties. No need to gripe about motorway prices when a total stranger foots the bill.

Back outside, warmed up and raring to go on, the Healey's engine fired in a second. I drove on eastwards. The sun was shining, the day was warm and my cause was just.

And I had a lead to follow.

Chapter Six

Traffic was light on the M4, relatively user friendly on the M25 and amazingly sparse on the M11. North of Ipswich I decided to take the country route, left the motorway and turned east. 15 minutes after 7 o'clock, I stopped at a pub in Saxted, on the main road through the village.

I sat in the orchard in what was left of the evening sunshine. In front of a half timbered, flint stoned, thatched cottage. I wasn't exactly on holiday, but I was light years away from side street encounters. In Suffolk, on a warm evening, in a garden soaked in the scent of lavender.

Twenty minutes later, I was in Halesworth, in the gathering twilight. I turned east and let the Healey gently roll down the Blyth valley to Broadmarsh.

No one is difficult to find in Broadmarsh. Everyone lives on The Street. That's all there is to the village. It runs about three hundred yards, from the parish church on the eastern boundary to the small triangle of village green at the western end. The houses on both sides of the road are a mix of genuine 17th century wattle and daub, small Victorian cottages, early 20th century arts and crafts style villas and a handful of 1950s bungalows. There is a pub, appropriately named the Blyth Arms. The village shop is housed in what used to be the blacksmith's forge. West End House faces the green and looks directly down The Street, back towards the church.

Uncle Sid saw me coming. He was in the front garden. As I got out of the car, he waved to me and called Auntie Joyce. She came out of the house, the biggest smile on her face. And I was a kid again.

This gentle, wise and gracious couple have been my guardians since I was five. All the best stuff I learned as I grew up, I learned from Auntie Joyce and Uncle Sid. Although separated by the width of the country, we are as close as it is possible to be. Bristol to the Suffolk coast is just a matter of geography. No emotional distance at all. We talk every weekend, even if only to check on health and the weather. Chrissie had visited earlier in the year, at Easter. I had spent last Christmas with them – the Christmas following Emily's death. Now, deservedly retired, Auntie Joyce is lead alto in the Walberswick Choral Society and runs the fiercely outspoken local WI. Uncle Sid worked as a turbine engineer at Sizewell Power Station until twelve months ago. Now he makes amazing things in his garden shed.

After a glass of wine and an interlude of

catch up chat, Auntie Joyce addressed the elephant in the room.

'So why are you really here?' she asked.

I bowed to the inevitable and answered the question.

'I'm looking for someone.'

Uncle Sid asked the next question.

'Around here?'

'A client of mine has gone missing. Her parents live in Ringsmere. I'm hoping they'll be able to help me.'

'Is she in danger?'

'Yes, she is,' I said.

They took this in. The three of us sat in silence for a while. Then Uncle Sid picked up the conversation again.

'Do you know where Ringsmere is?'

'North of here, towards Beccles.'

'Do you want me to take you?'

'No. I'll find my way.'

Silence descended again. Uncle Sid got to his feet.

'Come and see what I'm working on.'

He and I adjourned to the shed. It was the size of a single car garage and occupied a huge chunk of the back garden.

'And you actually want a bigger one?'

He pulled the double doors open.

'Ta dah!!'

Inside, on a bench running the width of the shed, was a monster array of woodwork and metal tools. In a corner, an oxyacetylene tank on a sack truck, goggles and a blow-torch hanging over it. And in the middle of the space, a very impressive sculpture. Bent, twisted, corroded bits of scrap metal, welded together with some skill and no less effort. A boat in full sail. Messy, brutalist, but formidable. I stared at it. Uncle Sid beamed at me.

'What do you think?'

I found my voice.

'Amazing,' I said.

He adjusted the spectacles on his nose and looked at me through the right bit of his varifocals.

'No, I mean it.'

I stepped into the shed for a close inspection.

'Where do you get the metal?'

'Gently Bentley Murdoch. He has a junk-yard down on the estuary.'

And junk some of it was. Radiator heating elements, steel chair seats, bits from an old filing cabinet, the top of an engine block, even a dustbin lid. I pointed to some beautifully hammered out metal plates.

'Where are they from?'

'The floor of a low loader.'

'And the sail?'

'I made it out of the side panel of a transit van.'

I stepped back to get the full picture again.

'Tate Modern here we come.'

'I did a six week welding course at South Lowestoft College.'

'I don't suppose you know how to unlock a mobile phone?'

Uncle Sid beamed at me once more, took off his varifocals, put them into the breast pocket of his shirt, cleared a bunch of tools off the saw bench and gestured to it. I sat down. He stood in front of me.

'All right, talk to me,' he ordered.

So I did. I told him about Deborah, but not about Daniel. About her empty house, and the photographs I had found there. About the interest from Grant and Copley, but not about what had happened to them. Uncle Sid listened without interrupting. But he had two questions to ask.

'Where are they now? Grant and Copley.'

I should have known I couldn't gloss over the ending to the story. Uncle Sid folded his arms across his chest and waited.

'Grant is in police custody,' I said. 'Copley is probably in hospital. I hit him with a steel rubbish bin and called an ambulance. I have his wallet and his mobile phone.'

Uncle Sid betrayed no surprise or alarm. Instead, he asked his second question.

'Do you think you'll find Deborah?'

It was the million pounder. And mine alone to answer. I couldn't ask the audience, go 50/50, or phone a friend.

'I believe that Deborah will be found,' I

said. 'Eventually.'

The implication was clear enough. Uncle Sid nodded, bowed his head for a second or two, stuffed his hands into his trouser pockets and looked down at the floor. After what seemed an eternity, he lifted his head again.

'Then let's hope and pray you are the first to do so,' he said.

Auntie Joyce called from the back doorway.

'Sid. Remember you're cooking tonight.'

'Yes, coming. The casserole's all done. Just need to put it back into the oven and heat it up.' He looked at me. 'My signature dish.'

Deservedly so. It was a culinary masterpiece. And enjoyed by all of us. The rest of the evening sped by. The conversation was warm and relaxed and funny. Full of anecdotes and the best of remembrances. Not one difficult moment.

Afterwards, we cleared the dining table and Uncle Sid announced he was going out for his walk. I looked at the clock on the sideboard. 10.20.

'Walk?'

'Yes, you know, like John Wayne in *El Dorado*,' Auntie Joyce said. 'The Deputy Marshall goes for his late night patrol.'

'I always went out with the dogs at this time,' he said. 'They're no longer around, but I got into the habit, so...'

He went into the hall, put on a fleece jacket and let himself out the front door. Auntie Joyce and I cleared the dining table and filled the dishwasher.

'I suppose Sid has asked you, if you really think you can find Deborah,' she said.

'Yes.'

'And you're not sure you can?'

'No I'm not.'

She looked at the dish I was holding.

'That has to be washed by hand.'

She took it from me.

'You are a good man Jack,' she said. 'You grew up caring about all sorts of things I barely came into contact with. You invest everything you do with a realism that's ... I don't know ... tender and hopeful at the same time. We live two hundred and something miles apart, but I swear I know when you're confused, or hurt, or in trouble.'

'You always did.'

'You're not sentimental. And I suppose that's good in your line of work. But you take a lot of punishment doing what you do. You take on more than you should and you give yourself away by the shovel full. You have been preserved, thus far, because you can give as good as you get, but most importantly, by your sense of honour.'

'Falstaff said – Honour is a mere scutcheon. I'll have none of it.'

'Falstaff only had Prince Hal's rejection to

worry about. You have such considerations as life and limb.'

'Have you been saving this up?'

'For the right occasion, yes.'

'And this is it?'

'Probably.' She put the plate down on the work surface. 'I'll do this in the morning.'

She closed the dishwasher door and pressed a couple of buttons. The machine hummed, gurgled and then burst into life.

'Let's go into the living room.'

She led the way.

'There's some cognac in the sideboard, if you'd like a nightcap,' she said.

'No thanks,' I said.

We sat down, side by side on the sofa.

'The point I'm trying so clumsily to make, is this,' she went on. 'I know how important right and wrong is to you. Sid is the same. So was your father. Neither of them ever had to think about the difference between the two. They instinctively knew what it was. You are cast from the same mould. *He knew the difference between right and wrong* would sit fair on anyone's headstone. But I don't want to see it on yours. And certainly not yet.'

She stopped speaking and stared at me. I needed to say something in response. So I tried.

'Firstly, I don't think you said anything clumsily at all. And secondly, I've been preserved thus far because I am careful. I promise you, I will continue so to be.'

That seemed to be enough. Her point made and the deal done, we lapsed into silence. Uncle Sid returned five minutes later. Locked the front door behind him and secured the rest of the house. Auntie Joyce said 'goodnight' and Uncle Sid followed her upstairs.

I sat on the sofa for a while longer. Considering.

Presumably Grant was still in hospital, with a couple of uniforms stationed outside his door. Hopefully, Copley was receiving medical care also. If such was the case, sooner or later he was going to get well enough to be able to call his boss. At which point, all hell would break loose. Contracts would be issued to the rest of the associates and then I'd then be on the run as surely as Deborah. I needed to unlock Copley's mobile, get into his contacts list and his mailbox. But that required the services of someone cleverer and sneakier than me. Meanwhile, the Thorntons were a priority.

I got up from the sofa and went to bed.

Chapter Seven

I woke to the sound of banging. My bedroom window was about twenty feet from the garden shed. And Uncle Sid was hard at work. Thursday morning. At 8.25...

Downstairs in the kitchen, Auntie Joyce apologised.

'He's unstoppable,' she said.

'Maybe you should ask yourself what he would be doing otherwise.'

'Doesn't bear thinking about,' she said.

We had breakfast in the dining room. The banging went on for another fifteen minutes, then stopped. Moments later, Uncle Sid joined us. He emptied the cafetière and ate the remaining two slices of toast.

It was time I set about some sleuthing.

Auntie Joyce provided me with the local phone directory. There was only one Thornton listed in Ringsmere. I called the number but a machine answered – apologising that Elizabeth and Bill Thornton weren't in, but giving me mobile numbers for them both. I missed Elizabeth's but I wrote Bill's down. I called it and he answered, from his office in Southwold.

I tried to tell him as little as possible – I

needed to give him the whole story face to face. He took on board that I was a private detective looking for his daughter and tried not to be alarmed. He said he was in his office all morning and would see me as soon as I got there. There was a moment when it seemed he was about to ask something else. He didn't and hung up.

I got ready to leave.

'Are you going like that?' Auntie Joyce asked. She looked me up and down and sniffed. 'Well?...'

'Well, considering I haven't got a change of clothes...'

'Or the basic requirements for personal grooming.'

She set about remedying the situation.

'Sid. Get him a spare toothbrush and razor. And one of your clean shirts. He can't go out looking like he was dragged through a hedge backwards.'

'Hardly...'

'I've been trying to make you look respectable for over forty years. I'm not having you disgrace me at this stage.'

I looked at Uncle Sid. He shrugged.

'You heard what she said.'

Twenty minutes later I looked at myself in the hall mirror. I had to admit to an improvement.

'Now you can go visiting,' Auntie Joyce said. And she opened the front door.

I drove east along the Blyth valley and got to Southwold in fifteen minutes. I found a place to park. And a bank, where I deposited twenty of Deborah's fifty pound notes to be transferred to Bristol. Then I went for a walk, while I rehearsed what I was going to say to Deborah's father.

It is impossible not to be seduced by Southwold. All the superlatives ever conjured up to describe the quintessential English seaside town are writ large here. If you were to make a hit list... Gather up sunshine, stunning coastline, colour washed beach huts, lighthouse, pier; add a touch of picturesque and quaint and a maritime history which goes back to the Domesday Book, then toss them up into the air; they would come down as Southwold.

I found the place I was looking for at the southern end of the High Street, just before it opens into the Market Square. *Huntley, Rafferty and Thornton* sat neatly above a second hand bookshop, on the first floor of what used to be an old wool warehouse – a handsomely restored regency brick building. At least, the latest Thornton sat there. Huntley and Rafferty were long gone. Deborah's father, a trifle ill at ease, waved me to a chair in his office and explained.

'Messrs Huntley and Rafferty set up business here in Southwold in 1885. The original

Thornton was my father. He became a partner here thirty years ago, after the grandson of the first Rafferty died. The last of the Huntleys died at his desk in 1996. I joined the firm seven years ago, when my father retired.' This was all stuff I didn't need to know.

I took a deep breath. 'Mr Thornton...'

'No no please. Call me Bill. Everybody else does. It's accepted as good form around here. May I call you Jack?'

'Yes of course.'

I looked at him. Not tall, maybe five seven, five eight. Slim build, grey hair, dark eyes. Pleasant and polite. But he looked like he was carrying the cares of the world on his shoulders. Perhaps he was, or at least had just cause to feel that way. Certainly, the things we were about to discuss were unlikely to lift the weight. The potted biography he had just given me, was a way of postponing, at least for a moment or two, the real conversation.

He sat down in the swivel chair behind his desk, shuffled some papers in front of him, then looked back at me.

'Is Daniel in trouble?'

Daniel. The first hurdle. He shifted in his chair, took hold of the lapels of his jacket, pulled them together and shrugged his shoulders, re-shaping himself into preparedness.

'Elizabeth and I don't really know our son as Deborah,' he said. 'And we haven't seen him since he moved to Bristol.'

'Out of choice?'

'Not entirely. We're trying to work through a ... period of adjustment. All three of us.' He repeated his question. 'Is he in trouble?'

'Deborah has disappeared,' I said. 'I'm trying to find her.'

'On behalf of whom?'

This was a bit tricky. I decided to be economical with the truth.

'A friend of hers. I'm not at liberty to reveal the name. I'm sure you understand client confidentiality.'

There was a desperate hush. I listened to the sound of traffic seeping up from the street. This was the most uncomfortable opening to any conversation in a long while. Clearly, Bill Thornton hadn't much of a relationship with my client as I knew her. There was a danger that neither of us would learn anything about Deborah Thorne on this day.

'This period of adjustment,' I said. 'Do you see an end to it?'

'We're not making progress.'

'Would you like to?'

'Of course.'

Then he got angry.

'Are you making some kind of judgement here? If so, I don't appreciate it. Am I sad about this? Of course I am. So is Elizabeth. We are confused, desperate, angry, furious. But we have no idea how to proceed. We are waiting for Daniel, Deborah to…'

He stopped. His anger dissolving as quickly as it had materialised.

'That was unpardonable,' he said. 'I had no reason to shout at you.'

'It's okay,' I said. 'You probably needed to shout at someone. I'm here and I'm not going to take offence.'

'Thank you. But I fear that raging is less than productive. Liz and I want to be part of this new world Deborah has created. But for some reason … we haven't been invited into it.'

I was wrong. Bill Thornton could learn something about Deborah today. In fact he needed to; if only to ease the weight on his shoulders. Of course, he'd then have a whole bunch of other stuff to concern himself with, but that might be easier to process. So I told him about the meeting with Deborah in my office. He listened without interrupting once. When I finished he asked a question.

'Are you telling me that nobody knows where Deborah is?'

'Yes,' I said. 'At least I hope that's still the case.'

'Because she is in danger?'

'Yes.'

He sat back in his chair and closed his eyes. He remained frozen in position for several seconds. Then he opened his eyes again and looked at me.

'Do you think you can find her?'
The million pound question again.
'The honest answer, Bill, is I really don't know. A lot of people set out to disappear. And they do for a while. Some of them are found. They don't cover their tracks well enough. They make mistakes and they lead me, or the police, or whoever, right to them. Deborah has no intention of being found. She has planned and worked and re-worked her disappearance. She did make a mistake leaving the birth certificate in her house. I'm here because I found it. But I got lucky with that. I still have no idea where to look for her.'
'And if you don't find her, the odds are that–'
'I couldn't give you odds on any outcome. I don't know who else is looking for her and what their resources might be. My guess is they're substantial. And these people, whoever they are, won't be inclined to give up. I don't know how much they know about Daniel Thornton. They don't know about you. If they did, they would have been here by now.'
I paused. He nodded, took a deep breath and waited for the coda.
'So I'm hoping you can tell me something about Daniel they don't know, which will help lead me to Deborah.'
I took the envelope containing the photo-

graphs out of a jacket pocket and pushed the pictures across the desktop.

'Do you recognise either of them? The woman, or the boy?'

He shook his head. 'No. Sorry. Who are they?'

'I don't know.'

'Where did you find the pictures?'

'In Deborah's safe.'

He looked again and shook his head again. 'Sorry...'

He passed the photographs back to me. I returned them to the envelope. And we both sat in silence again. Awkwardness was roaming the office like a caged tiger. Something had to give. Thornton looked at me, the same dead centre look his daughter had given me. Then confusion seeped into his eyes.

'I don't know where to begin,' he said.

'Begin at the beginning, go on until you come to the end and then stop.'

It took him a moment to recognise the quote.

'Alice in Wonderland.'

I nodded. Waited. Thornton rehearsed for a moment or two and then he began.

'When he was young, Daniel had a passion to set the world right. He qualified as a teacher. Did you know that?'

'I don't know anything about Daniel. So whatever you can tell me...'

'He got his degree in 1998 in Bristol. He

went on to the Graduate School of Education. Got his PGCE in June '99. I have to tell you, a one year post grad course is not for the faint hearted.'

'So I understand. My daughter is contemplating the same route. She's just about to start her final year at Bristol. She's doing Russian and French.'

'Daniel did Politics and International Studies.'

'Did he take a teaching job?'

'No. He decided to take a year out. He stuck a pin in the map of Europe and hit Switzerland. He went to Geneva. Two weeks later, he joined *Médecines Sans Frontières,* as a volunteer.'

'Without any medical experience?'

'You don't have to be a doctor to work with *MSF*. The organisation needs administrators, fixers, interpreters, drivers... Humanitarian aid is a complicated business these days. Adds up to a great deal more than simple doctoring.'

He paused for a beat or two.

'They sent Daniel to Kosovo.'

Not a man for doing things by halves, Daniel. First a Balkan war, then a gender change. Certainly not frightened by challenges.

'Apart from a text on Christmas Eve '99, we didn't hear from him for almost five months. We just watched the television news and imagined what he was doing. Prayed that he was still alive. Then in March 2000, he called us from an *MSF* aid station in Urosevac province. He had just been to Donjica. Do you remember the place?'

My knowledge of the Kosovan war was sketchy at best, but no one could forget easily the massacre at Donjica. It dominated news headlines for days and almost bounced NATO back into a repeat series of bombing raids.

'Was he there?'

'Yes. God knows what he witnessed. Three months later, after spending some days in a place called Lipojane, he was on his way home.'

'But not here? You weren't in Suffolk then.'

'No. Cambridge.'

He took a moment, glanced up at the clock on the wall behind me.

'Almost eleven,' he said. 'Look, you might as well know everything. This is going to take some time. There's a coffee shop in the square.'

We re-located to *Edna's*. A couple of dozen tables with chequered table cloths, in a cosy, sunlit, ground floor room. We sat in the bay window overlooking the square. Thornton ordered and I listened while he talked.

'My wife is an American. The daughter of Edward Daley Junior from St Louis. Through the considerable efforts of his father, the family firm made a fortune in the 1930s, out of washers and grommets.'

Not many people know what a grommet is. It was a funny word long before Nick Park's animated hero became a living legend. But I kept my face straight.

'Somebody has to make them,' I said.

'I suppose you would say that Elizabeth was an heiress. I met her at university in 1968. Back then, Forbes Magazine quoted her father's personal fortune at around thirty-five million dollars. Elizabeth was an only child. His devotion to her, was second only to his dedication to making money. Elizabeth was ... is ... a true Anglophile. She wanted to go to an English university. Edward decided it should be Cambridge. She accomplished the academic necessities, he paid for everything. However, as he once told me, he "cased the joint first". He bought the Charteris Estate – a Regency mansion and seven hundred acres; encompassing the twelve hectares surrounding the house, half a dozen farms and three miles of the River Nene. All of which came with a defunct earldom and a town house in Wisbech. Edward became, in essence, the resurrected Lord Charteris.'

Which was fascinating, but I wondered if perhaps we were wandering off the subject.

The coffee arrived. He poured and continued.

'Whilst not exactly the Duke of Westminster, Edward behaved like a minor version. He famously booked out the whole of a Cap D'Antibes hotel for the summer of 1970, so he could be sure to use it exclusively for ten days during late August. All was going swimmingly until the Haverford scandal. Ever hear of it?'

'No,' I said. 'Can't say I did.'

'The Haverfords were American old money from Concord New Hampshire. One night, they were guests at a party in the Daleys' summer home in Martha's Vineyard. An orgy of drink, drugs and up market bravado ended in murder. Charlie Haverford, the favoured son of the family, was found dead in one of the guest bedrooms. Edward's younger brother Harry, was arrested. Despite the efforts of a defence team which cost Edward Daley Senior a decade of profits, Harry was tried, found guilty and despatched to San Quentin. Stock in the family business nose dived. Harry committed suicide in his cell on Death Row. The old man took to drink and a spectacular bout of gambling. Elizabeth's father went back to St Louis, but could only watch as the business was taken over by competitors, broken up and sold off in bits.'

He paused and looked at me as if I was dozing off.

'I know this seems as nothing, compared to the accepted excesses of today. But this was buttoned up, uber-respectable, catholic

Massachusetts. The Kennedy homeland. Chappaquiddick, was just four years back in memory. Still haunting the clan and all those associated with it.'

I decided it was time to ask him if this potted family history was germane to our discussion.

'Please bear with me,' he said.

'Of course,' I said and took a deep breath. 'So this happened when? The mid 70s?'

'A couple of years before Daniel was born. Elizabeth and I were living in Northampton. Her father kept the Regency mansion, but he sold off the farms and most of the Charteris Estate to pay the remaining American debts. He sold the Wisbech town house and put the money in trust for Daniel. He died while Daniel was at university. He left Elizabeth the mansion and a substantial bill from the taxman. We sold off the rest of the estate to pay the Inland Revenue, moved to Cambridgeshire and lived in the house for a while. We tried to make the place pay for itself, but in the end, we decided to sell it. At which point, my father asked me to come here and join the firm. I'm glad I did.'

He sipped at his coffee, then looked at me over rim of his cup.

'I'm sorry. That's a long story.'

And so far, not much about Daniel. Although now it was clear where his money came from. Why he had a mortgage free house in Bristol and cash in the bank and how he could pay for his gender change.

The subject of which however, was rather too personal for *Edna's* bay window table. Thornton paid the bill. We left the coffee shop, crossed the square and walked along East Street, towards the beach. We looked out to sea, across Southwold Bay.

'There was a great sea battle out there in the summer of 1672,' Thornton said. 'Seventy-five Dutch ships surprised an English fleet at anchor in the bay. It was brutal and bloody. Not at all heroic. The fighting went on until dusk. For days afterwards, bodies and limbs were washed up onto the beach.'

'Who won?'

'Neither side, in truth. The Dutch lost more ships than the English and retired hurt. But the English fleet was so crippled, that the Duke of York was forced to abandon his plans to blockade the Dutch coast. I'm rambling aren't I?'

I looked at him.

'That's okay.'

And waited again.

'Daniel...' he said. 'Where were we?'

I reminded him.

'When he came home from Kosovo, did he talk about Donjica? Or the other place?'

'Lipojane. Not in detail. He didn't want to. So we never pressed him.'

'Did he take a teaching job?'

'No.'

'So what did he do?'

'He moved to west London. Bought a flat in Chiswick. He told us at one point that he was going to write about his time in Kosovo. Apparently, he kept a record while he was there.'

'A diary?'

'No. Some kind of journal.'

'Do you know where that is?'

'I have no idea. You obviously didn't find it in his house?'

'No.'

He turned away. I moved with him and fell into step as he began walking along the promenade. The beach was to our right. And, as befits a glorious August day, playing host to families making the best of the holiday weather. On our left, the beach huts stretched in line unbroken, towards the north end of the town. All conforming to what seemed the approved style. Grey or brown rooftops over shiplap boarding, seven or eight feet wide, ten feet deep, pediment porches on the front. All painted a base colour white, with highlights in blues, greens and reds. Not in bright primary colours, but tasteful, bleached-out pastels. With occasional Bohemian touches. Horizontal stripes, created by painting every other board in a colour. And flashes of art deco. A silver zigzag here and there, cabin names and numbers in sharp italics.

Thornton stepped onto a white porch under a pink and white striped pediment. He took a key out of the right hand pocket of his trousers and opened the cabin doors.

'Welcome,' he said and waved me inside. 'Make yourself at home.'

And like home it was. The pink and white theme continued inside the cabin. Pink throws lay across two custom made benches which met in a corner and made an L shaped sofa and served as two day beds. A small sideboard, another made to measure piece, with a pair of binoculars and half a dozen neatly piled magazines on top of it, sat underneath a three storey tier of bookshelves. A group of small seascape watercolours hung, carefully arranged, on the wall opposite the sideboard. And two, pink cushioned, wicker armchairs sat looking out to sea, one on each side of the door.

It was a calm, graceful, gently created space.

'This is Elizabeth's creation really,' Thornton said. As if this kind of quiet accomplishment was beyond him.

We sat down in the wicker chairs. He looked out to sea, across Southwold Bay and beyond. Then he spoke. In verse.

'Roll on thou deep and dark blue ocean, roll.
Ten thousand fleets sweep over thee in vain.

Man marks the earth with ruin, his control
Stops with the shore.'

Lines from a beach hut. Actually a passable title for a romantic poem. *Lines From A Beach Hut...*

'Byron,' I said.

He looked at me with some respect.

'You know it?'

'Is that so amazing?'

Suddenly he was embarrassed.

'No, of course not. I'm sorry. It's simply that ... er...'

I rescued him.

'My wife Emily, was a Byron fan. And over the years, I got seduced into reading him.'

'I did too, courtesy of Elizabeth.' He gestured over his shoulder. 'There's a volume on the shelves up there.'

He paused again.

'Deborah...' I said. 'We need to talk about the gender change. It may not have anything do with her disappearance, but at this stage all information is welcome.'

He nodded. 'Yes, of course.'

Then, resolutely, he began. And we were under way again.

'Deborah,' he said, 'told us what she was proposing to do in the summer of 2003. Here, in this beach hut. Sitting where you are. As you can imagine, it was something of a shock.'

'And up to that point?'

'We had no idea what was on her mind. She had never...' He changed the emphasis. 'We, had never talked about his. I always reasoned that Daniel had a conventional number of sexual and non sexual relationships with men and women.'

'Do you think that's how this is supposed to be defined?' I asked. 'In terms of relationships, sexual or otherwise.'

'No I don't. Not now. But at the time, I had no way of understanding the situation. I was simply trying to work it out. And I made a basic mistake. I asked...' He paused to get the definition clear. 'I asked Daniel, as he then was, if he was gay.'

'And he wasn't.'

'No. His passion to change gender had nothing to do with being gay. He just knew, he said, from around the age of twelve, that he was in the wrong body. He grew up with that conviction. Believing that one day, providing he remained balanced and rational and true to himself, he would be able to do something about it. And we're proud of him you know ... her ... Deborah. Her strength, determination, guts.'

He paused, lost in his recollection of it all.

'What do you think happened in 2003 that made him want to talk to you. Something to do with his experiences in Kosovo?'

'No. Something much more prosaic. He turned twenty-five. And NatWest sent him a letter asking him to come and discuss his options. Decide what he might like to do with the five hundred and eighty thousand pounds sitting in his account.'

'The Wisbech town house money, plus interest.'

'Yes.'

'His fighting fund all along,' I said. 'So to speak.'

'Daniel had been preparing for some time. He had been talking for a year or so with a clinic in Oxfordshire. Learning about what he was going to put himself through. Fortunately, the clinic worked closely with someone he knew. A Bristol psychiatrist he had met while he was at university.'

'Philip Soames.'

'Do you know him?'

Thornton didn't need to know Soames was dead, so I contrived to stay in the present.

'Deborah's therapist during the transition process.'

'How do you know him?'

That was easy to answer.

'When his mother died, he hired me to find a lost relative.'

'I see. But how did you know about his connection with Deborah? Such details are confidential surely?'

This was a bit trickier. I dredged up a little white lie. I told him I found a reference to

Philip in some papers in Deborah's safe and put two and two together.

'Clever of you,' he said.

'It's what I get paid to do,' I said, modestly.

He nodded. We lapsed into silence again. This time comfortable enough. It was simply that neither of us had any more to say. So I suggested lunch.

'No problem,' he said. 'I have arranged to have it catered. Liz will be on the way right now, with a hamper.'

'You specialise in alfresco dining by telepathy do you?'

He grinned. The first grin in our relationship.

'I called her mobile after you introduced yourself this morning. She said she would like to meet you, and suggested this rendezvous. A bit Noel Coward perhaps. But it is summer, we are at the seaside and Southwold is famous for its crab sandwiches.' He looked at his watch. 'She'll be here in about ten minutes.'

To fill the interim, I went for a walk along the beach. I hadn't established much in the last twenty-four hours. At least nothing, at first glance, that seemed to be useful. Daniel's Kosovo adventure however, strengthened my belief in my client's guts and determination. The latter, she had in spades. And that was what all of us involved in this case had to hold on to. Deborah's chances of coming through this, were greater than most people you'd meet in the normal run of things.

The trouble is, nothing is ever normal in the stuff that I do. The possibilities for error are huge, the margins for a satisfactory outcome are tiny.

I looked back at the promenade. A woman carrying what looked like a picnic hamper was walking swiftly along the row of beach huts. Bill Thornton stepped out from under the pink and white porch and waved at her. I decided to allow them a few minutes for him to précis our conversation. Maybe Elizabeth would be optimistic enough to see beyond the gloom. The reality was however, that no matter how well adjusted they both were, they had little of any cheer to look forward to. And meanwhile, they were depending on Jack Shepherd, investigator and knight errant, to make everything right. If possible. If he could not, then crab sandwiches and an afternoon at the seaside wouldn't amount to much at all. It was possible the Thorntons were on a hiding to nothing. In contrast to Jack Shepherd, who could always point himself home.

Bill Thornton was waving at me from the promenade. The crab sandwiches and an introduction to Elizabeth beckoned.

Chapter Eight

'What was she like?' Auntie Joyce asked.

It was just after 3.30. We were sitting in the garden, in the afternoon sunshine, eating the cake she had baked as promised.

'She is elegant, softly spoken and I suspect, very slow to anger. I liked her. Actually I liked him too.'

'How are they both, with all this?'

'The same as the rest of us. Confused and hoping for the best. They're a bit lost. Not surprising, considering this is way beyond anything they've experienced before. They deserve a happy ending.'

'Doesn't everybody?'

'Yes. But some more than others.'

'So what are you going to do now?'

I squinted up at the sky.

'Spend the rest of the day out here in the sunshine. Take you and Uncle Sid to dinner this evening. And go home tomorrow morning.'

Auntie Joyce saw straight through that piece of flannel.

'That's a very concise timetable,' she said. 'But it's not what I meant and you know it.'

The honest answer was, I had no long view

at all. No scheme, grand or otherwise. In the short term, the best I could do would be to get into Copley's mobile, check his messages and his contact list. Beyond that...

'If I had a halfway sensible plan, I would share it with you,' I said. 'But the truth is I don't have one.'

'Aren't you supposed to be a super sleuth?'

'Yes, well... You've found me out.'

'So what do you usually do when you get to this stage?'

'There's really not much method to what I do at any stage,' I said. 'I think for a bit. I ask questions. And sometimes the answers lead to more questions. The answers to which, on a good day, lead to me leaping into action. And that action leads to–'

That was enough. Auntie Joyce held up her hands and patted the air.

'All right all right…'

I finished as constructively as possible.

'Look ... I poke about, dig into things, hoping I'll unearth something which surprises everyone, particularly the villain of the piece. Who at that point, will be provoked into some action, desperate or foolhardy, and hand me something to work on.'

I looked straight at Auntie Joyce.

'That's it. I swear.'

'Sounds like you haven't a clue,' she said.

'Did you hear me say I did?'

Uncle Sid called out from inside the house.

'Anybody around?'

Auntie Joyce turned in her chair and shouted back.

'Out in the garden.'

Uncle Sid materialised in the dining room; framed by the French windows, cradling his laptop.

'Prepare to be amazed,' he announced.

'Where have you been?' Auntie Joyce asked.

'With young Gregory.' He turned and looked at me. 'He lives two doors along the street. He's fourteen and there's nothing he doesn't know about twenty-first century communication. He sent me a link.'

'To what?' I asked.

He waved the laptop at me.

'Get that mobile you stole from the man in the shopping centre and come with me.'

Uncle Sid went back into the house. I retrieved Copley's mobile from the Healey's glove compartment and joined him in the study. The laptop screen flicked from his home page to the inbox. He found the link. Picked up a mobile to pc usb lead and waved it at me.

'Young Gregory showed me how to do this. Give me the phone.'

I handed it over. He switched the mobile on, connected it to the laptop, double clicked on the link and we waited.

'Is this actually erm…?' I asked.

'It's the internet,' he said. 'Who worries about that? Listen, I may be fifty years older than young Gregory, but never I hope, too old to stay current.' He pointed at the laptop. 'Look at that.'

The screen offered a bunch of alternatives. Uncle Sid followed the instructions young Gregory had written down on a piece of paper. Less than two minutes later, the mobile screen flashed, the network jingle sang into life and Mr Copley's menu page lit up.

'Bingo,' said Uncle Sid. 'Phone unlocked.'

My uncle Sid, the silver phone hacker. All I could do was marvel.

He disconnected the mobile from the usb lead and passed it to me. A message in the window said *3 missed calls*. I dialled 121. The response was *you have no messages*. That was either a good thing, or a bad thing. It would have been useful to know who had called, although it might simply have been Copley's plumber. And answering the calls, had I been around to do so, would probably have been a mistake. I needed to go through the complete list of Copley's associates before I started talking to any of them.

I found my way into the menu and checked the outgoing call box. One call was logged to my home number, timed at 14.56 the previous day – the call I received just before I left the house. The message box was empty. There were fourteen numbers in the contacts box.

'Will you write these names and numbers down,' I said.

Uncle Sid fished a sheet of A4 out of a desk drawer and took a carpenter's pencil out of a pot on the desk. I went through Copley's contacts box, spelled out each name and recited each number. Grant's name was third on the list. Six of the names were solidly English, one was Welsh and one was Irish. Three other persons were listed by the initials 'H', 'M' and 'S.' The remaining two generated a little excitement. They were difficult to spell and impossible to pronounce. Vojislav Dujic and Josip Tudjman.

Uncle Sid stared at the names.

'Where do you suppose they're from?' he asked.

'Eastern Europe somewhere,' I suggested.

'Serbia possibly,' Auntie Joyce said, after we had returned to the garden and shared the question with her.

'Is that a guess?' I asked.

'Informed guess,' she said. 'I have a friend in the WI who is a Bosnian Serb. Mila Bulatovic. She was a librarian in Srebrenica. Survived the massacres and the reprisals of 1995. She escaped into Slovenia and got a boat to Italy. She was given asylum here in England because she had somewhere to stay.

Her daughter is married to the carpenter with the workshop at the other end of the street.'

'Do you think Mila would be able to locate those names to particular Serb areas?'

'I don't know. She might. I'll call her.'

'Invite her to supper,' Uncle Sid said.

On request, Auntie Joyce cooked bangers and mash with onion gravy. Mila's first dining experience on her arrival in Suffolk apparently. Alpha and omega for the rest of us too. Bangers and mash. No contest. Meal over, Uncle Sid organised coffee and cognac.

Mila was as laid back as anyone I've met. Mid 50s, tall and slim, with dark, bubbly hair and green eyes. And with a command of English – along with Italian and German apparently – which put my meagre French totally into the shade. The names were certainly Serb in origin she said, but locating names to areas was impossible.

'If you're British,' Mila said, 'You can reasonably expect to have a UK address. Most English people for example, live in England.'

'Except for those who live in Europe and the States and far flung places of the old Empire,' I suggested

'That's true,' she said. 'But almost all of those are ex-pats, who have chosen to live where they do. Millions of people in eastern Europe have no such opportunity. Ethnic

Serbs live all over the Balkans. And there are Albanians and Slovenians and Croats still living in Serbia.'

Uncle Sid passed Mila a cup of coffee.

'So where do these people call home?'

'That's the question that remains, despite years of ethnic cleansing. Do you know where Serbia is?'

'In the Balkans.'

'Where in the Balkans?'

Uncle Sid thought for a moment or two.

'I see what you mean.'

'Serbia is locked in the middle of a European nowhere,' Mila said. 'Hungary to the north. Romania and Bulgaria to the east. Croatia, Bosnia and Montenegro to the west. Albania and Macedonia to the south. Although that's not strictly accurate. Kosovo borders Albania.'

Auntie Joyce took a cup of coffee from Uncle Sid.

'And Kosovo has proclaimed itself a sovereign state,' she said. 'Because most of its population is Albanian. The heart of the trouble, right?'

Mila nodded and spooned sugar into her coffee.

'But the truth is, Balkan refugees live all over the world. An alien nation. A twenty-first century version of the infamous wandering Jew.'

I summed up.

'We know that Vojislav Dujic and Josip Tudjman have UK mobiles. Which means, if they don't actually live in the UK, at least they spend a substantial amount of time here.'

'So what do you do?' Uncle Sid asked. 'Ring them up and ask them where they live?'

'Barmy as that may seem,' I said, 'if I thought they'd give me their addresses, I'd do it.'

'There's always the possibility,' Mila said, 'that they are living openly somewhere. The internal affairs of Serbia and Kosovo are still a nightmare. Dujic and Tudjman could be living in a penthouse in Belgrade, or in a shithole on the Macedonia border and be equally invisible in either place.'

'But not in neighbouring countries?'

'The Croatian and Slovenian authorities are organised these days. Bosnia and Montenegro are getting there. But the reality is, hundreds of thousands of personal records have disappeared from offices all over the former Yugoslavia. And if Dujic and Tudjman have money, they could be living under the radar anywhere.'

Which is exactly what my client was attempting to do. Deborah was testing living under the radar to the limit. She had left a trail to follow – a house in south Bristol, her bank statements in the safe under the stairs, her notes in Philip Soames' office, her gender change history in a private clinic in Oxfordshire. Presumably she had a national insurance number. And somewhere, a doctor, or a dentist. There had to be places where she shopped, places where she was seen regularly, places where she was known and where she could be identified. But without breaking cover and mobilising the police forces of six counties I could only work in instalments.

It is largely true to say, that everybody trying to keep a low profile breaks cover eventually. Grant and Copley had done that. And I had a list of names and telephone numbers as a result. But that was the point. A list was all I had. And considering it was provided by a person with a job description which involved, as a core skill, hurting people, I wasn't exactly in the driving seat.

Mila raised her brandy glass.

'The best of luck with your search,' she said.

'Thank you,' I said.

She might just as well have been talking about the holy grail.

Uncle Sid escorted Mila home and went on to complete his late night constitutional. Auntie Joyce and I repeated the previous night's chores and tidied up again.

I remembered that my mobile had been switched off all day. I checked it for messages and immediately regretted doing so.

There were two words from a terse and seriously pissed off Harvey Butler.

'Call me,' was all he said.

Chapter Nine

I didn't sleep too well. To borrow, from Wordsworth, one of the few other pieces of romantic verse I know...

There was a roaring in the wind all night;
The rain came heavily and fell in floods.

There was a similar tempest in the bedroom also. I was still awake and punching the pillow around dawn. At which point I fell asleep and woke three hours later, feeling like someone had been trying to smother me.

Saturday morning. And outside, Wordsworth's day wasn't improving. In fact it was getting worse. The cloud cover was thickening as I looked out of the window; the world was darker than it had been when I went to bed and the rain was hammering down. Perfect weather for a five hour drive home.

'So stay here,' Uncle Sid suggested, over coffee, toast and scrambled eggs. 'Another day in sleepy Suffolk won't compromise your investigations surely. You're not overburdened with ideas after all.'

I was contemplating how to respond to that vote of confidence, when *BBC News* intervened. Auntie Joyce called to us from the living room.

'Chaps. In here. Quickly.' Then she shouted louder. 'Come on!!'

We joined her. She pointed at the TV screen.

The studio presenter had swung her chair to face the screen behind her and was introducing a Bristol reporter I recognised. She was standing in front of the 'Out Patients' department at Southmead Hospital. The studio presenter handed over to her and the screen mixed to a full shot. She began to talk.

'The administrators at Southmead Hospital in north Bristol, are launching their own investigation into these circumstances. A doctor, two nurses and a security man were injured in the incident. It appears that a patient, whose name the hospital trust and the police are not prepared to reveal, caused havoc on a ward he was transferred to, after receiving medical attention to serious facial injuries. Apparently, he got of bed and got dressed, intending to leave the hospital. Staff advised him against this. At which point he became violent, assaulted the nurse who was attending him, another nurse who attempted to calm the situation, and the ward duty doctor. Then he made his way to the entrance you can see behind me. He was intercepted just inside the doorway, by a security officer who was punched and thrown against a wall. The man was last seen running across the car park in the direction of Southmead Road. This is as much as we know at

the moment. More will emerge as the day goes on.'

The studio presenter asked if this sort of incident was rare. The Bristol reporter said such things happen more frequently than hospital authorities like to admit. But this one seemed to be more serious than most.

Auntie Joyce pressed the mute button on the TV remote. She and Uncle Sid stared at me.

'I don't suppose that...' she began.

'I didn't tell you everything,' I said.

'Obviously.'

'There was no point in worrying you unduly,' I offered, somewhat lamely.

'And now, we're not worried in the slightest,' she said.

There was a monster silence. She stared at me, with more menace than I thought the situation warranted. Out in the hall, my mobile began ringing.

The phone was sitting on the table by the door, next to my wallet, the brown envelope with the photographs inside, my car keys and Copley's mobile. The caller was Jason.

'Superintendent Butler has been chasing you.'

'Yes I know,' I said.

'He just called,' Jason said. 'Asked if I knew where you were. I gather he has left messages in the office, at your home and on your mobile.'

'Thank you Jason.'

He said it was all part of the service and then asked me where I was. I told him I was in Suffolk

'What are you doing there?'

'I'm just about to leave. I'll be back in Bristol late afternoon, weather permitting. It's pissing down here.'

'It's great here,' he said.

'Keep your own counsel Jason, will you please? Until we can talk.'

'Sure. Roger, wilco.'

'Later,' I said and disconnected the call. I walked back into the living room with the phone in my hand. Whereupon it rang again.

'I told you to fucking call me,' Harvey said into my ear.

'I was going to.'

'Once you had worked out a story you could regale with your face at least half straight.'

He took a beat rest, then got to the point.

'So this man who beat up a bunch of hospital staff at Southmead...' he said. 'Tell me about him.'

This was tricky. I began with, 'Why do you assume I?–'

Harvey shut me up.

'Never mind the bollocks. The 999 call was made from your mobile. So, either you stumbled across him and were too busily engaged on some nefarious purpose to wait for the ambulance; or you were responsible for his condition, but suffered an attack of conscience before becoming a fugitive.'

'Truthfully,' I said, 'it was a bit of both.'

'Who is he?' Harvey asked.

'Francis Copley. The Lexus driver.'

'So he found you?'

'Yes.'

Harvey heaved a sigh and mumbled something which sounded like 'Jesus Christ'. Then I heard the unmistakable rasp of grinding teeth, followed by a huge intake of breath.

'Where are you?' he asked finally.

'I'm in Suffolk, with my Auntie Joyce and Uncle Sid. Been here for two days. Say hello to Auntie Joyce.'

I handed the phone to her.

'Talk to the nice policeman.'

She did. Uncle Sid and I listened to her end of the conversation.

'Yes... Making some enquiries into a disappearance... I don't know... He hasn't said... I believe so, yes... Do you want to speak to him?... Yes, I'll tell him... A pleasure.'

She switched off.

'He wants to see you as soon as you get back to Bristol.'

'He was firm about that was he?'

She nodded. 'Seriously.'

'I'd better be on my way then.'

'Not until you have revealed all,' she said. She pointed to the sofa. 'Sit down.'

I did.

'Now, give.'

I did. Told them both everything. They listened. Enraptured, terrified and furious by turns. Auntie Joyce was the first to respond.

'So shall we examine this concept of worrying us?' she asked. 'Based on the knowledge we now have at our disposal... You are looking for a lady who was once a man, who is probably in mortal danger, along with you by association. Two enforcers have threatened to kill you. As a result of this encounter, one is, thankfully, in police custody. But the other, is at large in the community undoubtedly on some vengeance fuelled rampage. And two mysterious Serbian gentlemen, in all probability murderous gangsters, have placed you at the top of their hit list. Now correct me if I'm wrong, but "worried" would seem a hopelessly inadequate word to describe how we should feel about this... Sid?'

Astonished by her controlled tirade, he cleared his throat and swallowed.

'Absolutely,' he said.

When you're on a hiding to nothing it's best to acknowledge so.

'You're right,' I said. 'And I am not making light of the situation. Believe me, I never do. Even in the most routine of cases. But my client is in serious trouble. I have to find her and protect her and keep her safe.'

'Have you no other choice?' Uncle Sid asked.

'No. At least no other choice I can make.'

I looked at them in turn. The two people who had lifted me out of despair in the darkest moment of my young life. Who, with no children of their own, had rescued a frightened little boy, given him solace and care and more love than it was possible to dispose. I owed Auntie Joyce and Uncle Sid more than I could ever repay. And now I was frightening the hell out of them.

'Please try and give me the benefit of the doubt here,' I said. 'I promise you, all I'm trying to do is find Deborah. I will not deliberately put myself in harm's way. As soon as I know she is safe, I will go straight to Harvey Butler and tell him everything.'

They were both listening intently, but I turned to Auntie Joyce.

'We talked yesterday, about why I do what I do. Well, this is what I do. Though I swear, it's not a prime example of the norm. This case is a bit out of the ordinary. But I have to see it through.'

She give me her open, honest to goodness stare.

'Will you be careful?'

'Scouts honour.'

The silence which followed was eternal. Until Auntie Joyce wound up the conversation.

'That will have to do.'

She opened her arms. I got up from sofa

and stepped into them. She wrapped them around me and held me close. I looked over her shoulder towards Uncle Sid. He smiled and nodded gently.

I left Broadmarsh and drove up the Blyth valley towards Halesworth. I stopped in a lay-by, took the sim card out of Copley's mobile and threw the carcass into the river. Unlocked, the phone was dangerous. Using it would make me instantly traceable. But it might be useful to keep the information on the sim.

An hour later, I was on the A12 and driving south west to the M25.

The rain was relentless. Visibility was down to yards. Overtaking through rooster tails of spray was nothing short of reckless. The M25 was gridlocked, but at least, the rain began to ease. By the time I reached the M4, it had stopped altogether and the sky to the west was brightening. It was 1 o'clock and I had been on the road for three and a half hours. I put my foot down. The Healey responded, picked up speed and surged forward. Optimism was short-lived however. A lorry had jack-knifed a mile short of junction 15, ploughed into the central barrier and shed its load of corrugated iron sheeting all over the westbound carriageway. I was past junction 14 before I realised. I managed to crawl along to Membury

Services and into the rest area, to sit it out.

The restaurant fare wasn't altogether tempting. The tuna sandwich meal deal was a better option. I took the food and a copy of *Autosport* to a table near the traffic information screen, which was giving updates every twenty minutes on the clearing up operation at junction 15. I read the magazine from cover to cover. The lead article was bigging up Jenson Button's prospects at Spa in ten days' time, one of the low budget teams was in dire financial straits again, another row was brewing at Ferrari and Bernie Ecclestone, having given up his struggle to champion Bahrain, was claiming Qatar as the next new financial and ethically acceptable location for F1.

My mobile rang just after 4 o'clock.

Chrissie asked if I was free for dinner. I thought about it. A touch of improvisation was required here. I didn't have a plan for the next few days and I was growing to hate this struggling to work out what to do next. All I knew was I should keep a low profile, until I discovered how many Serbs and their accomplices were roaming round Bristol looking for me.

'Love to,' I said. 'But I don't know what time I'm going to be back.'

'You left Suffolk hours ago,' she said. 'You should be within hailing distance by now.'

There was a beat. The line crackled.

'I called Auntie Joyce mid morning,' she explained.

Another crackle.

'Dad. Can you hear me?'

'Yes.'

'Where are you?'

'Stuck on the motorway,' I said. 'Could be here for ages. By the time I get into Bristol, I'll be knackered and useless company.'

'Okay,' Chrissie said. 'But you're alright?'

'Absolutely.'

'Fine. Bye.'

She rang off.

The little white lies were mounting up. But so be it. And a plan was a plan, however hastily conceived. I picked up the mobile again and called Jason.

'Are you well?' he asked.

'I'm stuck on the M4, east of Swindon,' I said. 'I won't get into the office before the end of the day. Enjoy the weekend and we'll have a council of war on Monday.'

'Not around,' he said. 'In Wales from tomorrow, for a week. I'm going up to Snowdonia for some white water canoeing.'

That was good news. A bunch of Serbs and out of town contractors would be unlikely to find Jason in Snowdonia. And if they did, they'd be easy to spot. Like a privy on the front lawn.

'Have a good time,' I said.

'Sure to. Oh and er ... Ms Barnes just

passed the desk on her way in. Asked if I'd seen you today. Want to talk to her?'

'Yes, okay.'

'I'll transfer you. Take care.'

Linda asked me where I was. The question of the day is this. I told her I was on my way back from Suffolk. She asked me if I had plans for the evening. Only to rest and relax I said. She asked if I would like to do so at her place.

'Will this be a date?' I asked.

'Sunset with supper and wine,' she said. 'Would you like anything else?'

I hated to turn her down with white lie number twenty-seven. So I gave her an edited version of the story since Wednesday last.

'So?...' was all she said.

'Well, there may be a bunch of evil-doers turning the city upside down for me.'

'And there may not.'

'There may not. However, I am on the run. And I don't want to collect fellow travellers if I can avoid it.'

'So you need to lie low.'

'Until I can work something out.'

'Then lie low here,' she said.

I considered the proposition for a moment or two. Linda supplied the rationalisation.

'You know this house. It's ideal. Out of the way, tiny road, cul de sac. And you can hide your not entirely un-recognisable motor car here too. I have a garage.'

'So have I.'

'Just the place. *Oh there it is. The man's back in town, clearly*. Let's face it Jack, the Healey is more conspicuous than you are.'

She was winning this hands down. I made one last rear guard effort.

'I do not want to put you in danger,' I said, emphasising every word.

'We're both grown-ups. Well, I'm a bit more grown up than you are. And you need help. Besides, where are you going to stay? Some motel on the A38?'

'This is just a little more serious than being grown up.'

'You're big and strong and tough and you'll look out for us both.'

'You don't need me, you need Jack Reacher.'

'Oh for fuck's sake, just come and stay here,' she bellowed down the phone.

Even the toughest blow hard should know when he's licked.

'Okay, okay. Thank you.'

She took a deep breath. 'Good. Straight here.'

'I have been summoned to talk with Harvey Butler,' I said.

'So call him from my place,' she said. 'He'll be at home watching *Points West* by the time you get back into Bristol. Anything else?'

'Ringing off now,' I said.

'Later,' she said and beat me to it.

I sat still, staring down at Jenson Button's face on the front cover of *Autosport*.

'I'm not certain this is a good idea Jens,' I said.

Chapter Ten

At 4.35, the TV monitor told me that westbound traffic was moving again.

I set out for Portishead. A bursting at the seams, old dockside town; now reinvented as a desirable dormitory settlement, complete with Waitrose and executive waterfront homes. The over-hyped centrepiece is Port Marine, newly fashioned out of the old harbour, and for some reason trying to pretend it's a Cornish fishing village.

Linda had moved into the best bit of old Portishead – the Woodhill area – three months earlier. I skirted the town centre and found Channel Bank. I drove up the hill and on to Woodlands Road, which runs east, precariously close to the Severn Estuary cliff tops. The entrance to Linda's property is about half way along the road, sharp left through a gateway. I turned into the small parking space in front of the two-storey 1930s art deco house, which from this point of view, always seems to be hanging over the cliff edge.

Linda's Golf was parked by the front door. She stepped out of the house, walked to the garage door and heaved it upwards. I drove into the garage.

'Welcome,' she said, as I climbed out of the Healey.

'Thank you,' I said.

She looked terrific. In lightweight, tan chinos and a cream silk shirt, not tucked in, the hem clinging neatly to her hips. The shirt was tailored to fit, the chinos were a bit tighter than chinos should be, but she wasn't making any mistakes. Linda doesn't have to work at being sexy. Dressed up or dressed down, she simply always is. She seems to function by instinct, in a languorous slow motion. Something we'd both acknowledged for years but, somehow, had managed to orbit around. Now there was no need to and we both knew it. But the next step in the relationship was crucial.

She lead the way into the house, from the tiny oak front door down half a dozen steps into a living room with a great view. 'Remember that?' she said.

Basically, all of the Bristol Channel. We stood side by side, looking through a twelve foot square window, at nothing but water below us. The weather was glorious now and standing close to the glass I could see to the left, as far downstream as the mouth of the estuary and to the right, upstream to the first of the Severn bridges.

'What do you think?'

'I think it looks great now. But what about

between the September equinox and mid April, when the wind is blowing force 8 and the channel is actually whipping up against the window?'

'I'll love it to bits.'

'Yes,' I said. 'I think I would too.'

Linda had chosen the furniture carefully, to fit the space. A made to order beechwood framed sofa and two armchairs, upholstered in fabric – a herringbone pattern in shades of cream. A low table, bookshelves and a small sideboard in matching light oak. The dining table sat under a casement window overlooking the garden at the side of the house, which sloped gently towards a stone wall bordering the edge of the cliff top.

Inland, there was a kitchen to the left of the front door, a walk-in larder next to it and above, a bathroom and two bedrooms, one of which replicated the sensational view below.

'Can you really afford to live here?' I asked.

'Just about,' Linda said. 'I'll be alright if I find a couple more clients and do less work for you.'

I did my best to look hurt.

She looked me up and down.

'Is this it?' she asked.

'What?'

'The complete Jack Shepherd? No suitcase and no change of clothes. If only I'd realised...'

‘I did leave Bristol in a hurry three days ago.’

‘Three days in the same clothes?’

‘Trousers, yes. This shirt is courtesy of Uncle Sid.’

‘I suppose he did his best... Oh God no... You haven’t been in the same underwear since?...’ She shuddered. ‘No don’t answer that. Sainsburys. Still open at this hour. Or there’s Tesco.’

I don’t buy my groceries at Tesco. Or anything else for that matter. I certainly can’t be persuaded to look upon Tesco as a fashion house. On the other hand I’m no denizen of the designer outlets – as my recent foray into Cabot Circus can attest to. I decided that Sainsburys it should be.

‘Get into the shower,’ Linda said and pointed along the hall. ‘I’ll sort out your wardrobe and I’ll be back in half an hour.’ She took a long look at my trousers. ‘They’ll have to do.’

She went downstairs, found her handbag and car keys, opened the front door, then yelled back up to me.

‘There’s a dressing gown hanging on the door in the spare bedroom.’

The front door closed.

I decided to phone Harvey before I did anything else. I found my mobile and called his. He wasn’t best pleased.

‘I’m off the clock,’ he said.

'You told me to call.'
'No. I said I wanted to see you. Face to face, in person, in my office.'
'Well that's the point, you see.'
There was a pause. I listened to the buzz on the line until Harvey came back to me.
'Let me guess,' he said. 'You are hiding from Francis Copley, whose current purpose is your apprehension and the subsequent application of brutal and insensate violence.'
'In a nutshell.'
'We have the ending to the life of Philip Soames as evidence of this work.'
'Unhappily.'
'Where are you?'
'Not far away.'
'Okay. I'll set up a meeting place and call you Monday morning. Stay out of trouble until then, if you can.'
He rang off. I got into the shower.
Ten minutes later, dry, pink and shiny, I found the dressing gown on the bedroom door. Actually, a monstrous, fluffy, white bathrobe. Not Linda's surely. For a moment I wondered who it was who last wore this. The secret huge man in her life. No slippers to match however. I put my socks on, immediately appreciated how silly I looked and took them off again. Barefoot, I padded downstairs to the living room.
Sunset, supper and wine, Linda had

promised. The premier, heady ingredient was developing outside the window. There was a yellow haze hanging over the Welsh coastline, which deepened into a pale orange as I watched. Sunset over Magor doesn't sound much, but there was a soft edged stripe of gold sliding towards me across the channel, widening as it travelled. As if it would keep on going until the light enveloped me, like the Richard Dreyfuss character in *Close Encounters*. I re-focussed on my reflection in the window, glowing orange. The room behind me seemed to be glowing too. I heard the front door open and seconds later Linda stepped into the picture. Or rather, she materialised into it. Altogether other-worldly.

'I promised you a sunset,' she said.

I turned back into the room. She held up a Waitrose carrier bag.

'Mission accomplished. Make yourself presentable, then come and help me with the stir fry. We're having pork.'

She handed me the bag and swayed off towards the kitchen. I adjourned to the bedroom and examined the purchases. Grey socks, blue socks, a choice of briefs or boxers and a couple of soft cotton denim shirts by a young designer who had made the *Observer* colour supplement a couple of weeks earlier. I eschewed the boxers, chose the blue socks and decided on the blue shirt with a signature design on the inside of the collar and the cuffs. I found a clothes brush and spent a couple of minutes attempting to make my trousers presentable. Satisfied that I had done all I could, I reported to the kitchen.

'That's better,' Linda said.

She dropped a handful of pork cubes into the wok on the hob. They hissed and sizzled. She picked up a wooden spatula and began to stir.

'So give me something to do,' I said.

'This is a double wok operation,' she said 'That one…' She nodded to a smaller wok sitting on a chopping board on the worktop in front of me, '…has peppers, carrots, broccoli and bean sprouts in it. Crush that clove of garlic and mix it in.'

I did. The pork fried on for a couple of minutes.

'Okay,' Linda said, 'Put the wok on the gas and stir away.'

We did synchronised stirring for another couple of minutes.

'Add the stir fry sauce,' she said.

I poured the sauce over the vegetables.

'Another minute or so,' she said.

The aromas were amazing – pork frying in olive oil, vegetables in stir fry sauce and a lingering smell of garlic.

'Going solo now,' Linda said. 'Let me have your wok.'

She poured the vegetables over the pork

cubes. The big wok sizzled again and steam hissed upwards into the cooker hood. She picked up a bowl of rice noodles and tipped them into the wok and handed me the spatula.'

'Keep going until I tell you to stop.'

I stirred for another minute or so. Linda took a couple of warmed plates out of the oven and counted down. Moments later, the stir fry pork, vegetables and noodles were dished up. Along with a bottle of white burgundy.

We sat at the dining table to eat.

'Wait,' Linda said, 'The big finish.'

She pressed a tiny rocker switch on the wall to the side of the window looking out into the garden. A row of small dado lights set along the base of the cliff top wall, glowed softly.

'Voila…'

Sunset, supper and wine.

Followed by coffee, conversation and music.

Linda held up a bunch of CDs.

'Duffy, Nora Jones or Alison Krause?' she asked. 'Or if you like, we can go back a bit. Bonnie Tyler, Bonnie Raitt...'

'Duffy,' I said. 'What have you got?'

She turned over one of the CDs and began reading the track list.

'*Stepping Stone, Mercy, Warwick Avenue…*'

I held up my hand. 'Okay. No contest.'

She put the CD in the player and joined

me on the sofa.

'You know, you're really too old for Duffy,' she said, as we listened to the title track.

I stared at her.

'Mid 40s...' She shook her head sadly.

'Just four years older than you.'

'Its okay for old broads,' she said. 'But not for old men.'

'You mean, people will point me out in the street? I'll be named and shamed, like some sort of mid-life crisis offender? *You do realise that he's a big fan of Duffy don't you?*'

'It's a risk, let's not deny it,' she said.

'I'm not ashamed of my musical taste. I acknowledge I never embraced Irish folk, punk, or gangsta rap. But I'm not just an ageing rocker. I got heavily into 2-step garage.'

It was her turn to stare.

'What?'

'2-step,' I said, 'is the generic name for all kinds of irregular rhythms that cross the beat and don't conform to garage's traditional four on the floor pulse.'

I had her complete and undivided attention.

'A typical 2-step drum pattern, features a kick on the first and third beats of the bar and a shuffled rhythm, creating a lurching 'falter-funk' feel... Do you want me to go on?'

'Oh absolutely.'

'Resulting in a beat distinctly different from that present in hardcore house or techno.'

I beamed at her.

'Where did you pick that up?' she asked.

'Studied it,' I said

'Bollocks.'

'Abuse is no basis for reasoned argument.'

'You got that stuff from the net.'

'Er... If pressed...'

'Yes, but why?'

She sat back, tilted her head and looked at me suspiciously.

'What else are you getting from the world wide web that I don't know about? I admit I'm genuinely impressed that you remembered all that 2-step stuff, but why the hell go there in the first place?'

'Mentioned in a book I was reading. It was a slow day, so I looked it up.'

'And you've immersed yourself in 2-step ever since.'

'Not immersed no. But I have listened to Oris Jay and Woody.'

'I see...'

'And you should know that 2-step made it into the mainstream in 2000, when Artful Dodger Featuring David Craig, got to number two in the charts with *Re-wind*. Although that was actually a crossover. 2-step fused with R & B...'

That was as much as I was going to get away with. She waved her hands, like she was swatting wasps away from her face.

'Enough, enough!! A girl invites the man in her life to supper and in return, he takes her on a tour of obscure musical sub-genres.'

'Am I?'

She looked at me.

'What?'

'The man in your life.'

There was a long silence. Her eyes never left mine.

'Is this the time to confess?' she asked.

'I will if you will,' I said.

'Okay...' She took a deep breath. 'There is no other.'

She waited for me to respond.

'We've shared a lot in the past twelve months,' I said.

'You rescued me from the clutches of the city crime boss,' she said. 'Just a small thing I know but–'

'And you picked me up when I was down. You helped me make sense of the nonsense. I stopped feeling sorry for myself and I focussed. We are close.'

'So does that mean?...'

She didn't complete the sentence.

'I don't know,' I said. 'Maybe it does.'

'So, what's the worst that can happen? It doesn't work.'

'No the worst that can happen, is it does work and then it doesn't.'

She took a beat.

'Okay,' she said. 'One step at a time. Let's see how this works.'

She eased a couple of feet towards me, swung her right leg over my knees and sat straddling my lap. She took hold of my face in both hands, pressed my neck gently back against the sofa cushions and leaned into me. She kissed me. I opened my mouth and her tongue found mine. And it all started to work. I put my arms round her waist and held on. It was a long time before we started breathing again.

Linda sat back. 'Step one,' she said. 'And that seemed to work.'

'How many steps are there to this?'

'I can't imagine.'

'Maybe we'll know when we get there,' I suggested.

'Yes,' Linda said. 'So let's not rush.'

She looked at me for a long, long time. I manage to hold her gaze. Then she straightened up. Raised her arms and linked her hands behind her head. Which meant that all the crucial bits moved in that languorous slow motion thing that she does. Her breasts strained against the silk shirt as I watched, transfixed.

'I want to enjoy getting there,' she said.

I couldn't manage to say anything. She grinned at me.

'Shall I get up now?'

'I think you'd better.'

'We've got the rest of the weekend,' she said and swung to her feet. 'I'm going to clear up.'

I got to my feet as well. She held up her right hand.

'It's just a matter of filling the dishwasher. There is brandy in the sideboard. Help yourself.'

The rest of the evening passed in a fusion of music, conversation and wine. Just before midnight, I followed Linda upstairs. Escorted her to her bedroom door. I opened the door. She stepped in front of me, then turned and leaned back against the door frame. Graceful, relaxed and sexy.

'I think this next bit should be step two,' she said. 'And maybe not now, tonight. If that's alright with you.'

I told her it would be.

'Goodnight then,' she said.

She straightened up and kissed me. Not like earlier. Not a 'here we go into the relationship' kiss, but a 'this is going to be special, give it time' kiss.

She backed into her bedroom and closed the door.

I looked down at the pattern on the carpet for while. Then followed it to the spare bedroom.

I slept like a man without a care in the world.

Chapter Eleven

The bedside clock read 9.05 when I woke up, rolled over and looked at it. There was something strange about the face. It was different. Then I realised where I was.

Linda, dressed in light grey track suit trousers and white tee shirt, was sitting in the living room, reading *The Guardian* Saturday review section. There was a cafetière of coffee and a plate of croissants on the dining table.

'Good morning,' she said. 'Did you sleep well?'

'Careless and dream free.'

'That's good.'

She stood up, dropped the newspaper onto the sofa, moved into my arms and kissed me. Her hips did a 'meet the day' wiggle, then she towed me across to the table. I sat down. She picked up the cafetière and poured me a cup of coffee. I reached for a croissant.

'How long have you been up?'

'Up and out. An hour or so. It's a lovely day.'

'So what do you usually do on such a lovely day?'

My mobile rang from somewhere. I tried to locate the source of the sound.

Linda pointed across the room.
'On the window sill,' she said.
I picked up the phone. Adam's home number was printed in the window. Chrissie was on the line.
'Good morning,' I said.
'Morning Dad. Where are you?'
I looked out of the huge window. The sun was bouncing sky blue light down on to the channel. The surface of the water sparkled.
'Looking at a great view,' I said.
'Where?' she persisted.
'Portishead.'
'What are you doing in Portishead?'
'I just told you, looking at–'
'Don't be obtuse Dad.'
'As in blunt, or as in slow of perception.'
'As in dodging the question.' There was a pause, then she said, 'Oh my God. You're at Linda's.'
It was my turn to fall silent. She gave me a few seconds then she went on.
'Is that where you are?'
'Yes. That's where I am.'
'Since yesterday?'
Across the room, Linda was waving at me. I held the phone behind my back and mouthed 'what?' She pointed at the phone, then opened her palms and wiggled her wrists, like a conjuror warming up for a magic trick. I decided to take no notice. I put the phone back to my ear.

'Linda is offering me sanctuary.'

Chrissie refrained from the proverbial ironic reply. I took the opportunity to expand.

'I am lying low,' I said. 'There are some people watching my house.'

Chrissie took that seriously enough to stop imagining what Linda and I might be engaging in.

'What people?'

'I don't know.'

'Dangerous people?'

'I fear.'

'Oh for Christ's sake…'

She lapsed into silence. Working out all the implications. So I offered a summary of the situation.

'I have been hired to find someone,' I said. 'Other people are looking for her as well. They have now discovered I am on the case and consequently, they're trying to find me too. The bonus is, these people don't know what I look like. So ... as long as I don't do any recognisably Jack Shepherd things in public – like hang around at home or drive my car to work – I should be safe and relatively free to go about my business.'

Chrissie listened to that piece of nonsense with more generosity than it deserved. In times past, she would have run out of patience halfway through and given me a bollocking. But now she tends to process my understatements pragmatically. She doesn't approve of what I do, but she is trying to understand why I do it. In return, I am trying to share stuff with her in the way I shared with Emily. Part of Emily's legacy to us was an expectation that we would be honest with each other. Most of the time we manage to achieve this. But Chrissie is no pushover and she doesn't smile sweetly and wave me on regardless.

'And how long will this state of affairs persist?' she asked.

'To be truthful, I don't know. My client paid me for a week's work. I owe her another forty-eight hours. If I don't find her I'll get help from Harvey Butler. He's kind of in the loop. And at that point, this requirement to sneak around should go away.'

'Okay,' she said. 'I'll believe that, for now.' Then abruptly, she changed the subject. 'Come to lunch.'

'May I invite my host?'

'Of course. Put her on.'

I held out the mobile to Linda.

'Chrissie wants to talk to you.'

Linda put the phone to her ear and said 'hello' to Chrissie. She listened for a moment or two, smiled and said 'thank you' Then listened some more, nodded, as if in silent agreement to something, closed the call and handed the phone back to me.

'Lunch at 1 o'clock,' she said

'Is that okay with you?'

'Yes of course.'

'What else did Chrissie have to say?'

She grinned at me. 'Girl talk. Privileged information.'

A lazy breakfast segued into a couple of hours with *The Guardian* – this punctuated by intermittent cries of scorn, frustration and finally rage, as the paper chronicled the story of yet another government minister outlining the latest coalition 'big idea' and another desperate opposition spokesperson attempting to ridicule the misbegotten enterprise. Finally, Linda threw the news section across the room.

'It's the same bloody litany of misery every weekend,' she said.

'You have to read the *Mail* to feel secure in the gated middle class estate,' I said. 'Do you really want to do that?'

She got to her feet.

'I'm changing for lunch.'

I had nothing to change into, so I skimmed the colour supplement while Linda swopped the track suit trousers for tight blue jeans and added a light weight denim jacket to the tee shirt. I stared in admiration. She acknowledged the attention, stepped into a pair of comparatively low heels and flowed towards the front door. I followed, eyes glued to her backside.

Linda unlocked the Golf and eased herself

in behind the steering wheel. I tried to relax in the front passenger seat. But as soon as we got into traffic I became restless. After a few minutes she got fed up with me.

'Is it my driving?' she asked.

'No,' I said. 'I just want to be sure we're not being followed.'

At 12.45, we drove into Clevedon and parked by the Marine Lake. No one swung into the car park behind us. I got out of the Golf and sauntered on to the promenade, attracting no attention whatsoever. From where I stood, I could see Chrissie's house up on Dial Hill. I looked around. Apparently, there was no one remotely interested in me down here. I sauntered back to the Golf.

We navigated our way along Beach Road, past the entrance to the pier and up to Castle Vale. Linda drove past Chrissie's house, with me searching doorways and parked cars for men with broken noses and wide shoulders. She turned the corner into Vale Drive, stopped and parked under a tree. No one materialised from any direction. I got out of the Golf and walked to the end of the street, crossed over Hill Terrace, sat down on a stone bench and looked out to sea. I sat alone and unmolested for three or four minutes. That was enough rope surely. I got to my feet and walked back to Linda, who had climbed out of the car. She pointed the key fob at the at the driver's door. The car bleeped, the headlights flashed and the doors locked. She looked at me across the car roof.

'Well? Satisfied?'

'Yes.'

Together we walked back to Chrissie's house. No car cruised up alongside us, no one stepped out from a gateway. This was the most peaceful street in town.

Until we rang the doorbell.

Sam bellowed a greeting from inside the hall. Linda looked at me. I realised I hadn't told her about the dog.

'That's Sam,' I said.

'Don't worry, I like dogs.'

Adam swung the front door open and Sam launched himself into the garden. He saw me and leapt across the space between us. We did a reprise of our encounter earlier in the week. I back pedalled onto the lawn.

I heard Adam shout, 'Sam! Come here Sam!!'

But Sam was having a great time and oblivious to all exhortation. The wrestling match ended with me grabbing his choke chain and hauling him into a sitting position in front of me.

'Now stay,' I ordered.

He stayed. Mouth open, tongue hanging out. He snorted and shook his head. His ears flapped and his dog tags jingled.

'Hello Sam,' Linda said.

The dog turned his head and looked at

her, for a moment contemplating another round of excitement. Adam beat him to it.

'Sam. Come here.'

Without demur, Sam got to his feet, executed a silky 180 and trotted back to the house.

'In you go,' Adam said.

I joined Linda by the door. Adam smiled at us.

'Now that's over...' he said, 'Welcome.'

The roast beef was terrific. And after lunch we went for a walk. All five of us. Linda borrowed a pair of trainers from Chrissie.

On the sea front, the pier was bustling with visitors, making the most of the last week of the summer holidays. The tide was high, leaving little room on the beach for buckets and spades and digging in rock pools, but there was no shortage of kids making the best of it. We walked round the beach, past the re-painted, cast iron Victorian band stand and on to Marine Lake.

Poet's Walk – named after Coleridge, Wordsworth and Southey – climbs the hillside at the west end of the lake and runs southwest along the cliff tops above the Bristol Channel. It ends by looping round the tiny, ancient church of Saint Andrew and its stunningly set graveyard with widescreen views over the water. If you could choose your last resting place, then surely this would be it.

The channel sparkled silver grey in the sunshine. We stood high on the hill above the church. Sam mooched about on doggie business, sniffing the ground and following tracks; every now and again looking back over his shoulder, to ensure that all of us were still together.

'He likes it up here,' Chrissie said.

'Not difficult to see why,' I said.

Sam found a stick. He brought it to Adam, put it down on the grass in front of him and looked up, as if butter wouldn't melt. Adam picked up the stick and threw it. Sam hared after the stick and disappeared over the brow of the hill. Adam followed. Linda picked up her cue and chased after Adam.

Chrissie hooked her left arm into my right, leaned her head against my shoulder and looked out at the horizon.

'How are things with you and Linda?' she asked

'What "things"?'

I looked down at the top of her head. I shook my shoulder and her head bounced. She straightened up and looked at me. I repeated the question. She looked at me, drenched in amazement.

'You know exactly what I mean,' she replied. 'What is the situation?'

'Is that really the sort of question a daughter should ask her father?'

‘Then there is something going on.’
‘There is nothing going on.’
‘Of course there is,’ Chrissie said.

She looked at me fiercely, daring me to deny it. So I gave her my best ‘I have no intention of dignifying this interrogation with an answer’ stare. It wasn’t the response of a man confident in the unassailability of his position. And Chrissie knew it.

‘I’m not asking for chapter and verse,’ she persisted. ‘I’d simply like to know the er ... current situation.’

‘When I know what is, you’ll be the first I’ll call.’

She blew out her cheeks in exasperation, freed her arm and thumped my shoulder with it.

‘Remember,’ she said. ‘We agreed that you would share stuff with me. Like you did with Mum.’

‘I never shared anything like this with your mother.’

She stepped back and gathered herself for a change of tack. She gave me the beautiful, open look that was pure Emily. And now she was serious.

‘It’s taken a lot of harsh words, months of mending and hard work to get to now... So talk to me and I’ll listen. If not about Linda, about the case.’

I took some time working out what to say. Chrissie waited. I offered the best explanation I could.

'Chrissie... I've always believed I am sensible enough to know when to keep my own counsel, when to seek advice and when to ask for help. And this sharing thing has to have substance. Your mother and I, always talked when there was something to talk about. Seldom, when there was nothing worth bringing to the table – unless I needed another take on some half-arsed theory I was working on. As to Linda and I, right now, what's going on is...'

I tailed into silence. Chrissie appeared not to be listening. Suddenly she sighed.

'We missed a whole chunk of good stuff, didn't we? You and me. Caught up in missions of our own.'

I nodded. She talked on.

'The sulking and the silences. The arguments. The rows, the fight ... and then the storming out. The...' she searched for the right word... 'severance. Mum was hurt. Much more than she ever let us know.'

'She knew stuff would mend. And it did.'

'Thankfully. But too late. There should have been more time for the three of us. Not just eight months. I mean, how long is that?'

'We did the best we could,' I said.

'I know,' she said 'But with cancer, the best, however good, is never good enough. Is it?'

We stood in silence. Close. Absorbed by

the moment.

Sam trundled back across the hilltop, followed by Linda and Adam. He reached us, stood at our feet and stared up at us.

'I think he wants to go home,' Chrissie said.

Linda drove us back to Portishead, late afternoon. We climbed out of the Golf in front of her house.

'How about a drink?' she asked. 'I don't mean here. You remember the old Royal Hotel at the end of the road?'

'It's still in business?'

'Yes.'

We walked to the pub.

The Royal did a roaring trade during the days when the steamers ran a regular service across the channel from Portishead to Barry. Standing just back from the dockside, the pub served food and drink to hundreds of passengers a day, travelling to and from south Wales. The *Balmoral* and the *Waverley* have been refurbished and restored to their late Edwardian glory. And they still visit the channel ports, on both sides, even travelling out to Lundy. But not to the old regular timetable, and no longer in and out of Portishead.

Years and changes notwithstanding, the Royal is still there, at the dockside end of Woodlands Road. With a new bunch of regulars from the desirable end of Portishead. No longer hosting the clamour of voices and accents, the agglomeration of day trippers, brothers and sisters, uncles, aunties, in-laws and even business people, who decided they had time to cross the water and could ignore the Severn bridge and the tolls. The Royal has had a coat of paint since I was last there twenty years ago and the inside has been re-modelled in 21st century Harvester style. The bar is highly polished faux light oak and the drinks on offer are different. A selection of beers, light years away from Whitbread Tankard and Courage Best. Belgian lager, new world wines, alcopops, bottled cocktails and designer water.

I like Belgian beer and Linda found a Californian chardonnay that was okay. We sat by a window overlooking the water. The view was great, but the old ambience and the even older landlord, were long gone. Mercifully, the place was quiet – too early for the executive binge drinkers – and the old steamer pictures and histories were still on the walls.

We watched from the lounge as the horizon turned yellow, then orange, then magenta. We finished our drinks and by the time we stepped outside, the world was moonlit. The sky was cloudless, pocked with stars – pin points of sharp, bright light. We walked home, hand in hand, for all the world like new lovers.

'Thank you for the day,' Linda said.

Outside her front door she said, 'Don't switch any lights on when you get into the house.'

I looked around me. 'Are we hiding from someone?'

'Indulge me...'

We stepped into the living room and came face to face with what looked like an old Hollywood movie plate shot. Framed by the picture window, moonlight bounced off the surface of the channel and lit up the world like it was day. The water was luminous. In the background, lights dotted the Wales coastline like manmade star clusters. We stood, side by side, mesmerised.

'Stunning,' Linda breathed. 'Happens every full moon, as long as the clouds are high.'

There are moments absolutely impossible to ignore. And this was one of them. Linda took the lead.

'Step two,' she said. 'If that's alright with you?'

I didn't answer the question. I couldn't. Linda decided that meant yes. She lifted the tee shirt over her head and dropped it onto the floor, shook her hair back into place, reached out and began to unfasten the buttons on my shirt. She pulled the shirt out of my trousers reached around my back and drew me into an embrace. I responded and pressed myself against her. She rotated her hips gently. The bedroom was miles away and we were past the point of no return. We made love on the floor, in front of the huge picture window, lit by moonlight.

After it was all over, Linda was the first to speak.

'I love you. You know that,' she said.

I turned to look at her.

'Does that spoil things?' she asked.

'No,' I said.

'I was so afraid that ... when we did this, it wasn't going to work. And I want it to.'

'So do I.'

And then suddenly it was okay. Everything. She sat up and faced me, her back to the window, silhouetted against the moonlight.

'Then ... I want us to be ... well us,' she said. 'But together. I want to be part of you and what you do.'

'Okay.'

'I've known you a long time, Jack. Sharing, isn't something you're good at.'

'You've been talking to Chrissie.'

That was a pretty disdainful remark. But Linda surfed it with ease, as if she hadn't expected anything other than such a crass evasion. It behoved me to apologise.

'I'm sorry,' I said. 'And it's true. I'm not

good at sharing.'

She looked at me for a long time.

'This isn't a contest,' she said finally. 'And you're not under siege.'

'I know. A question of old habits I guess. Born out of doing a job in which I spend long periods keeping secrets.'

'Did you keep secrets from Emily?' she asked, then suddenly looked startled. 'Sorry, sorry. My turn to apologise. That was none of my business.'

'No, I'll answer,' I said. 'I tried not to. I shared all the good things and some of the problems, but not always the details. But I never dissembled. At least, not knowingly.'

'Can it be like that with us?'

'I think so. Come back here, I can't see your face.'

'That's just as well, because I'm going to cry. And it's not a good look. Some people cry beautifully, but I don't.'

'Cry away,' I said. 'I don't care. Just come here and do it next to me.'

She did. And we lay side by side. Outside, the moonlight just went on and on.

Chapter Twelve

I woke the following morning in yet another bed. My fourth of the week. Alone. Linda wasn't there. Up and out again apparently. So I had time to rationalise.

I made some coffee and sat down in the living room to think. I swiftly came to the conclusion that there was, after all, no point in keeping a low profile. Everybody involved in this case was hiding from everybody else. Deborah was hiding from Grant and Copley, probably two Serbs, and the person she had hired to find her. I was hiding from Grant and Copley and probably two Serbs. Copley was somewhere, nursing his broken face and hiding from me and the police and, because he was on a losing streak, probably two Serbs. The one plus, was that Grant was effectively on remand, and presumably, as soon as he was well enough to be moved, on his way to the medical wing of Horfield Prison.

So... We could all stay where we were and sit tight. But to what end? None of us was going to make any progress that way. We might as well all agree to meet and slug it out.

I resolved to go back home and back to

work and advertise that I was back in business.

Linda came back from the Channel Bank Deli with a selection of Danish pastries and pain au chocolat.

'We're going out after breakfast,' she said.

'Okay.'

'And ... I know we have obsessed about you keeping your head down, but I've been thinking about it.'

'So have I,' I said and offered her my rationalisation.

'That's substantially how I looked at it,' Linda said.

I poured us both some coffee.

'How are you on the countryside?' she asked

'Terrific on a sunny day. Why?'

'A client has given me two tickets to the Great Western Show.'

'That's more than mere countryside,' I protested. 'It's farmers and prize bulls and tractors and probably morris dancing.'

'Members tickets,' she said. 'Access all areas, including the members bar and restaurant.'

I began to waver.

'And a free five course lunch. Which I am assured is very good indeed.'

Linda stood up and posed provocatively.

'I'm prepared to take off my clothes, if it helps.'

It was a couple of hours before we left the house.

The showground is in Wraxall Vale, near Tyntesfield House. We were waved into the Members Car Park by a Members Steward and directed to the Members Hospitality Area. We booked a seat for lunch at 1 o'clock and sought out Linda's client, Heather. She was doing duty in the Information Centre, which sat between the First Aid Station and the RSPCA display tent.

'You will have to excuse me,' Heather said, 'but there's a bit of a crisis. A toddler has wandered off, somewhere behind the small show ring, and we are organising a search party.'

'Can we help?' Linda asked.

'Help. Yes, yes of course, indeed you can, thank you so much.'

Heather spread a map of the showground in front of us.

'Can you go and have a look in area F?' She pointed to the map. 'The little girl was last seen to the east of there. She's likely to be off the beaten track. She would have been found by now if she was wandering around alone in a busy area. She's four years old. Her name's Elaine.'

Heather picked up a couple of walkie-talkies and pressed the squawk button on each. She demonstrated one of them.

'That's the talk button. That's the volume control.'

She handed them over to us.

'How long has she been missing?' I asked.

'About fifteen minutes.'

Area F was full of kids' rides and roundabouts. We stood in front of the Teacups and consulted the map. Then Linda looked up and beyond the carousel.

'There seems to be a double row of trailers back there. Generators, exhibitors' trucks, that kind of thing. The sort of place where a four year old could get lost, don't you think?'

It was worth a try. We took the Teacups as a central reference point, with me working to the right of them and Linda to the left. I found Elaine three minutes later.

She was standing in the middle of a quadrangle of grass, bordered by trailers and motor homes. She was holding a rag doll and a toffee apple.

She was staring at a huge dog. Some sort of Rottweiler Mastiff cross, tethered to a chrome trailer hitch and asleep on the grass.

I was about twelve feet behind her when she heard me approaching. She turned round and smiled. I nodded at her, trying to stay quiet.

'Big doggie,' she said.

She swung back and looked at him.

The walkie-talkie crackled into life. Linda's voice buzzed out.

'Jack? Nothing this side of the Teacups. I'm working my way–'

I switched off. But too late.

The dog woke up, lifted his head and registered our presence. He was sleepy and he began with a yawn. He rolled onto his belly. His lips slid back across his teeth and the yawn morphed into a snarl. He straightened his back legs and his hind quarters rose up into the air.

The rope tether was longer than the distance between the dog and the girl. I put the walkie-talkie down on the grass and called to her softly.

'Elaine... Can you step back towards me?'

She didn't seem to hear.

The dog transferred his weight forwards and heaved himself upright. He shook his head, like a swimmer with his ears full of water. His muzzle oscillated and sprayed spittle. Then he barked and launched himself at Elaine.

I was closer to her than he was and, mercifully, Elaine's knee jerk reaction was to step backwards. I swept her into my arms and turned away as the dog's jaws opened and then closed on the tail of my jacket. I strained forwards, the dog pulled backwards and ripped a mouthful of jacket away. The onward force pitched Elaine and I forwards onto the grass. I landed on top of her. She shouted in pain and started to cry.

The dog spat out the chunk of jacket and hurled himself at us again. I barrel rolled us away from him a split-second before he reached the end of his tether. He was in mid air as the rope straightened like a steel rod. His neck jerked backwards, his bark turned into a scream then a violent choke. He crashed to the ground and his head bounced a couple of times.

I sat up, hanging on to Elaine, who was crying fit to bust. She was still clinging on to her doll, the toffee apple had disappeared. She was bleeding from the side of her mouth. She had obviously bitten her lip when I landed on top of her. There was a mud stain stretching across her right cheek from her bleeding lip to her ear. But otherwise she was okay.

I held her close. She panicked and tried to squeeze out of my grasp. There was nothing I could do but hold her tighter. I got to my feet, my arms wrapped around her and looked for the walkie-talkie. I located it, freed my right arm, picked the handset up and switched it on.

'Linda. This is Jack.'

Elaine was still crying and Linda could hear her.

'Is that her? Is everything all right?'

'Fine. Meet me at the Teacups.'

Which was also fine, in principle. But I couldn't walk out from behind a row of trailers, in a torn jacket with a squirming, bawling four year old in my arms. God knows what the reaction would be. So I sat back down on the grass, relaxed my grip a little and gave Elaine some room to squirm. She responded to the release of pressure and her panic began to subside.

Five or six yards in front of us the dog lay still. Elaine's attention was drawn to it and as she became interested, the crying diminished into a burble and finally into hiccups.

The walkie-talkie burst into life again.

'Jack. I'm at the Teacups. Where are you?'

'Doesn't matter, we're alright. Sitting on the grass, waiting for Elaine to calm down. Call Heather. Get Elaine's mother and a First Aider to the Teacups. Don't worry, the girl's okay. A couple of grazes that's all. We'll be with you in a few minutes.'

We got to our feet.

'We are going to find your Mum,' I said. 'Do you want me to carry you?'

Elaine nodded. 'Yes,' she said. Then added, 'Please.'

I picked her up. Sitting in my arms, she swung round and looked back at the dog.

'Is the doggie alright?' she asked.

'We'll see later,' I said. 'Come on.'

The St. John's Ambulance man said that Elaine was none the worse for her adventure. Elaine's mother thanked me for what I had done. Linda said I looked terrific with a chunk missing from the tail of my jacket. I used another £69.95 of Francis Copley's money to buy myself a new one – a dark green lightweight fleece.

I talked for a while with Julia, the Inspector doing duty in the RSPCA tent.

She agreed to do the paperwork necessary to get an initial investigation into the incident with the dog. I decided to go back to the trailer.

There was a man sitting in a chair on the veranda outside the trailer door. He levered himself upright as I approached. He was wearing a shiny black suit. The jacket was tight around his weightlifter shoulders and tapered to his hips. His head was shaved. He was big and ugly and he looked bored. Part of his job description however, was to be polite – at least on first acquaintance.

'Can I do something for you?' he asked.

His lips rolled back and a kind of grim, mini smile tried to grow. He looked like he flossed with a tyre lever.

'Is this your trailer?'

'No.'

'Do you have a dog?'

'No.'

'Is the owner in?'

'Yes.'

'Do you think I can talk to him?'

'I'll ask.'

Without taking his eyes off me, Shoulders stepped back a couple of paces, reached for the trailer door handle, turned it and pulled the door ajar. He called inside.

'Mr S. We have a visitor.'

There were a few seconds of anticipation, before Lloyd Starratt pushed the door open and stepped onto the veranda. He was mad as hell about something and when he saw me, his mood didn't improve.

'What do you fucking want?' he demanded.

'Where's the dog?'

'What fucking dog?'

'The dog that was tied to the trailer hitch half an hour ago.'

'There is no dog.'

'Obviously not now,' I said. 'But there was before.'

'Fuck off,' Starratt said and went back into the trailer. Shoulders stepped down from the veranda and stood full square in front of me.

'You heard what Mr S said.'

Clearly. And I couldn't misread the vibe coming from Shoulders, silently reinforcing the message.

I said 'goodbye' as politely as I could. Shoulders nodded his thanks. I turned around and walked away from him.

Back at the RSPCA tent I told Julia about Starratt.

'Doesn't surprise me,' she said. 'We have

investigated two incidents in the past eighteen months in which he was involved. Perhaps this time…'

'The dog wasn't there when I went back. It may be dead. I think its neck was broken.'

'So... He will just get rid of the body and we won't have any evidence to go on.'

'Isn't there a doggie DNA test? There might be some spit on what's left of my jacket.'

'There is a kind of DNA test. But it's basically to determine what breed, or mixed breed, a dog is. It doesn't get much more forensic than that. We might get some sort of classification from the spit on your jacket, but not a great deal more. Anyway, without the dog or Starratt's co-operation, we'd get nowhere.'

I took that in. She handed me a business card.

'Let's keep in touch anyway,' she said. 'You never know…'

Linda and I adjourned to the Members Restaurant for lunch.

The soup wasn't great but the other four courses more than made up for the starter. The rioja was good too. All in all, just reward for our efforts earlier in the day. I managed to avoid the morris dancing, although I was introduced to Lucifer, a Highland bull judged the 'Best In Show', who did his lap of honour around the show ring to thunderous applause.

'What a magnificent beast,' Linda said.

'This is his third win in a row,' Heather whispered with some reverence. 'He's worth four thousand five hundred guineas.'

Linda spent a little less than that. She bought a Mexican chiminea – a clay, tear drop shaped construction on short legs, with a fireplace in the base and a chimney like an upside down funnel.

I stared at it.

'For autumn evenings in the garden,' she said.

We got it into the back of the Golf and left the showground at half four.

'It's been a good day,' Linda said. 'A great lunch, I've bought something for the garden, we have marvelled at Lucifer and you have been heroic.'

That was an issue. Heroic or otherwise, my second encounter with Lloyd Starratt within the space of six days was bothering me. I would hope to enjoy a long life without ever coming into contact with him or his brother. It might be argued that the nature of my work makes such rendezvous inevitable. Not so. I never meet scum like the Starratts by coincidence. And certainly not in the course of a Sunday afternoon in the country.

Linda must have noticed me frowning.

'Something bothering you?' she asked. 'Jack...'

I realised she was talking to me.

'Sorry.'

'Well?...'

'What?'

'I asked if something was bothering you.'

'Kind of,' I said. 'I've had a busy week. One of the most eccentric of my career. With a cast featuring a trans-gender client, a dead psychiatrist, two London enforcers, the Starratt brothers and a couple of unknown Serbs.'

She looked across the car at me.

'They are not all connected surely?'

'Everything's connected. Nothing happens out of the blue.'

'I don't believe that.'

'There's a whole bunch of stuff swirling around out there. Most of it passes unnoticed. It's just a question of emphasis.'

Linda was still looking at me.

'Eyes on the road please.'

She looked ahead again.

'So explain,' she said.

'When something you've never really thought about happens to you,' I said, 'you immediately recognise that it's also happening to other people. Hundreds of them. Your senses about whatever it is, sharpen up and you see the event differently. You fall down and break your arm and then you see a whole bunch of other people with their arms in slings, wandering round the shopping mall. That's not co-incidental. You're not suddenly drawn to people with broken arms. Simply alerted to them, because you have the experience in common. I wouldn't have gone to see Auntie Joyce and Uncle Sid three days ago, if I hadn't discovered my client's parents live in Suffolk. I wouldn't have met Lloyd Starratt's dog today, if we hadn't gone to the show.'

'No mystery there surely.'

'That's the point. This stuff happens. In sequence. And in context. And therefore, it's not random. My client, the Starratts, Grant and Copley, the Serbs and the death of Philip Soames are all elements in one scenario. All part of the same "whodunit".'

Linda changed down a couple of gears, turned right and headed along the Gordano road. We crossed the M5 and she pointed the Golf in the direction of Portishead. Then she spoke again.

'So...' she said, 'We would not have ended up screwing on my living room floor, if you had not agreed to work for Deborah six days ago?'

I looked at her. What could I do but stick to the premise?

'Well ... yes,' I said. 'But we would, I hope, have done something similar at some other time soon.' I dug the hole deeper. 'As the result of another series of circumstances.'

She looked at me.

'How romantic is that?'

'It's not un-romantic,' I suggested.

Linda stared ahead again, now concentrating on the traffic approaching the centre of town.

'Look at it this way,' I said. 'Deborah brought us together.'

She didn't say anything.

'Does it matter how it happened?' I asked. 'It did. And it was terrific. Wasn't it?'

'Yes. Of course it was. I just didn't expect such a ... rationalisation.'

'To be fair,' I said, 'I didn't bring it up. You did.'

'Oh and that's really helping too,' she yelled at me.

The final three minutes of the journey passed in silence. We climbed out of the Golf. She slammed the driver's door and stared at me across the car roof.

'Sorry for shouting at you,' she said and led the way into the house.

Inside the living room we faced each other.

'I should go home,' I said.

Linda shrugged.

'If you wish.'

'Tomorrow's Monday. God knows what the week has in store. I have a list of stuff to do. I need a change of clothes…'

'Sure,' she said. 'Yes, right.'

'Linda...'

She held up her hands, palms outwards

'Jack, it's been good. I enjoyed the weekend. We have plenty of time to work on this.'

I found my car keys. Linda opened the garage. I kissed her and got into the Healey. The engine fired after a couple of revolutions and I eased the car out on to Woodlands Road.

I was home twenty-five minutes later.

Chapter Thirteen

Monday morning. 9.15.

The duty PC on the gate at Trinity Road Police Station let me in without a murmur.

'Please park to the right sir,' he said. 'I'll call reception.'

The duty desk Sergeant smiled a welcome.

'You are expected in CID, Mr Shepherd.' He pointed across the lobby. 'Take the lift. DS Hood will meet you on the third floor.'

He did. I stepped out of the lift, almost into his arms.

'Morning Jack,' he said.

The politest bunch of coppers you could wish to meet. But they were just the warm up act. Harvey Butler was sitting in his office at the end of the CID room. He was the star turn and considerably less affable.

'Ready to co-operate, are you?'

'Since when was it my practice to be difficult?'

George Hood grinned and asked me if I would like some coffee. I looked at him with suspicion.

'It's not from the machine in the corridor,' he said. 'We have a state of the art De'Longhi

Dulce Gusto. Straight white?'

'Please,' I said.

'I'll get DC Shackleton on the case.'

He left Harvey's office.

'Coppers drinking designer coffee,' I said.

'DC Shackleton has an account at John Lewis,' Harvey said by way of explanation.

Not entirely explicit, but I assumed DC Shackleton had bought the coffee maker and presented it to the office.

Harvey leaned back in his chair and motioned me to one of the chairs in front of his desk.

'Sit down,' he said. 'I take it, you've decided to come out of hiding.'

'I reasoned that staying out of circulation was counter-productive.'

'You mean you need help.'

He stared at me and raised his eyebrows.

I live in the expectation that one day I will get the jump on Harvey, but so far, in the nineteen years I have known him, he had always proved to be the patient, intuitive, detective his rank and reputation merits. I have often been less than truthful with him, I have ignored him, disobeyed him and on occasions come dangerously close to breaking the law, but in the end, I have never been able to out-manoeuvre him. He is quite simply, the cleverest copper I know.

'I have a list of phone numbers I would like you to check for me,' I said.

'Being, as we are, at your personal beck and call,' he said, without a trace of irony.

I conceded the only way was to be simple and straightforward.

'I should tell you about Francis Copley,' I said.

'Indeed you should.'

I took a beat. Harvey nodded in encouragement.

'Copley found me. I tried to lose him. Failed to do so. He caught up with me. There was a confrontation. I relieved him of his wallet and his mobile phone.'

'You mean you stole them?'

'Yes.'

I fished Copley's wallet out of a jacket pocket and passed it across the desk. Harvey looked at it, then back at me.

'Where is the mobile?'

'In a river in Suffolk. I took out the sim card and threw the phone away.'

'So we can get Copley's contacts from the sim card?'

'I've already done that.'

Harvey held out his hand. I gave him Uncle Sid's A4 sheet with the list on it. He stared at me.

'The sim card?'

'Can I have your agreement that you will trace the numbers for me?'

He looked at the paper and read the list of names.

'Who are these two characters, Dukik and Tugman?'

I corrected his pronunciation. 'Dujic and Tudjman. Probably Serbs.'

'And what do they have to do with this?'

'I've no idea.'

Harvey sighed. I went on.

'Cross my heart and hope to die. Two names in Copley's mobile. That's all I know.'

Hood came back with coffee in a cream coloured mug, shaped like a letter U. Another step on the road to sophistication.

'You'll enjoy this,' he said.

Harvey addressed his sergeant.

'George. Our private investigator requires the assistance of the public sector. Do we feel disposed to help him?'

'I would say,' Hood said, 'that depends on what he is offering in return.'

'Not a great deal actually,' Harvey said.

'Those phone numbers could be useful to you,' I suggested. 'Some of them are listed only by initials because he doesn't want to give away full names. Which may mean they are people of significance.'

'By that, you mean of significance to us,' Hood said.

'Yes.'

'That's your pitch is it?'

'Yes.'

'Because you don't really need us to find these people,' Hood said. He picked the piece of paper off the desk and looked at it. 'Just ring the numbers. And when Messrs "H" and "M" and "S" answer, they will reveal who they are.'

'Maybe,' I said. 'But...'

'He doesn't want to give himself away,' Harvey said to Hood. Then he re-focussed on me. 'Is that not so?'

'I don't want to call any of those people. I just want to know who they are, what they are and if possible, where they are. Then I can figure out what to do next. Grant and Copley began with Soames, for some reason. Then they moved on to me. As to the others, I've no idea who the hell they are, but somehow, they have a connection with my client. I don't mind them coming after me – that's probably what it's going to take – but I don't want them to know I'm on their case. Yet.'

I stopped and waited for a response. Harvey and Hood stared at me. I continued.

'You can trace every number on that list.'

'The trade off being,' Harvey said, 'we might discover some major public enemy among Copley's contacts.'

'Grant and Copley were hired by someone local, right?'

'That's what we assume.'

'So you need to know who he is,' I said. 'He could be on the list.'

'He probably is. Okay George, get it organised.'

Hood went out of the office with the list. I took my first sip of coffee. It was very good. I took another. Harvey waited. I put the mug down on his desk. He picked it up and shoved a coaster underneath it.

'Sorry,' I said.

'Anything else we can help you with?' he asked.

By which, he meant he had finished buggering around and wanted this conversation to produce something of substance. I asked him if he was looking for Copley. He told me Hood had put DC Shackleton on to it. An important cog in the machinery, DC Shackleton.

'He's young and he's bright,' Harvey said. 'A bit of routine sleuthing will be good for him. So far, all we have on Copley, is a minor assault charge.'

'What about the torture and murder of Philip Soames?'

'Possibly. But in the absence of evidence, all we know is that some person or persons unknown, took Soames out at high tide – presumably in a boat – and dumped him mid channel. Using what kind of boat and from where, we have yet to discover. If we assume Soames was delivered to the boat by Grant's Lexus, then it was done from this side of the channel. We've looked at the CCTV footage of the approaches to both Severn Bridges from the Welsh side and there's no Lexus to be seen. Which suggests that Grant and Copley are indeed based this side of the water. However, as we have no idea where the Lexus is now, there's no fast track in that direction and no trail back from the body. The wounds tell us how Soames died. We know he had been dead for at least twelve hours when he was found. But that's all we've got.'

'Has Grant said anything?'

'His jaw's wired up. He's not doing much talking at all.'

He changed the subject.

'So Sherlock... Tell me what you did from the moment you left Copley in Cabot Circus.'

He folded his arms and waited. I took another drink of coffee. And gave him chapter and verse. About Suffolk, the Thorntons, Mila and the Serb names. It took a while. I added the interlude with Starratt for good measure. Harvey listened without interrupting once. When I finished, he summed up.

'So you are, to all intents and purposes, no further forward than you were when last we met?'

'I have a list of phone numbers,' I said.

'And a jacket with a tear in the back.'

Hood came back into the room.

'Not exactly names to conjure with,' he said. 'But interesting.'

'You have our complete and undivided

attention,' Harvey said.

'Okay... Some of them are known to us. Three of the names are from west London. Boasting convictions for activities which include blackmail, extortion, GBH and robbery with violence. The Welshman, Owen Rhys, is a bit of a glory boy from Newport. One conviction for beating up a lady bartender in Bedwas. The Irish connection is another hero, called Michael O'Donnell. He likes to insist that his infamous career is behind him. He now runs a security firm in Lisburn – actually a bunch of doormen and bodyguards. The three names not known to us, belong to Copley's brother in law, his sister and his grandma. Again all in west London.'

He paused.

'Which leaves us with?...' Harvey asked.

'The Serb numbers no longer exist. The phones have been ditched. Probably the instant Dujic and Tudjman discovered Copley had mislaid his. They weren't contract numbers anyway. Pay as you go phones, probably bought off a supermarket shelf. 'H' and 'M' are women. Hilda and Marion. What they and Copley get up to, is open to the floor...'

He paused again. More dramatically this time. Harvey sighed impatiently.

'Which leaves us with 'S.' Get on with it George.'

Hood looked straight at me.

'This gives some credence to your theory Jack. 'S' is a man all three of us know and revere. Lloyd Starratt.'

I looked at Harvey. He looked at me. We both looked at Hood, who nodded, as if confirmation were needed.

'Lloyd Starratt,' he repeated.

'Any more of that coffee George?' Harvey asked.

Half an hour later, the three of us had compiled all we knew about Lloyd Starratt. DC Shackleton had printed out a hard copy of his police record. A bunch of arrests but no convictions. Amazingly. Rancorous and malevolent bastard though he was, constantly in the headlines and on the police radar, nothing criminal had stuck to him in thirty years. He was getting away with it handsomely.

'George,' Harvey said. 'Assemble a list of all the known associates of every current member of the Starratt clan. Find out where they are and what they're doing.'

Then he looked at me.

'And a little assistance from you would be appreciated. I want to know where your client is. I want to talk to her.'

I opened my mouth to speak. Harvey raised his right hand and pointed the index finger at me.

'I don't want any bollocks about protection and confidentiality. The lady may have nothing to do with these inglorious people. I fervently hope that's the case. But if she is on the run – and from the likes of Starratt, Grant and Copley – then she needs more than just your help. Face it Jack.'

He waited for a moment.

'Now you may speak.'

'A week ago, my client hired me to find her. I've made no progress in that direction. But she will contact me again, sometime in the next twenty-four hours.'

'Why?'

'Deborah hired me for seven days. The time runs out tomorrow morning. She's organised and methodical. She'll call me.'

'So, give us permission to bug your phones,' Hood said. 'Office, home and mobile.'

'No. Not until I've talked to her again.'

'We can link your client to Philip Soames.'

'But not to his death.'

'You don't believe that and we know you don't,' Harvey said.

'He was her shrink. That's all so far. Besides, Soames had seventy something other clients.'

'Grant and Copley came looking for Deborah,' Harvey said.

'I won't give you permission.'

'Then we'll get a warrant.'

'You haven't got enough grounds for a warrant.'

Harvey ran out of patience. He stood up and yelled at me across his desk.

'Don't fuck about with me Jack!'

I stood up and faced him.

'All I'm doing is protecting my client.'

'Obstructing the course of justice is what you're doing. We have a dead body, two assaults, no three if you count the Southmead unpleasantness, and a contractor on the run. Add the Starratt clan to the recipe, along with two mysterious Serbs and your terrified client – who is probably superglued to the whole thing – and I have more than enough to take to a judge, the Attorney General and the Home Secretary.'

'Okay, so do it.'

I turned to leave. Harvey stopped me.

'Wait a minute. Sit down again.'

I sat down. Harvey looked across the room at Hood, who was now stationed in the doorway.

'Talk politely to Gloucestershire Constabulary George. Find out how much they'll allow us to do on their patch. The Starratts are obviously misbehaving. And if they do something silly, somebody ought to be around to catch them at it.'

Hood left the office. Harvey dropped back into his chair, propped his elbows on the desk, put his hands together, interlocked his fingers and tucked them under the end of his nose. He sighed, disengaged his hands, then re-connected them underneath his chin.

'Are you really going to make this difficult?'

I nodded.

'It will end in tears,' he said.

'Maybe.'

There was a long pause. Time enough to walk twice round the office. I found something to say.

'When Deborah contacts me, I'll do my best to convince her to call you.'

Harvey grunted.

'Do more than your best. Because if I have to bug your phones and put a round the clock watch on you, I will.'

He meant it. I knew he meant it. He knew I knew he meant it. We had come to the end of the discussion. Harvey held out his right hand.

'Give me Copley's sim card.'

I handed it over and walked out of the office.

Chapter Fourteen

Suddenly I couldn't think of anything to do. Out of purpose, out of sorts and out of ideas. An investigator measuring his chances of success in slender degrees of hope. Waiting for his client, whereabouts unknown, to call him and help out.

I drove to my office on automatic pilot. There was a note from Linda, pushed under the door. *There are two trans-gender help organisations in the city. One in Cotham and one in St Pauls. Why don't you try them? Phone numbers below. Sorry we ended yesterday so stupidly. Later. Love L.*

I read the note a second time. It was reasonable to assume that, in her five months in Bristol, Deborah had hooked up with other trans-gender people. And on reflection, how many of them could there be? But that was a bargain basement assumption. Why should trans-gender women feel compelled to link up at trans-gender gatherings? Presumably none of them wants to be defined forever, by some designer medical interregnum. Whatever has been done, has been done and is over. I decided that wasn't too patronising, given that it was a rationalisation from a position of some ignorance. But Linda was right. Getting a basic inside track, could help me get closer to the emotional and intellectual responses of my client. And maybe that would help find her. Or at least, give me some confidence to engage with her, if and when, she got back in touch.

A machine answered the first number I called, telling me that Jenny wasn't available, but I should try her mobile, or alternatively, call Sylvia on hers. Both mobiles asked me to leave messages. I decided not to. In this case, introductions should be live. I dialled the second land line number. Annie Marshall answered. I introduced myself.

'My name is Jack Shepherd. I am a private investigator. I have a client who has gone missing. I believe she may be in grave danger. I need help to find her.'

Annie was less alarmed by this unsolicited call than I feared she might be. She answered directly.

'And how do you think I can do that?' she asked.

'May I give you a name?'

'Yes.'

'Deborah Thorne.'

There was a long pause before Annie came back to me.

'Tell me a bit more,' she said.

I gave Annie a description of Deborah and

a précis of the conversation in my office six days ago. I told her about the trip to Suffolk and the meeting with Deborah's parents. It was enough to convince her I was serious. She asked me about *Shepherd Investigations*. I gave her the office address, phone numbers and a brief biog. She said she would come and see me. I offered to go to her.

'No,' she said. 'I would rather meet you at your place of work. Later today perhaps. Shall we say mid afternoon?'

We agreed on 3 o'clock.

'See you then,' she said and rang off.

I leaned back in my chair, surveyed the room, then noticed the front of the right hand desk drawer. Jason had repaired it. The lock wasn't there any longer, but he had re-filled and sanded the holes and replaced the handle.

I decided that coffee was a good idea, but there was no milk in the fridge.

With Linda absent, I went down a floor to purloin some from Patrick. He was listening to Meatloaf's *Paradise By The Dashboard Light*. I told him I preferred his current hard rock phase. He said he was contemplating a foray into disco. I begged him not to do it. Back in my office, I made some coffee, filled a mug and drank it, filled the mug again and drifted into consideration of Lloyd Starratt. I needed to know more about him.

I called Adam at the *Post*.

'Is he part of your investigations?' he asked.

'He might be.'

'God, you do pick 'em.'

We did a deal. Lunch for information. We met in the Landoger Trow in Queen Street. The literary inspiration of Robert Louis Stevenson, the place he re-created as the Admiral Benbow in *Treasure Island*. It's a long journey from 18th century pirate haunt to 21st century gastro pub, but that's progress for you. Adam was at university with the current manager.

We ordered the Monday house special and sat down with our beers in a corner of the lounge. Adam pushed an envelope file across the table.

'Hard copy of all the *Post* has on Lloyd Starratt and his kith and kin.'

I opened the file and read the pages.

The Ma Barker of the outfit was eighty-two year old Aurora, the mother of the Starratt boys. She lived with Lloyd in some splendour – he had called the farmhouse Southfork – waited on hand and foot by her adoring number one son. Lloyd farmed three hundred and twenty acres north of the village of Parkend, slap bang in the middle of the forest. The youngest Starratt, Ronnie, worked as the farm manager. The only member of the clan not on a police database, he was apparently making the place pay. There was money at Southfork and Lloyd was more than happy to wave it about. *Starratt Haulage,* presided over by the number two brother, Hughie, boasted a warehouse and half a dozen trucks quartered in Cinderford. Never likely to rival Eddie Stobart, the company did most of its business, trundling around South Wales. Hughie's wife, Brenda, owned a pub in Lydney and ran another in Coleford. Marvin's business, currently being supervised by his cousin Jared, was roof tiling. Jared's cousin Marlene, was married to Ronnie, and ran a low-rent escort agency housed above a bookmaker's in Blakeney, on the eastern edge of the forest.

'It's a glorified knocking shop,' Adam said.

Maybe. It was certainly the kind of enterprise that would sit comfortably within the Starratt business portfolio. But nothing to generate the interest of the regional crime squad, or threaten the godfathers of organised crime. The Starratts were as unlovable a bunch of undesirables as you could wish to avoid. But murdering psychiatrists, hooking up with hit men and doing business with mysterious Serbs was substantially out of their league.

Adam had done some thinking.

'This business with Lloyd and his brother and his dog is personal,' he suggested. 'It's your thing surely, not your client's. Lloyd happened to be at court, circumstances at the showground led you to his trailer. No surprise at all that he was in both places.'

'It's not him that's the common denominator, it's me,' I said.

'Okay. But that doesn't mean the events have anything to do with the case you're working on. You were at court supporting a former client. A couple of minutes earlier or later in the lobby and you'd have missed Lloyd. At the show, you went searching for a lost child. If you hadn't pitched up at the Information Tent, you wouldn't have got involved.'

'Grant and Copley tortured and murdered Philip Soames,' I said. 'Lloyd Starratt's phone number is on Copley's sim card. So are the numbers of two Serbs here in the UK. My client worked in Kosovo, witnessed a massacre and now she's on the run.'

'Incidents Jack. Not necessarily coincidents.'

The Monday special arrived. We ate in silence for a while. Then Adam put down his knife and fork.

'Alright... The real problem here, the key to all this, may not be who murdered Soames, or why Grant and Copley were looking for Deborah, or what the hell Starratt has to do with anything.'

He put his elbows on the table and leaned towards me.

'Focus on the Serbs and ask three questions. Who are they? Where are they? And what are they doing? Then ask yourself another. Given that you're convinced all the aforementioned are connected, who is the person most likely to know the answers to those questions?'

I swallowed the last mouthful of the Monday special.

'Deborah,' I said.

Adam nodded.

'So your mission Jack…'

I was back at the office by 2.30. Linda was still out. Or rather she was out again. There was another note, poked under my door. *Back around 6. Can we have dinner?*

The phone on my desk rang at precisely 3 o'clock.

Jason's oppo, Alex, said that Annie Marshall was in the lobby. I asked him to send her up and stepped out of the office into the corridor. Twenty yards away, the lift banged, clunked then started to whir. Ten seconds later, there was another clunk and the whirring stopped. The lift doors opened to reveal Annie in a blue summer dress, belted around the waist and at least three inch heels. I raised my right arm in acknowledgment. She smiled and waved back, stepped out of the lift and walked towards me. Cool, poised and elegant. Tall, like Deborah. Five feet eight or nine.

She held out her right hand.

'Annie Marshall,' she said.

I joined her right hand to mine and shook it.

'Jack Shepherd,' I said.

I released her hand and waved her into the office. I followed and pointed to one of the client chairs.

'Please sit down.'

I took a long look at her from my side of the desk. She had streaked blonde hair, blue eyes, mature laughter lines, cheek bones that were more prominent then mine – as if she had recently lost some weight – and a slim line chin. She sat in the chair, crossed her right leg over her left, let the material of her dress settle just above her knee and, totally unabashed by the scrutiny, waited for me to complete the assessment.

I sat down in my chair and then she spoke.

'Do I pass muster?' she asked.

'First impressions count for a lot in my line of work.'

'Of course they do. You are an investigator, don't worry. The first time my wife saw me in a dress and pearl earrings, she smiled, looked at the wallpaper behind me, then back into my eyes and suggested she made some tea. She went into the kitchen and stayed there for ages, all the time engaged in a huge effort to work out what to say next.'

'What did she say?'

'She said, "Right. Now I must think of you

as a woman."'

'And was that okay?'

'Yes it was.'

'And was this a genuine trans-gender moment or an early cross-dressing experiment?'

'It was a trans-gender moment. I never was a transvestite. Not in any demonstrable fashion anyway. Have you heard the joke?'

'Which joke?'

'What's the difference between a transvestite and a trans-sexual? About three years.'

I laughed. She grinned back at me.

'Actually,' she said, 'these days there's some debate about "trans-sexual." It's a description, not a condition.'

I considered the proposition for a moment or two.

'So, you're not a trans-sexual, you're a trans-sexual woman,' I said.

'In truth, all the labels get in the way. I accept that they are the result of a long time spent by people trying to create user-friendly definitions. But if gender ceases to become the focus and people can stop explaining what it means, then the "trans" business can be considered over and lives can begin anew. I am a woman. End of story.'

She took a deep breath.

'Sorry. I'll climb down from the soap box now. What do you want to know?'

That was a hell of a question. The answer

was, anything and everything. Anything that would help me find Deborah and everything that would help to stop me making foolish assumptions.

Annie helped out.

'Okay. There is a process applied to all of this, from the beginning to the end. A clearly signposted route. Which begins with the big decision; to change gender.'

I nodded. 'Okay...'

'You have to know why you want to do this and explain everything to your GP. Then, all being well – by that I mean if the GP believes you – the next step is a referral to a psychiatrist. The psychiatrist has to believe you too. If he does, then he will refer you to a gender assessment clinic or another psychiatrist specialising in gender identity. In my case and in Deborah's, it was Philip Soames, here in Bristol. This is a major examination. If you don't pass, it's the end of the line. A resolute and unchangeable mindset is required. Any display of hesitation, or inconsistency, or recognisable delusion, will bring everything to a grinding halt.'

'But if you get through it?...'

'If the psychiatrist believes you, he will diagnose "gender dysphoria" and prescribe a course of hormone treatment.'

'Which begins the physical process of turning you into a woman?'

'Effectively. You combine breast augmentation with electrolysis to get rid of face and body hair. But most importantly, you put on your frock and set about living as a woman.'

'And all the while, the psychiatrist monitors the process.'

'Yes.'

'Then what?'

'Well ... that's where some people stop. They decide that passing as a woman is enough.'

'But actually being a woman...'

'Is the real issue. You can't be a woman with a penis. To complete the change, it has to go.'

She let the pause fill. Then she spoke again.

'Shall I go on?'

'We've come this far...'

'Empathy from relatives and friends, is an absolute requirement. But this isn't something that can be shared, obviously. So what follows, is called the Real Life Test. You must live as a woman in every way, for two years.'

'With no down time as a man?'

'None at all. There are more psychiatric assessments during this period. If you make it through, you get your surgery. And then ... well you can imagine.'

'Actually I don't think I can imagine it.'

And I didn't really want Annie to explain. But she felt she needed to.

'To begin with, it's as basic as you would

expect. The removal of the testicles and the erectile tissue of the penis. Obviously that's not very tricky, it's an amputation. It's the next bit that's clever.'

I couldn't believe that Annie was being so matter of fact about all this.

'Clever?...'

'There's a big hole left between the rectum and the prostate. This is lined with the penis skin and the scrotum to make the vagina.'

She smiled and turned the palms of her hands upwards.

'And that's it. A gender change.'

And having gone through all that, something of a triumph. To know everything about the process and to understand what has to happen, is one thing. But to look forward to it... That must take a special kind of resolve.

'The bonus is,' Annie said, 'once the surgery is complete, all the bits work.'

I stared at her. She grinned back at me.

'Have I embarrassed you?'

'No. I'm just reflecting that if I had said something like that it would have been deemed smutty.'

'Not by present company,' Annie said. 'Anything else?'

'Your voice.'

'Hours of lessons with a voice coach. Contrary to legend, you don't go up two octaves when you have your testicles cut off.

You have to work at it.'

'May I ask you some other stuff?'

'Out of what? Curiosity?'

'Curiosity sounds better than prurience.'

'I like a man who suspects his own motives,' Annie said.

'It's a side effect of what I do,' I said. 'Collateral damage.'

She smiled again.

'Ask away.'

'How long have you been a woman? I mean, how long have you lived as a woman?'

'I'm 49. I had the surgery six years ago.'

I must have looked surprised.

'You're wondering why it took so long.'

'I think the decision is immensely brave,' I said. 'At whatever time in life you take it.'

'My rationalisation is that, emotionally, I've always been a woman.'

'Was that a problem?'

'Weirdly, no. You might assume it would be. You know, a kid on his own; avoiding all the rough and tumble stuff; hopeless at sport; passionate about art and drama.'

'It's an archetypal picture.'

'Not mine. I played rugby at school. And then at university. I re-built an old Norton motorbike my Dad kept in a shed at the bottom of the garden. Basically my interests are still the same. I didn't give up motorbikes for chick stuff. I was a girl, born into a boy's body, who liked to do what boys do.

My early life wasn't tormented by demons and dark thoughts. I'm not sure there was ever a really miserable Alan, desperate to become a re-constituted Annie. I just knew, that given time, there would be something I would have to do. I decided on the surgery. Now I'm a different shape and I'm rather proud of it.'

'You have every right to be. You look terrific. Am I allowed to say that?'

'Don't be coy, you're letting yourself down.'

'I've only known you twenty minutes.'

'I've been propositioned on much shorter acquaintance. I don't mind you, or anyone, inspecting the equipment. I am a woman and my femininity is no more of a mystery than anyone else's.'

'You're tall,' I said. 'Slim hips and long legs.'

She nodded in acknowledgement.

'And no cellulite,' she said.

Something that hadn't occurred to me. Men don't get cellulite.

'That's a bonus,' I said.

'Here's the thing,' Annie said. 'The bottom line is, no one should worry about their femininity, or their sense of themselves as women. In my case, it just took a while to straighten things out, as it were.'

'You got married. To a woman. That's a resolutely male thing to do.'

'Yes.'

'And you didn't have second thoughts?'

'I was in love with Mel. I still am. We still live together. And we have two children.' She gave me an old fashioned look. 'You're trying very hard not to be surprised by all this.'

'Sorry.'

'Mel claims she knew, long before the pearl earrings moment, that I was trying to work something out. When I finally told her and she got over the immediate shock, she said she was relieved to know what it was.'

'What about the kids?'

'Because I did all this so late on, they were grown up and hardly fazed at all. At the time, Charlie was nineteen and at university in the US. He's still there, working in Silicon Valley. Holly was seventeen and doing her 'A' Levels. She's now in Yorkshire, designing wind turbines. We are a very well adjusted bunch, considering.'

Annie was genuinely relaxed. We were both enjoying this conversation. But at some point we had to begin talking about my client. Annie got to it before I did.

'So what happened when you met Deborah for the first time?'

I took some time over my response. I struggled to slide into the next chapter. Annie waited.

'You are having trouble here,' she said

'Yes. There's no easy way to say this, so ... Philip Soames is dead.'

Annie shifted her position in the chair, put her hands on the arm rests and sat up straighter.

'From what?' she asked. 'He wasn't ill, was he?'

'He was murdered.'

Annie looked at me without blinking.

'Why?'

'Some people are looking for Deborah.'

'People, what people?'

'That's the problem. I think only Deborah knows who they are?'

'Then it follows you should ask.'

'Let me tell you the rest of the story,' I said.

Annie listened patiently while I did so. When I finished, she got to her feet.

'Do you mind if we go for a walk?'

We walked out into the sunshine and over the re-furbished footbridge into the park.

'I've known Deborah since she came to Bristol,' Annie said. 'Which was what?... Four or five months ago?'

'About that. Did you meet up at any time in the years before? When you were both clients of Philip?'

'No.'

'In the last four months, have you met any of her friends?'

'No.'

'Did she ever talk about anybody?'

'She must have I suppose, but I don't

remember who. I don't think I can recall any names.'

'A woman in her mid or perhaps late 30s. With a child.'

Annie screwed up her face in concentration.

'No. I'm sorry. I've known her since just before Easter. It has taken me the whole of that time to learn as much about her as you have done in less than a week. I don't think I can add anything.'

'I found two photographs in Deborah's house. Presumably taken by her. The woman and the child are on a beach. In Devon.'

Annie stopped walking. I turned to face her. She stared ahead for a moment or two, then looked at me again.

'Devon,' she said. 'Actually, south Devon. Once ... once Deborah talked about ... oh God what was it? About... No, the conversation wasn't in fact about Devon. It was about the surgery. The date of the surgery. We were comparing notes, I guess, about the experience. She mentioned, no more than an aside really, that she had been on holiday in south Devon, just days before going into the clinic... And er...'

She gave up struggling with the story.

'Sorry ... I really can't remember any more.'

'It may just be enough,' I said. 'Can I crave your indulgence for another fifteen, twenty minutes.'

'Yes of course.'

Back in the office, we looked through Philip Soames' notes. Deborah had seen Philip three days after her surgery on July 25th 2006. So she must have been in south Devon, with her friend and the child, around mid July. Annie agreed with the assessment.

It wasn't much, but it was new information. Not gold maybe, but a little richer than base metal.

'Is it too early for a drink?' I asked.

Annie looked at her watch.

'It's quarter past four,' she said.

I fished a bottle of Laphroaig out of the bottom drawer of the filing cabinet.

'Now that is disappointing,' Annie said.

'I'm sorry. Don't you like whisky?'

'Yes I like whisky. It's just that the bottom of the filing cabinet is a bit of a cliché.'

'It helps with the Chandler thing I'm trying to get going,' I said.

Annie grinned.

I poured the drinks, sat down again and we talked. About her journey, about her family and about her real happiness with who she was now. About me and what I do and why I do it. About my days in the police force, about Emily and Chrissie. Like we were new best friends. And then about Deborah again. It was Annie's turn to ask the million pound question.

'Do you really think you can find her?'

'No self-respecting private investigator likes to admit when he's beaten. But I have no idea where she is. Right now, I feel less worried for her than I did. We have a bunch of sensible coppers on the case and they can deal with the UK bad guys. I don't know anything about the Serbs. But the police can put Deborah into protective custody and do something about them – if she'll talk.

'That still bothers you.'

'I'm making assumption after assumption. All of them ending in the idea that Deborah is hiding from Dujic and Tudjman. But I could be wrong. The whole business is just plain untidy. I hate it. I need Deborah to come out of the woodwork and talk to me.'

'If she does,' Annie said, 'tell her we have met and talked. Tell her everything we talked about. It may help. God knows you have earned your money. She will recognise that surely and perhaps...'

She changed up a gear.

'Ask her to call me. She may do so. And, who knows, I might be able to make a difference.'

The phone on my desk rang. I craved Annie's indulgence and picked up the receiver. Linda was calling from next door.

'Am I interrupting?' she asked.

'No no, it's fine,' I said. 'Come and meet Annie.'

I replaced the receiver.

'That was Linda. Next door. My accountant.'

Linda knocked politely on the door, opened it and stepped into the office.

Annie turned in her chair. I introduced them. Annie looked at her watch. Linda apologised for interrupting. Annie stood up.

'You're not interrupting anything. We have finished. Good to meet you.' She turned to me. 'Remember. Tell Deborah to call me. See you later, I hope.'

She nodded at Linda as she left the office. Linda watched her go.

'Very smart. Is she ... a trans-sexual?'

'I have been told that "trans-sexual" is an adjective,' I said.

'I see. She's a trans-sexual woman.'

'Just a woman.'

'You're being very correct,' Linda said.

'I'm learning to be.'

It was early, but we were both hungry and there was a Mexican restaurant open on the other side of the Cumberland Basin. We walked to it. On the way, Linda gave me a rundown of her afternoon.

'Lunch in the council chamber. Followed by two hours of hype and nonsense from the directors of a new initiative. More half arsed proposals for regional expansion. All involving collaborations between the public and private sectors, ho ho ho.'

'These men are philanthropists,' I said.

‘How can you be so cynical?’

‘These men,’ she countered, ‘are on the make. Once again. With more schemes to get local government to pay for their personal aggrandisement.’

‘Aggrandisement…’

She looked at me, as though disappointed that I wasn’t taking this seriously.

‘Councillor ShitBrain from Henleaze took centre stage. He came up with a barmy scheme for the redundant electronics factory along the river from here. Another bloody retail outlet. He’s even got a name for it. Phoenix Park. And he was supported in this crass proposal, by a group of people who want to build a bunch of starter homes on the brown field site behind it.’

‘Well that’s a good thing. Isn’t it?’

‘You may think so. But there’s a reason the site has been derelict for so long. There was a paint and dye factory there for thirty years. The ground is toxic. The developers can’t afford to clean it themselves, so they want the council to help out.’

‘They won’t get that surely? I mean nobody’s got any money.’

‘Ah well, that was the point at which the council Finance Director got to his feet and made a speech about promoting growth. And they went on to debate this in all seriousness.’

She stared at me. Inviting me to say something. So I asked a question.

'Why were you at this gathering?'

'I'm a member of Business West. I get invited to these gigs.'

We had reached the door of *Cantina Casita*. I opened it.

'Oh yes,' Linda said, 'Lloyd Starratt was there.'

Leaving me to assimilate that minor bombshell, she swept into the restaurant.

Linda had chicken enchiladas. I had tacos dorados. And we had a couple of bottles of Corona. As we ate, Linda explained that Starratt, being a substantial local entrepreneur, had been an invited guest. He had shown up in an expensive suit – all swagger and bonhomie – and worked the room.

'I have to tell you, he's good at it,' she said. 'Especially with those who can't distinguish charm from smarm. He announced his whole hearted support for the Phoenix Park scheme. And graciously accepted the applause that followed. The slimy bastard has more front than a row of houses.'

I bit into the last taco. Linda changed the subject.

'Did your friend Annie help?'

I swallowed.

'Yes. Thank you for pointing me in her direction. She knows Deborah. The connection may be enough to persuade Deborah to open up.'

'And if it isn't?'

'Then I will admit defeat.'

Linda ate her last mouthful of chicken and wiped her lips with her napkin. 'Which will leave Deborah where?' she asked.

I picked up the glass of Corona, drained it and put it back on the table.

'I have absolutely no idea,' I said.

Linda and I walked back to the office and this time talked about us. We came to the decision to let whatever was happening, continue to do so, without questioning and tinkering. It wasn't going to go wrong. We had simply to leave it alone and let it go right.

There were two messages on my answering machine. The first, from a man called Leonard Hopkins, asking me if I could call him. The second, from Harvey Butler saying he had some information to impart. I called him first. His office phone diverted to his mobile. He was at home.

'We've checked with the Borders Agency,' he said. 'They have no record of Vojislav Dujic, or Josip Tudjman. Neither of them are in the UK as bona fide refugees or potential immigrants. Which leaves us with two matters for debate. Either they're here illegally, or they have genuine passports and they're enjoying our hospitality, like every other tourist. Serbs can visit the UK and stay for six months without visas. And if Dujic and Tudjman have Croatian passports, they don't need visas at all. They could have driven in through any channel port, waved their passports at the appropriate desk and passed into the UK with no fuss or bother. Sorry Jack.'

Dispirited, I called Mr Hopkins. He said he was receiving threatening emails and the police weren't doing anything about it. Could I? I told him it wasn't the sort of work I did. He said something about "another waste of time" and rang off.

I looked at my watch. 7.15.

Linda materialised in the doorway.

'I've got to go. Homework to do for tomorrow.'

She stepped to the desk, leaned over it and kissed me.

'Sleep well,' she said.

Then she was gone. Leaving Jack Shepherd, super sleuth, on his own, with no idea of what to do next. I was beginning to regret refusing to allow Harvey to bug my phones. I had to get a fix on Deborah somehow and I had turned down the means to do it.

I decided to go home too.

Chapter Fifteen

Deborah called at 10 minutes past 8. The ensuing conversation had its ups and downs.

I went through the investigation so far, day by day and discovery by discovery. Except for one item I reserved for later – the photographs on the beach had to come as a surprise, at the most useful moment.

Deborah reacted like a celebrity whose ghost writer had got all the facts of her biography absolutely correct, but given away far too many secrets. She took a long time to recover her composure. Unlike her approach to our original meeting, Deborah hadn't rehearsed this encounter. Or at least, she hadn't allowed for the deluge of stuff I was pouring down the line. I prodded away at the most sensitive element in the story.

'Grant and Copley were hired to persuade Philip Soames to provide information about you,' I said. 'Somehow, from somewhere, they found out you were a client of his.'

'I don't know how,' Deborah said.

'Copley is from west London.'

'And I used to live there, yes.'

'So it's not unreasonable to ask if you have any previous connection with him.'

'I don't know Copley. Or Grant.'

'Do you know Lloyd Starratt? It's possible he hired Grant and Copley. Why would he do that?'

'I don't know. I can't answer any of these questions.'

'Deborah…'

She was growing impatient. And I was losing ground. The week's work I had done was being eclipsed by a bunch of 'I don't knows'. And we hadn't got anywhere near Dujic and Tudjman yet. She snapped back at me.

'What have you told the police about me?'

'Very little. Not enough to encourage them to look for you. Although they now have all of Philip's case notes. They know I'm stalling and it won't be long before they run out of patience.'

'What happened to your much prized client confidentiality?'

'Philip was tortured and murdered,' I said. 'Given those circumstances, it took no time at all for the police to get a warrant. They are looking for a motive. You and I both know what that is. It's the search for you.'

There was a sustained silence. I counted my way through it, timing the hiatus to my next line.

'We have to meet,' I said.

Another pause. This time I waited for Deborah to speak.

'No,' she said.

'Then there's nothing more I can do,' I said.

And disconnected the call.

And waited.

It was six minutes before Deborah called back.

'I'm sorry,' she said.

That was a step forward, so I moved carefully on.

'I need to ask you about Dujic and Tudjman,' I said. 'Don't say "I don't know them". Think for a moment, then tell me why they might know you. Go back to your time in Kosovo. Who might Dujic and Tudjman be?'

That was a useful question. Deborah thought about it.

'Members of some Serb militia group,' she said. 'Kosovan vigilantes, ex-policemen, criminals who saw opportunities in the misery and the massacres. There are shed loads of possibilities.'

And Dujic and Tudjman weren't necessarily on the run. Whatever they might have been ten years ago and whatever they were doing now, they weren't in the UK as political refugees. Or because they didn't want to be in Serbia.

So I ploughed on. I asked Deborah if she had been in touch with any Serbs since she came back to the UK. She said 'no'. I asked if she had any residual relationship with anything Kosovan. She said 'no'. I asked her if she was still in contact with *Médecins Sans Frontières*. She said 'no'. The conversation was hurtling towards a precipice, with a huge sign on the edge reading 'Nothing to Learn.'

So I jumped on the alternative band-wagon. I told her about Annie.

'You really have been working for your money,' Deborah said.

'Annie said the same thing. And she also suggested you should talk to the police.'

'At the risk of sounding like a broken record...' she said.

We were never going to find an ending that would play, so it was time for the photos business. I told Deborah about finding her safe and breaking into it. I went through the list of the stuff I had found. There was no response from her end of the line.

'Who are the people in the photographs on the beach?' I asked.

'I won't tell you,' she said.

'Because, if I can find them, I can find you.'

She didn't deny that proposition. She was quiet for a long time. Making her mind up about something. I waited.

'I'll call you back in fifteen minutes,' she said.

'Okay.'

I put the phone receiver back in its cradle.

Poured myself a large brandy and sat down on the living room sofa.

I had been making assumptions about Dujic and Tudjman ever since I had discovered their names in Copley's mobile. Because they were Serbs and because Deborah had been in Kosovo. That was all. I had no evidence of any connection between them. The Serbs were in the UK on business. And given their association with Copley, their business was probably less than legitimate. So what? Maybe they weren't the issue here at all. It was the woman and the child who were causing Deborah concern.

Speculation is essentially a fruitless exercise. Developing a theory has purpose and direction, pondering is something else entirely. Up to now, this investigation had been a fishing expedition. And I hadn't caught anything of substance. I had driven five hundred miles, asked a lot of questions and assembled skip loads of information. Which was just so much crap, unless I could make something of it.

The alternative, was simply to leave the stage. Bring down the curtain on the last performance and go on to the next show. I had a week's wages in the bank. There was no need to send my client an invoice. And Copley had covered my expenses. In fact there was enough left for dinner and a bottle of champagne.

But the bottom line was, I had not found my client. And that was the job.

Or at least, how it had started. Sure, I had failed in my quests before. I was no stranger to wreckage and unhappy endings. But I had seen all of them through to the end, however bitter.

Impossibilities take a bit longer...

The telephone rang again.

'I want you to stay on the case,' Deborah said.

I processed that information. Deborah waited for me to respond. When I didn't, she asked if I was still there. I said I was.

'Use the money in the safe in my house. Take as much you need. You have been brilliant so far. I didn't imagine, for one moment, you would find out so much about me.'

'Tell me about the woman and the boy on the beach,' I said.

'No.'

'Okay, you're trying to protect them. I understand. From what? If it's serious, let's go to the police. Get their help.'

'No.'

She ordered a change of subject.

'I don't want a conversation about the police. Not now.'

'Alright,' I said. 'So... Are we going to continue this in the conventional manner? Are you going to tell me where you are and what you're doing?'

'No, the original rules apply. I can't help you with this. That has always been the point. Otherwise, we would not be talking. All this would be at an end.'

'At least give me your mobile number.'

There was a long exhalation of breath down the line. Then another long pause.

'Deborah?...'

She came back to me.

'I want your word you will not give this number to anyone else.'

'You have it.'

She gave me the number; asked me if I could remember it. I recited it back to her.

'Write it down somewhere if you have to,' she said. 'But please don't put it into your phone. Or anywhere it can be traced.'

She rang off, before anything else could be discussed. I took the receiver away from my ear and stared at it for ages. The line buzzed on, unconcerned. I disconnected the call, went into the kitchen and made some coffee, wandered back into the living room, poured some more brandy and returned to the sofa.

I talked with myself for a while. Once again, a plan was needed. However optimistic.

Of all the characters in this drama, Lloyd Starratt was the most accessible. At least, in the sense that I could find him. I decided to believe the supposition that he had hired Grant and Copley. That being the case, so far his best laid plans had failed substantially. He hadn't found Deborah, Grant was under arrest, Copley was in hiding and Starratt himself was on the police radar. I could take some measure of credit for the scenario and that helped me feel better.

Feeling positive was next up. And with that, came a plan of sorts. Which could conceivably work – if I stayed in one piece and avoided getting stomped on by people such as the man outside Lloyd's trailer.

A trip to the Forest of Dean was required.

I hadn't been in the forest for years. To get there, you have to fork out a small fortune to cross the River Severn, or spend twice as much on petrol, driving north and west and then back south again. Bristolians don't have the Forest of Dean high on their list of places to frequent. Like Londoners don't visit the Tower of London – they live next door to it, they know it's there and it's expensive to get in to. This corner of Gloucestershire is more tatty than romantic. What remains of the forest itself – almost fifty square miles of dense woodland on the banks of the River Wye – is magical. But the 21st century has imposed itself resolutely. Local industries have died and jobs along with them. People born and bred in the forest, stay because it's all they know. They join the dole queues and live on benefit. Long established, ancient communities have withered away. While, in contrast, the wild boar continue to flourish. The sitting Tory MP doubled his majority at the 2010 election. Add to that, a bunch of in-breds like the Starratts, who all have the same chin and who have survived by shortening the odds and playing the percentages and the history comes up to date.

Tomorrow's job, was to raid the piggy bank for the funds necessary to cross the Severn. Then drive into the forest and beard the lion in his den.

Chapter Sixteen

Tuesday morning. The second Tuesday on the case.

I decided I didn't need to burgle Deborah's safe again – at least not yet – and spent a couple of hours with Adam's notes and the road atlas, trying to pinpoint the locations in the Starratt empire. I found all the places listed. The Starratts flourished, in all their tainted glory, like feudal barons in a medieval kingdom.

I crossed the Severn Bridge just before 10 o'clock, in glorious sunshine. Paid to get into Wales and then drove north, back into England. Through Chepstow and on up the A48 towards Lydney. Turned northeast into the forest and headed for Parkend.

A couple of miles later, I pulled into a lay-by, screened from the road by a fringe of trees and lined on the other side by a farmer's hedge. I climbed out of the Healey and looked around. The day was warm and the lay-by buzzed with activity. There was a hum from insects in the nettles. Bees were busy, darting in and out of a bunch of wild roses, their heads open to the sunshine. A butterfly settled on the Healey's driver side wing mirror. I watched her open her wings in slow motion, then dip from side to side like a fighter pilot saluting. She was light grey and blue and white and luminous in the sunshine. Her wings flapped twice, she rose, then dipped, turned and flew into the trees by the road.

I found a gap in the hedge, stepped into it and took time out for a pee. I heard a car pull up behind me. I ignored it, finished what I had started, zipped up and stepped back. The barrel of a hand gun was poked into my right kidney.

A voice, thick and nasal, spoke into my right ear.

'Don't turn around until I say so.'

The owner of the voice sucked in breath, then spoke again. I waited.

'Now. Turn around now.'

I did. Francis Copley stood stock still, bloodshot eyes looking at me from behind a nose like Charlie Cairoli's. Worth a huge laugh and a round of applause, if it wasn't for the 9mm Browning automatic he was pointing at me. He sucked in breath once more, through thick, bruised lips. He let it out again, slowly and gently. His nose currently wasn't up to the job.

The Lexus was parked behind him, engine idling.

Copley eased the Browning's safety catch off.

'I knew if I hung around your place long enough, we'd eventually get to be alone somewhere,' he said.

He sounded like Melvin Bragg with a bad cold. With his left hand, he pointed to the offending proboscis.

'This hurts like hell and the painkillers don't help.'

'Just reward for your misdeeds.'

Copley grimaced. At least I think he did. Difficult to tell in the mess of nose and lips. Maybe it was a smile.

'Be cheerful as long as you can,' he said.

'I try to stay bright,' I said, 'Whatever the company.'

Copley ignored the jibe.

'We have things to talk about before ... well, before what happens after that,' he said. 'But not here.'

He waved the Browning in the direction of the Lexus. I looked at the car. It had a new registration number.

'Go on,' he said. 'You first.'

I led the way to the Lexus and stopped facing the radiator grill. Copley moved to my left and opened the driver's door. He took a couple of steps back and opened the passenger door behind it.

'Come round here and get into the front,' he ordered.

We climbed into the Lexus, in formation, like dance partners. The moment I landed in the driving seat, I felt the Browning in the back of my neck, pointing at me over the head rest. We closed the car doors on the same beat. The pressure of the gun barrel went away, as Copley slid to his left and positioned himself in the middle of the rear seat. Then I felt the gun once more, against my left cheek.

'Now then,' he said. 'I'm going to sit back a little and let you drive. But I can't miss from half a yard. So take it easy and we'll get this first bit done without mishap. Alright?'

'Yes.'

It was all I could manage to say. He was a few lines of dialogue away from shooting me, at least, but my mouth was dry and my heart rate up thirty or forty beats.

'So off you go. Slow and sedate. It's a lovely day and we're in no hurry. Out of the lay-by and turn left.'

It was an automatic gearbox. I slipped the lever into drive, eased the Lexus out of the lay-by and onto the road. Half a mile later, I was ordered right, then in a mile or so, left onto a narrow lane with grass growing along the middle. The lane crumbled into a track, the grass grew longer and a minute later I drove the Lexus into a farmyard. Copley told me to switch off the engine.

'Leave the key in the ignition,' he said.

He moved across the seat and opened his door.

'Okay, your turn.'

I opened the driver's door and we slid out like we had got in, synchronised, one behind the other.

'Take a couple of paces forward,' Copley said.

I did. There were two big stone barns in front of me. The one to the left had holes in the roof and no doors and windows. Inside it, I could see an old John Deere tractor with no wheels, sitting on its springs and a collection of pieces of knackered and rusting farm machinery. The barn to the right was in better condition. A restored roof and windows and big double doors. And it was being extended. The foundations of an adjoining building to the right, about the same size as the existing one, had been completed.

Copley noticed me looking at the work

'Eighteen inches of hardcore in the bottom,' he said. 'Easy enough to scoop out six feet of it. And when it's back in place and level … who's going to know. There's a team coming to pour the concrete later in the week. The weather forecast is bright and sunny.'

He stopped talking, to let the information sink in.

'Now turn around.'

He was about eight feet away, still pointing the Browning at me. Couldn't miss from there.

‘That’s fine,’ Copley said. ‘Let’s talk.’

He backed up to the Lexus driver’s door, still open. He eased himself onto the seat, his feet on the ground outside the car.

‘I’ll sit, if you don’t mind,’ he said. ‘I have moments when I get a bit dizzy.’

He had added another couple of yards to the distance between us.

‘Whose place is this?’ I asked him.

He didn’t reply. I persisted.

‘Belongs to Lloyd Starratt, doesn’t it?’

He still didn’t reply.

‘He hired you to find my client. Why?’

Now he replied.

‘He hired Grant. Grant hired me.’

‘Why?’

‘I don’t know. He didn’t say.’

‘How did you get to Philip Soames?’

He waggled the Browning at me.

‘Enough of this,’ he said. ‘Where is your client?’

‘I have no idea,’ I said. ‘One of the conditions of the engagement.’

He grimaced again. I decided it was supposed to be a smile. I let it subside, then went on.

‘Look. You have a 9mm automatic and you’d have to be the worst contractor in the business, to miss from there. I have no wish to become part of the foundations behind me. Deborah is hiding out somewhere. She hired me to find her, working on the assumption that if I could do that, then so could you. I haven't found her. And it's what I do. I'm good at it. So...'

There was a pause. Copley raised his left hand and gingerly pressed what was left of the bridge of his nose. He tried to sniff. It hurt and something rattled. Then he took his hand away and re-focussed on me.

'Is that it?'

'Let me sum this up for you,' I said. 'Yes. Absolutely. Yes.'

Copley stood up. Obviously in pain. He closed his eyes, dipped his head, lifted it and opened his eyes again. Anger blazed across the yard. He bellowed at me.

'Don't fuck me about!!'.

He raised the Browning and fired a shot over my right shoulder. The bullet hit the wall of the barn behind me and ricocheted off somewhere into the distance. Then he extended his right arm and aimed at the gun at my forehead.

'This can be so simple,' he said. 'Just tell me where your client is. Then we'll get this unpleasantness over with.'

Suddenly, he swayed on his feet and lifted his left hand to his head again.

'Oh Christ,' he said.

I launched myself across the space between us, dipped my shoulder and slammed into his chest. He went backwards like he was being pulled on a bungee rope. Into the car and onto the driver's seat, still hanging on to the Browning. The back of his head bounced off the steering wheel. He straightened up and looked at me.

I balled my fist and hit him hard on what was left of the nose.

There was no resistance. What I hit disintegrated with a soft, squelching sound. I drew my fist back, covered in blood and bits of soft tissue. Copley screamed in pain, turned ashen in an instant, passed out and fell towards me. I caught him, straightened him up again and pushed him back into the seat. I grabbed his legs and swung them into the seat well and leant his neck against the head rest.

He had dropped the Browning. I picked it up, ejected the clip and stowed it in the inside pocket of my jacket. I checked the glove box, empty except for the car manual. I went through all Copley's pockets – a grim reprise of the last time I did this. I looked under the seats, in the compartment between the seats, and the door storage spaces. There were no more clips to find.

Copley came to, threw up down the front of his jacket, then passed out again.

I found my mobile and dialled 999. Explained that the man I was with had serious facial injuries and was drifting in and out of consciousness. I gave the best directions I could to wherever the hell we were.

There was a dismal pattern emerging here. Hitting people in the face, then phoning policemen and paramedics. I stood and waited, the Browning in my pocket, staring at Copley.

He woke up once more. I shifted into his line of sight and told him an ambulance was on its way. He tried to say something, but words wouldn't form. Blood burbled out of his mouth. Then he passed out again. For some reason, I checked the Browning was still in my pocket.

It was a desperately long twelve minutes, before the ambulance arrived. The paramedics took one look at Copley and set to work immediately. He was ready to leave for the hospital as a local police patrol car turned into the yard.

WPC Renshaw was in her late 20s. Slim, faired haired and around five feet six. Her partner PC Walton was slim and fair haired too, a bit older I guessed and the same height as me. Both were concerned and keen to work by the book, anxious that their approach should be user friendly and on message. All was going swimmingly, until I explained that the man the paramedics had just rushed away had tried to kill me. And not just today, on a previous occasion also. User friendly turned to suspicious, then to genuine alarm as I produced the magazine clip and the Browning.

'Have you got an evidence bag?'

PC Walton ducked into the patrol car, fished about and found one. He held the bag open and offered it to me. I dropped the Browning and the clip into it.

'That may have been used in the murder of a man called Philip Soames, in Bristol last week. The policeman in charge of the case is Superintendent Harvey Butler. I'll happily go with you to the nearest police station. We can sort out things from there.'

PC Walton sealed the bag and stared at the contents. WPC Renshaw coughed politely. I looked at her.

'Is the Lexus yours?'

'No. It belongs to Mr Copley.'

'Did you come here with him?'

'Some of the way, yes.'

PC Walton had recovered his composure and now joined in the discussion.

'What do you mean by that?'

'My car is in a lay-by a couple of miles away. I stopped there. Mr Copley appeared, waved the Browning at me, made me get into the Lexus and drive it here.'

'Why?'

I went through the chain of events, the conversation and Copley's offer to plant me in the foundations of the barn extension.

I stopped when I got to the end of the story. WPC Renshaw and PC Walton stared at me for ages. Directly above our heads, I could hear a skylark.

'You come with me,' WPC Renshaw finally instructed. 'PC Walton will drive the Lexus.'

Twenty five minutes later, we were all sitting in the canteen at Lydney police station; WPC Renshaw staring at me across a plastic topped table, PC Walton fetching the tea. Harvey had been informed of my escapade and George Hood was on his way from Trinity Road. WPC Renshaw's radio crackled into life. She answered it. Where I was sitting, it was impossible to distinguish what was coming from the other end. So I waited. PC Walton arrived with the tea. WPC Renshaw ended the call and looked at me.

'Mr Copley will be alright. Once they've mended his nose again.'

'Make sure you hang on to him this time.'

PC Walton snorted into his mug of tea. I couldn't tell if he was disgusted by the irony or thought it was funny.

WPC Renshaw's radio burst into life again. She nodded her way through more incomprehensible stuff, then switched off and got to her feet. PC Walton looked at her.

'We have to go,' she said to him. Then turned to me. 'May I respectfully request you stay here in this room until Detective Sergeant Hood arrives.'

'You may,' I said. 'And I will.'

The young coppers left me to myself. I

waited, as patiently as I could. Not something I'm good at. The clock on the wall said five minutes to noon when Hood and the indispensable DC Shackleton walked into the canteen.

Hood introduced him. 30 years old or thereabouts, curly brown hair and hands the size of goalkeepers gloves. I stood up. Shackleton offered me his right hand, clamped it around mine and shook. I got pins and needles in my fingers.

'Pleased to meet you,' he said. 'You're a bit of a legend at Trinity Road.'

'And you're the coffee king,' I said.

I freed my hand from his, trying to smile. Hood noticed and grinned.

We all sat down. Under the table, I clenched and un-clenched my fist and waited for the feeling to come back.

'So...' Hood began. 'Not content with making our lives miserable, you are now freelancing in the neighbouring police authority.'

I opened my mouth to speak. Hood held up his right hand.

'We have joined your crusade against Lloyd Starratt,' he began. 'But for this to be crowned with success, we need the Gloucestershire Constabulary to smile upon everything we do on their patch.'

I opened my mouth again. Hood went on.

'I haven't finished. You appear to be doing your best, to strangle this relationship at birth. And re-arranging Francis Copley's face again is not the way to go. I appreciate he was no oil painting to begin with, but Accident and Emergency has enough to do, without you persistently adding to the load.'

'He started it,' I said.

Hood didn't reply. He stared at me, sighed and got to his feet.

'Come on then. Show us this place of Starratt's.'

Shackleton and I stood up again.

'Can we pick up my car on the way?'

We called at the lay-by, picked up the Healey and I led the way back to the farmyard. We gathered in front of the barns. Shackleton stared for a long time at the restored building. He walked up to one of the windows, pressed his face against it and looked inside. I watched, intrigued. Hood looked at me and nodded approvingly, like a fond parent watching his child do his party trick. Shackleton turned back to face us.

'Hay bales up against the windows. Blocking out the light. Why would someone do that after he had put new windows in?'

'He wouldn't,' I said.

'Unless he had something to hide,' Hood said.

He moved towards the barn. Inspected the big double doors, chained together and padlocked.

'Question,' Shackleton said. 'How to get in without the owner knowing?'

'Let's take a look around the back,' Hood said. He looked at me. 'Are you coming?'

'What, stay here and miss all the fun?'

Shackleton led the way. He chose the left hand side and walked through the passageway between the two buildings. Hood and I followed.

The area behind the barns looked just like another piece of farmyard. Except that it wasn't. It was tidy. And empty. No bits and pieces, none of the usual farm yard detritus and no machinery. Except for a red, two wheeled cart, parked tight against the wall, in front of a door. It was a big metal beast. Eight feet high, ten feet long and six feet wide. Resting at the front on its tow hitch.

Freshly laid concrete stretched from the back of the barns for about thirty feet, to a tall thick hedge, which actually bordered the whole chunk of land. The hedge stretched from left to right as we looked at it, then back on both sides, past the barns, to the entrance yard. The entire site was enclosed and camouflaged from the outside world. And there were a couple of other structures. To the left, behind the un-restored barn, sat two steel ship containers, re-painted green. Presumably used for storage.

Hood consulted Shackleton

'What's beyond the hedge?'

Shackleton dug into the inside pocket of his police jacket and took out an iPhone. He pressed buttons for fifteen seconds or so. The gadget sang and bleeped. He flicked his right index finger across the face of the screen, looked at the result, then showed the screen to Hood.

'Two fields between here and Southfork,' Shackleton said. He pointed over the hedge. 'The place is about three quarters of a mile, as the crow flies.'

Hood looked around him.

'How many vehicles can you get in this space do you think?' he asked.

Shackleton put the iPhone back in his pocket.

'Fifteen, maybe twenty,' he said. 'Depending on the size.'

Hood nodded, looked round the whole area again, then focussed on the piece of engineering.

'It's a Grain Cart,' I suggested.

'Proper name, Chaser Bin,' said Shackleton.

Hood and I looked at him. He shrugged.

'My uncle's a farmer,' he said.

'Can we move it?' Hood asked him.

'We'll never manage to drag it,' Shackleton said. 'But the Volvo's got a tow hitch. If I drive and you two push, we'll get it clear of the door.'

DC Shackleton was the Man, so neither

Hood nor I could gainsay. He skirted the extension and went to fetch the Volvo.

'He's got a degree in communications sciences,' Hood said. 'Being fast-tracked. Word is, he's been watched by OE15. A bunch of funny people at the Home Office.'

Shackleton drove the Volvo into the yard, U turned and backed up to the chaser bin tow hitch. Hood grabbed the handle of the turning bolt and began spinning it clockwise. The cup on the chaser bin hitch rose. Shackleton backed the Volvo tow hitch ball under the cup. Hood turned the handle anti-clockwise and the cup dropped neatly onto the ball. Shackleton unlocked the tow hitch brake. Hood and I got into position behind the bin.

'I'll hit the horn when I want you to push,' Shackleton said and got into the Volvo.

He gently revved the two and a half litre engine, the horn barked, Hood and I pushed and moments later the chaser bin was clear of the re-conditioned door. Shackleton locked the tow hitch brake again and we gathered in front of the door. There was a long steel bolt bar across the door, pushed into the wall on the right hand side of the door frame. Hood hauled it backwards and the door swung open towards him.

He pulled the door wide. DC Shackleton and I followed him into the barn.

And found ourselves standing in what

looked like a circus ring.

We stood in the centre of the barn, in the shaft of daylight which lanced in from outside and looked round three hundred and sixty degrees. We were inside a circle of hay bales, five or six metres in diameter; complete except for two gaps – in front of the doorway we had just come through and the padlocked double doors opposite. Aisles led to the doors like exits from an arena. In front of the hay bales, there was a ring of chain link fence, three feet high. And behind the fence, space where the audience bleachers would be if this was a circus ring. More hay bales were piled in the corners of the barn and up against all the windows.

'What the hell is this place?' Hood asked.

Shackleton was thinking. Hood and I waited.

'I think it's a dog fighting ring,' Shackleton said.

He looked at me.

'You know Starratt. You've met one of his dogs. What do you think?'

I thought it was the most frightening proposal I'd heard in a long time. But I did know somebody who could give us a second opinion. I found my mobile and called Julia, the RSPCA Inspector I'd met at the Great Western Show.

She was in her office. I described the mis-en-scene and its location on Starratt land.

There was a couple of seconds' pause when I finished, then she spoke.

'Hang on a minute.'

She put down her phone receiver and moved away from it. I heard her voice again, distant, talking to someone else in the office. Meanwhile, Shackleton was taking pictures with his iPhone. Julia came back to me.

'We think your DC Shackleton is right. It is a dog fighting ring. And we have some new information here that may lead to something. Will you and your two policemen come in to see us?'

I relayed the request to Hood. He nodded.

'We'll be there in an hour or so,' I said.

I ended the call. Once Shackleton had completed his photographic essay, we moved out of the barn and locked the door. Hood stared at the chaser bin.

'Can we get it back into the same position?' he asked. Then he looked at Shackleton in apology. 'Sorry...'

The bin was reversed back across the doorway. Almost inch perfect. Leaving no sign at all of the barn invasion. A couple of minutes later, I got into the Healey and followed the Volvo out of the yard.

Chapter Seventeen

The Bristol RSPCA headquarters is south of the city centre, in St Phillips. Julia met us in the lobby and took us up a flight of stairs to a large open plan office. She introduced us to Chief Inspector Andrew Overton, head of the Special Operations Unit, who ushered us into a smaller office to the left of the stairwell. The five of us sat round a table and filled the rest of the space in the room. There was a laptop, a blue folder and a couple of DVDs on the table.

Overton picked up one of them.

'This was sent to us three weeks ago. Anonymously. In a padded envelope, post-marked in Newport. See if you recognise anything.'

He slid the DVD into the drive slot of the laptop.

'The pictures have been transferred from footage shot on a mobile phone.'

We all watched the laptop screen. The pictures were shot from a distance, and from some very odd angles. From behind cars and behind people's backs – presumably the operator was being careful. But there was no mistaking the location. The farmyard, the restored barn, a digger to the side of it, the car park behind it, crammed with expensive metal. I looked at Hood and Shackleton. They nodded in agreement. We continued to watch as people got out of their vehicles and moved into the barn. The pictures ran out and the DVD froze.

'Nothing from inside the barn?' Hood asked.

Overton shook his head.

'No phones, cameras, recorders of any kind are allowed into one of these events. Everyone is body searched at the door.'

He waited for one of us to say something else. Julia prompted Hood.

'Is that where you have just been?' she asked.

'Yes,' Hood said.

'Is it Lloyd Starratt's place?'

'We believe so.'

'Tell me about the interior again. Does it look as if it's ready for business?' She turned to me. 'Jack?'

'I don't know,' I said. 'I mean, what state of readiness does it have to be in?'

'Was the ring set up?'

Shackleton took his iPhone out of his jacket pocket and looked at Hood.

'Sure,' Hood said. 'Go on.'

Shackleton showed his pictures to Julia and Overton. When they had scrutinised the folder, Overton talked to all of us again.

'Looks to me like it's ready for action. We don't know how long ago the DVD footage was taken. Whoever sent the picture didn't say. But he, or she, did say, that there was another event planned. There was a hand-written note in the envelope.'

'Have you still got it?' Hood asked.

Overton opened the blue folder and pushed it across the table. The note was in ink and written in neat, capital letters – *THIS WILL HAPPEN AGAIN SOON*. Hood leaned forward and read it. Then looked across at Overton.

'That was all?'

'Yes. Which is why we have kept it to ourselves so far. You know how investigations have to be conducted Sergeant. It takes a long time to gather enough evidence to get to the stage when we can ask you for help. We can't steam in mob handed like the police – if you'll forgive me. However, it looks like you three gentlemen have just found what we need. Thank you.'

Julia took up the story.

'We have all been on Lloyd Starratt's case for a long time. We know he keeps a number of dogs which only just avoid infringing the Dangerous Dogs Act. None of them makes the banned breeds list. And that's the problem. He doesn't keep American Pit Bulls, Blue Nose Pitbulls, Japanese Tosas – there's a list of a dozen or so. Any of his dogs walking down the High Street on a lead would pass for anybody's family pet. By that definition the law is useless.'

DC Shackleton interrupted.

'But surely, the act deals with more than just a list of breeds. The legislation covers any dog, which in the opinion of the Secretary of State, is bred for fighting.'

Overton ploughed into the discussion.

'Or has the appearance of a dog bred for fighting,' he said.

'So...' Shackleton said, 'That gives you room doesn't it?'

'No. You can train a Cocker Spaniel to be aggressive. But do you think anyone is going to look at a little creature like that and say he looks the part? The law should be based on deeds, not breeds. When a house is burgled, you arrest the burglar. Not the crow bar he jemmied the door with.'

'Okay,' I said. 'We all know who's to blame here. It's the Lloyd Starratts of the world.'

Overton went on.

'Absolutely. No legislation will keep any animal or person safe from dogs with irresponsible owners.'

He got out of his chair, walked to the office door, opened it and called into the big room.

'Rufus...'

'Moments later a huge, bronze German Shepherd trotted into the room, stopped, looked at Overton and sat down.

'Good boy,' Overton said. 'Lie down.'

Rufus stretched out flat on the carpet.

'He comes to the office with me every day. Sits by my desk while I work. Goes out with me on calls. Does he look dangerous?'

'No of course not,' Hood said.

'Are the German Shepherds your Dog Unit works with dangerous?'

'No. Although, hopefully, to malefactors they can appear dangerous.'

'So there you are,' Overton said. 'Don't blame the breed. The hard cases and thugs involved in dog fighting can trash the reputation of any dog. Rottweilers were bred as sled dogs. They have immense strength, they can pull carts. They have beautiful faces and instinctively beautiful manners. But at some point, some arsehole with a tattoo starved one, stuck it outside in a kennel, threatened it and turned it mean. So the Rottweiler isn't trusted. Like a bunch of other genuinely friendly dogs. But you can't go round taking Bull Terriers and Doberman Pinschers away from responsible owners.'

'Did you get a good look at that dog outside Starratt's trailer?' Julia asked me.

'Yes. But all I could tell you was I thought it was some kind of Mastiff. I don't know if I was anywhere near any kind of breed recognition. Elaine wasn't frightened of it.'

'Her family has two Collies. Of course

she's not frightened of dogs. She is used to well socialised animals. So she didn't understand the danger. Didn't recognise the threat signals given out when the dog woke up. The dog on the other hand, knew that aggression was the way to get what it wanted. When Elaine didn't back off, it attacked her. That wasn't the dog working on instinct, whatever breed it was. The sad, bloody beast was taught that.'

'So what do we have to do?' I asked.

'Change the legislation,' Julia said. 'Make it tougher. And give us more powers to nail people like Lloyd Starratt.'

There was a long pause. Julia sighed.

'Yes, this is old ground I know.'

Down at my feet, Rufus started to snore gently. Overton grinned.

'Have you got another five minutes?' he asked Hood. 'I'd like to show you something else. I think it's part of this investigation.'

Hood said we had all the time in the world. Overton took the DVD out of the laptop and replaced it with the other one from the table.

I wasn't prepared for what I was about to see. And it turned my stomach over.

The pictures were taken in the Forest of Dean. RSPCA Inspectors digging soil out of two shallow graves. Uncovering the corpses of three dogs. Gaping wounds on their necks and shoulders. Fur and skin ripped from their chests and flanks. Brutal, sickening and finally, impossible to watch. I got up and left the room and found my way to a toilet.

A couple of minutes later, as I was washing my face, Julia found me and apologised.

'But I can't say I'm sorry we made you look at that stuff,' she said. 'Now you know what we're up against.'

'Why were they buried? Surely it would have been sensible to burn the corpses.'

'Yes it would. We suspect that on this occasion, the dogs died on the way home from a fight. So they were dumped.'

'How did you find them?'

'Straight out of *Midsomer Murders*. You know, the scene. The one where the local shopkeeper's dog finds something half buried on his morning walk through the woods.' Her voice softened. 'Are you okay? You look a bit green.'

I pulled a paper towel out of the wall dispenser and dried my face.

'You know, our purpose isn't just to save animals – although that's what we are forced to try and do. Our job is to find the people who do these barbaric things and prosecute them. In essence, it's so simple. Stop them doing what they're doing and the problem will go away. I can tell you, hand on heart, that I would joyfully embrace not having to do this job. If overnight, it was rendered unnecessary and I found myself out of work,

I would raise the biggest cheer ever heard on God's green earth.'

I dropped the paper towel in the plastic bin under the dispenser. Julia held the door open for me.

'But then, all of us in the charity business have the same unredeemable mantra– "If only we didn't have to do it". I apologise again, for the outburst. We get too involved sometimes.'

We went back to the office. Shackleton was sitting on the floor with Rufus. Overton was talking to Hood.

'In the past, we've been assisted on raids by officers at Trinity Road from a unit called ST5.'

'Yes I know it. I'll talk to them.'

'Can they get some surveillance in place quickly? This next event may be in a couple of days.'

'The sooner the better I should imagine,' Hood said. 'Less expensive if we don't have to hang around.'

The two men shook hands.

'Thank you,' Overton said. He looked round the office. 'All of you.'

Shackleton got to his feet. Rufus looked up at him.

'Bye Rufus,' he said.

'Say goodbye Rufus,' Overton ordered.

Rufus barked once and got to his feet. We filed out into the main office. Rufus escorted us to the head of the stairs.

I drove across town. Realised I hadn't had any lunch and picked up a tuna sandwich and a salad. I was back in my office at 3.15. There were no messages on the answering machine. I made coffee, ate the sandwich and pondered.

It was obvious I had to suspend operations on Lloyd Starratt. We all had to let this planned dog fight go ahead. And if Starratt was caught in flagrante, so much the better. He would have the guardians of law and order swarming all over him, like flies on the dog turd that he was. And that could only enhance investigations into the whereabouts of Dujic and Tudjman.

So, what else to do?... I locked on to a revolutionary idea. Call my client. I did, got the default message from the service provider and rang off. Called again, this time checking the display on the handset, to make sure I wasn't hitting the wrong buttons and leaving a message for a stranger. I told Deborah that Francis Copley was out of the picture, that we were making progress with Lloyd Starratt, and that I would get back to her in due course.

A minute's work done and I was back in limbo again. Which led me to further contemplation and to considerations of south Devon. I needed a new road atlas for the office. As big a scale as possible.

I decided to avoid the miseries of the approaching late afternoon traffic, walked round to the Nova Scotia and took the harbour Ferry into the city centre. I paid £3.50 and we chugged gracefully through the sunshine. Giving me time to work out what I was really after. Fifteen minutes later, I disembarked at Castle Park, crossed the kids playground and walked into Broadmead.

In W H Smith, I bought the three ordinance survey maps which cover the south coast of Devon.

OS maps are brilliant for beaches. Cliff faces, shale, shingle, pebbles and, what I was looking for, sand. There's actually not much of that in south Devon.

A spectacular coastline it is, but not the first choice for a bucket and spade holiday. Apart from Seaton and Sidmouth, west of Lyme Regis it's mostly pebbles all the way to the English Riviera. Torbay has a sandy beach. But that gives way to shingle and the rocky bays and soaring cliffs round Brixham. On past Dartmouth and all the way round Start Bay it's the same. No sand. And from Start Point, westwards, past Salcombe and on to Plymouth, there is only one real sandy beach. Or rather a cluster of them, around the gloriously named Bigbury on Sea.

I had maps spread over the floor and across the top of my desk, when Chrissie arrived. With Sam. He bounced into the office and Chrissie called for him to 'Sit'. He did. On Totnes. Which didn't matter much, because Totnes doesn't have a beach.

'Not barging in are we?' Chrissie asked.

'No, you're not. Great to see you.'

'We've just spent an hour running round the Ashton Court estate.'

I tried to gather up the maps on the floor – at least those Sam wasn't sitting on. As every activity in his life equates to play, he thought this was some new game and it was ages before any semblance of order was restored.

'Are you thinking of buying a boat?' Chrissie asked.

I looked at her. She went on.

'Or a cottage by the sea perhaps?'

Sam slid into the seat well under my desk and lay down.

'This is research,' I said. 'Into the sandy beaches of south Devon.'

'There aren't many of those.'

'So I've discovered.'

'And the best is at Bigbury on Sea.'

'Do you know it?'

'I've been there. With Adam. He knows the place really well. He's at the paper. Do you want me to call him?'

Chrissie caught Adam in the lobby of the

Post building, on his way out of the door.

'I'll be with you in half an hour,' he said.

I took the beach photographs out of the desk drawer and passed them to Chrissie. She studied them,

'Could be,' she said. She gave the picture of the boy back to me. 'Look at the sand.'

There was a lot of it. The boy was surrounded by sand. Firm dark sand. The sort of sand that is regularly covered by the incoming tide. Chrissie handed me the other photograph.

'Now look at that one again.'

The woman was sitting on her beach towel, on the same kind of sand. Behind her the shoreline cliffs. I looked at the picture of the boy again.

'Notice,' Chrissie said. 'No sea anywhere. In either picture.'

'Well there wouldn't be in the photograph of the woman,' I said.

'Absolutely. But what about the boy? Where is he standing?'

'The background's different. And the tide's out. So he's on another part of the beach. Maybe at a different time of day.'

'Supposing he isn't?'

'But he is. Obviously.'

Chrissie grinned at me.

'I don't want to say any more. I might be wrong. When Adam arrives, show him the pictures cold. Don't give him any clues. Just tell him south Devon. Let him come up with his own assessment.'

I stared at the pictures again.

'They're not taken in different places,' Adam said. 'They're reverse points of view. The one of the woman is shot looking up the beach, the one of the boy looking out to sea.'

'Can't be,' I said. 'There's a wall or a cliff behind him.'

'It's an island,' Adam said.

I looked at the picture again.

'Behind the kid. Burgh Island.' He pointed at the desk top. 'Look at the OS map again. The Torbay and Salcombe one.'

All three of us gathered round my desk. Sam shuffled forwards and poked his head out of the seat well, decided that nothing interesting was happening after all and dropped his head back on to his paws.

On the map, Adam traced the coastline westwards from Start Point.

'Look... No sandy beaches until you get to Bigbury. And there, out at sea, across two hundred yards of beach, is Burgh Island. Just a big rock really. With a hotel on it.'

He picked up the photograph of the boy.

'The background's out of focus but... Behind him, is the base rock. To his left, is the slipway up from the beach. Can I use your pc?'

'Sure.'

Moments later Burgh Island was on the screen. A stunning shot, taken at high tide, from the hillside above Bigbury beach. The island was just that. Two hundred yards from the shore and surrounded by water. Adam tapped the keyboard and the picture was replaced by another, taken from the same place, at low tide. And we were looking at the beach. Unbroken, rich, bronze sand.

'For a couple of hours, twice a day, the island is surrounded by water,' Adam said.

On the island, just above the slipway, the Burgh Island Hotel sat in restored art deco splendour. Adam gave us a potted history.

'The original house was built in the 1920s. By an Edwardian captain of industry, for his Bohemian wife and her friends. Almost as far west as you could get from London. A luxury gaff, away from the prying eyes of his business competitors. A bolt hole for the artistic and the extra-ordinary. A place where it didn't matter who your companion was, or what your sexual preferences were. Flappers and bright young things, played and drank and danced to swing bands from London clubs.'

I looked at the screen for a long time. They must have had great parties. 'Now restored. A hotel where you still dress for dinner.'

'How do you know this place?' I asked.

'We ate there once upon a time,' Chrissie said, 'A couple of summers ago. No more than lunch, I hasten to add.' She nodded at Adam. 'This man has occupied a suite there however.'

'Back in 2008,' Adam said. 'A weekend bash, at the invitation of the only truly rich person I know. Hamilton Bainbridge. Known as Hammy to his friends. He's a broker. Sort of. He fiddles with money.'

'The appropriate choice of word,' I said.

'I shared a room with him, first year at university. I saved his life.'

'What?'

Adam looked at me and grinned.

'That's how he's always looked at it. We were both on the swimming team. He turned up for training one day, pissed. Dived into the shallow end of the pool, hit his head on the bottom and floated back to the surface. Unconscious, face down in the water, blood pouring from his forehead. I got him out of the pool, woke him up and staunched the bleeding. He has cherished that moment. Emails me a couple of times a year. And we catch up at places like Simpsons and the Savoy. He's actually one hundred and fourteenth in line to the throne.'

I stared at him. 'Why haven't I heard this story before?'

'Just a bygone deed of heroism I never talk about.'

He looked at the photographs again.

'So who are these two?'

'I don't know,' I said 'But, suddenly, I'm getting closer. I think the pictures were taken by my client. On holiday.' I pointed at the pc screen.

'There, at Burgh Island, maybe.'

Expensive maybe, but it was the sort of place Deborah could afford. Exclusive. And that was good too, given the date. Deborah had been living as a woman for eighteen months at that point. Coping with all the complications and the uncertainties and the terrifying prospect of the surgery she was about to undergo.

'So,' Chrissie said, 'If you need peace and tranquillity and uncomplicated days, Burgh Island is the place.'

'And if the three of them did stay there,' Adam said, 'the hotel will have names and addresses. Information they may pass on to you... If you give them reason enough.'

We all sat in silence for while. Then Adam spoke again.

'Okay,' he said. 'Who's for something to eat and a night on the town?' He looked at me. 'Jack?'

'Even if I thought you were being remotely serious I'd still say no. A takeaway, home, bath and early bed for me.'

Adam called to the dog.

'What do you think Sam?'

There was a grunt, a rustling and a scraping and Sam came out from under the desk.

Tail wagging, ready for anything. Chrissie told me to sleep well and the three of them left the office.

I tidied up the maps and sat at my desk for ages, suddenly overwhelmed by tiredness. Nine hours ago, I had driven over the Severn Bridge to find Lloyd Starratt. Instead, I had met Francis Copley, two paramedics, a bunch of Gloucestershire coppers, Bristol coppers, RSPCA inspectors and a German Shepherd called Rufus. Along with Chrissie, Adam and Sam. The most people I had ever encountered in the course of one working day.

And now Linda. There was a gentle knock on the office door. I invited her in. She was wearing another stunning business suit, this time a navy blue number.

'Have you been out impressing people again?' I asked.

'I guess some of us can afford to sit at a desk all day.'

She took a step forward and tilted her head to one side.

'You look terrible,' she said. 'Are you alright?'

'I will be. Given a moment or two of TLC.'

'Oh dear,' she said. 'That's a little unsubtle. You must be desperate.'

She stood in front of my desk. I got to my feet, moved round to join her. She swung to face me, leaned her backside against the desk and let it take her weight.

'So?...'

I kissed her. She opened her mouth, arched her back and gently rotated her hips. It was a while before we finished. I stepped back.

'Better?' she asked.

'All the difference in the world.'

'So where have you been all day?'

I told her. She grew more astonished as the tale progressed.

'I have a drinks date with a client in a few minutes,' she said. 'But we can meet later.'

I shook my head. 'I need a few hours to myself. And a bit of thinking time. Do you mind?'

'Of course not.' Linda opened the office door. 'See you tomorrow.'

She glided out into the corridor. I picked up the laptop and the OS maps, found my car keys and moved to the door.

The phone on my desk rang. I turned and stared accusingly at it for a couple of seconds. Yes or no? Had to be yes. There's always the possibility that the call at the end of the day will be the one which breaks the case. I put the laptop down on the desk and picked up the receiver. Some manic tosser in a call centre asked me if I was aware that sixty-five percent of small business persons were under insured. I told him I was amazed at that statistic and put the receiver down.

I drove home though Clifton away from the traffic, and then east into Redland from the Downs. With a short stop at the Shing To Takeaway, to pick up beef in black bean sauce, fried rice and vegetables.

While I was eating I watched a double bill *Dad's Army* – the immortally funny episode with the grenade down Jones' trousers and the heart breaking 'brief encounter' story. That was the highlight of an eighty-five channel choice. I tried to get interested in the new ITV, post watershed thriller, but lost interest during the first commercial break, which arrived less than eight minutes in.

I called Chrissie. We talked for half an hour or so. Then Auntie Joyce rang moments later. She sounded relieved to find me still in one piece. I told her that all was well and all the bad guys – save the two Serb gentlemen – had been dealt with. Had I found Deborah? Not exactly, but we were now communicating by phone. Auntie Joyce suggested I might consider updating the Thorntons. So when she rang off, I did. At least I spoke to Elizabeth. Bill was out at some local business do. Supernaturally boring was Elizabeth's take on it. She thanked me for all that I was doing. Deborah had called. Once and briefly, but it was enough to know she was well. I told her I was pleased. She thanked me again.

I was in bed before 10 o'clock.

Chapter Eighteen

Over breakfast, I made a decision about south Devon. On offer, was a two and a half hour drive, to persuade a bunch of people who didn't know me from a hole in the ground, to talk to me. The hotel staff might not fess up. But they would have to respond to the police. So, breakfast over, I drove to Trinity Road to talk to Harvey.

He made a massive effort to suppress his amusement when I asked for his help. We sat in his office, drinking more cups of DC Shackleton's freshly brewed coffee. If attention could ever be assessed as both rapt and ironical at the same time, then Harvey was accomplishing it. When I finished pleading, he sat up straight and looked me right in the eyes.

'Are you not at risk of betraying client confidentiality here? Personally I don't give a toss – "information information information" is my motto. But with you, it's a matter of integrity; embedded deep. You'd better be careful this doesn't get out. All the people queuing up to offer you work will lose confidence.'

He was really enjoying this. He had an axe

buried in my head and he was managing to grind it at the same time.

'Are you making progress on the Philip Soames business?' I asked.

My attempt to deflect his purpose didn't bother him at all.

'Are you offering to help?'

'How? I don't know any more than you do.'

'So what are you offering? In return for the favour you're asking.'

'I've done my best to give you Lloyd Starratt,' I said. 'I've hoovered up a couple of west London enforcers...'

'Indirectly...'

'And now, finding my client will help with everything else. In particular, the Philip Soames murder.'

'We don't know that.'

'Jesus Christ Harvey!...'

He stared at me. Then down at his desk, then out of the window, then back at me. He blew out his cheeks. I pressed on.

'I need your help,' I said. 'That's all. I'm not asking you to break any rules. It's a genuine, routine piece of police work. You can do it in moments.'

Harvey folded his arms across his chest and nodded his head.

'Go and see DC Shackleton. Tell him I said it was okay.'

He un-folded his arms, sat back in his

chair and waited for me to leave. But I had to establish something else.

'Can I have your assurance that you won't act on the information DC Shackleton will gather? At least, not before I can.'

Harvey chose his words carefully.

'We may decide not to waste police time and resources looking for someone who is, at the moment, of no direct interest to our investigations.'

'Thanks,' I said and got to my feet.

'However...' Harvey continued. 'If, at some time in the near future, we deem the information useful to us...'

He gave me his best 'understand what I mean' stare. I left the office and went in search of DC Shackleton.

I showed him the photographs and told him the story. He called the Burgh Island Hotel and talked to the manager, who passed him on to the owner, who consulted his wife, the co-owner, who agreed they should all help. As soon as they could, but not immediately. There were two weddings and an evening function to get through today. Shackleton ended the call.

'We'll do this by email,' he said. 'Give them twenty-four hours. Don't worry. We'll get you what you want to know.'

He scanned the beach photographs and Deborah's picture into his computer. I gave him a list of questions to ask the hotel staff.

I was back in my office by 11 o'clock. The phone began ringing as I opened the door.

'I'm working up a story about the Starratt clan,' Adam said. 'I cast the net a bit wider than the bounds of the *Post* archive. And I found something which might give you pause. Latterly, Lloyd Starratt has been given to good works.'

I sat down in my chair.

'Difficult to imagine I know,' Adam said. 'But his deeds are writ large.'

'Where?' I asked.

'In the *Chepstow and Wye Valley Gazette*.'

'So not that large then.'

'Nonetheless, worthy of note. I'll email you a folder. Take a look at it.'

I switched the laptop on and set about making coffee. Not up to DC Shackleton's mucho gusto standard, but drinkable enough. I took the mug back to my desk, sat down and called up my email inbox; downloaded Adam's file.

And worthy of note it was.

The South Wye Valley Comprehensive School sits on rising land north of Chepstow. Separated from a 60s built council estate and its primary school on the outskirts of the town, by what was once two acres of meadow. Owned by Lloyd Starratt. And now transformed, through the generosity of its benefactor, into a playing field, to be shared by both schools. A cricket square in the middle, a four hundred metre running track, two football pitches, showers and changing rooms. The inaugural football fixtures were scheduled for the first Saturday of the autumn term, but meanwhile, midway through the previous summer term, there had been a bit of a do. A marquee, a barbecue and *Ballistic* – the band from South Wye Valley Year Twelve. Children, parents, local dignitaries, teachers, and school governors, celebrating the completion of the work, with a cricket match between parents and the South Wye Valley First Eleven.

A reporter and photographer from the *Gazette* had chronicled the event. The article glowed with praise for the project. An album of pictures were taken. And there was Lloyd, posing and posturing and milking the occasion for all it was worth. He had even made a speech, thanking all those who had come together to make it all possible.

Albeit coming from Lloyd, the un-knowing reader would have given way to emotion and felt a lump in his throat. However the more cynical among us could have been forgiven for feeling their gorge rising and searching for the sick bag.

Lloyd was at it. In spades.

The phone rang again.

'Have you got the stuff?' Adam asked.

'Only Lloyd Starratt could morph from philanthropist into dog-fight promoter.'

'And I've just discovered something else. The primary school, Meadow Estate, has been in "special measures" for three consecutive Ofsted inspections and is now deemed a failing school. The local education authority, in cahoots with the Minister for Education, has informed the governors they intend to turn it into an Academy. Do you know how academies work?'

'Tell me.'

'Well essentially, they're self governing. Most are constituted as charities, or taken under the wing of already existing charitable organisations. There's a bunch of those around the country, running groups of academies. This, that and the other trust. Academies operate independently of the local education authority. Usually funded by some version of a public private partnership. These private sponsors are charged with bringing, and here I quote, *qualities of success* to academies, to be *creative and innovative* and to change the *long term trend of failure in the schools they replace*. That's the mission.'

'So the story with Meadow Estate is?...'

'The governors feel they're being bullied by chief wizard Michael Gove. The teachers think they're going to lose their jobs. And a group of parents have got together to oppose it. But here's the thing. One of the would be investor sponsors in the Meadow Academy Charitable Trust, is Forest Holdings. Of which the CEO is? One guess only...'

'Lloyd Starratt.'

'Every egg a bird.'

'So what does he get out of the deal? I mean, he can't claim to have a track record in educational reform.'

'Apparently, in return for a minimum investment of ten per cent of the academy's capital costs, the sponsor is able to influence the process of establishing the school, its curriculum, ethos and any specialisation.'

'Such as?...'

'Take your pick. Science, business and enterprise, sport, technology, the performing arts. You remember the evangelical christian greengrocer?'

'Boss of some chain stores, yes. He got into trouble.'

'He was accused of promoting the teaching of some obscure evolutionary doctrines in his academies.'

'Leaves the field wide open for Lloyd,' I said.

'It's all glorious bollocks,' Adam said. 'But more than likely to happen. Think about it Jack. Lloyd Starratt running a school.'

I couldn't bear to think about it. It was unimaginable, untrammelled absurdity.

'So are we on a crusade to put a stop to this foolishness?' Adam asked.

'Absolutely,' I said.

'I'll keep digging,' he said. 'In the meantime, I'm going to talk with the parents action group. Write something about them. Big them up a bit. Talk to you later…'

He rang off.

I shook my head. Tried to clear it of all thoughts of Lloyd Starratt the educator. I was having no success, when the phone rang again. It was Julia.

'We have just heard from ST5,' she said. 'Their intelligence leads them to believe the dog fight is happening tomorrow afternoon.'

'They got on to that quickly.'

'They were most of the way there apparently. They have someone under cover, who has someone among Lloyd Starratt's cronies. They just weren't sure about the location. You gave it to them.'

Suddenly I felt five hundred per cent better. I must have been deep in thought for a while, because Julia asked me if I was still there. I asked her what the next step was.

'The raid is organised.'

'Can I be there?'

'Officially, ST5 won't let you go along. But as it's a combined operation, we can. As a support investigator. Maybe with the video team.'

'You record the raid?'

'In all its hideous drama. We have to have evidence.'

I began thinking about this. Julia came back to me.

'Do you have a strong stomach?'

'No. You saw yesterday. I'm one of the great throwers-up.'

'You don't have to be there,' she suggested.

'Yes I do. What's the schedule?'

'There'll be a briefing at 10 o'clock tomorrow morning, at Trinity Road. Andy will describe what we think is likely to happen in the barn. The DI heading the ST5 team will then go through the whole operation in detail. The police team will include two marksmen with rifles. We will have two vets with us. The problem is, nobody is quite sure when the event gets under way. We have to get into the barn before the whole gruesome business begins. But preferably, once there is a full house. We need to nail the organisers, and be able to prosecute everyone there, including the punters. If there is nothing happening, we won't be able to. It's not against the law for a bunch of people to gather in the country for some private doggie celebration.'

'How many are there likely to be? Do you know?'

'Twenty-five or thirty. And there may be a number of fights on the bill.'

'So what is the main attraction. The fighting, or the betting?'

'The betting is as ferocious as the action. Bets can be huge. Four or five hundred on a dog. This is a business Jack. And it turns over a small fortune for the promoters.'

In this case, Lloyd Starratt and his band of heroes.

Julia asked me, once again, if I wanted to be involved in this. I assured her I did. She asked me to be in her office at nine tomorrow morning and ended the call.

The euphoria of five minutes ago had evaporated. Suddenly I was thinking of Sam and Rufus and the joy they bring to all of us. Dogs give unconditionally. Sure, they expect to have a roof over their heads. To be fed and played with and exercised and allowed to sleep soundly and unafraid. But for that small outlay, the humans get massive returns. Friendship, love and a relationship which last the dog's lifetime. We bring dogs into our world and they live with us on trust. It's a very simple deal. The minimum requirement is that we return the love they inspire.

I needed a distraction. Some entertainment.

Considering an early afternoon screening at one of the multiplexes, I went out and bought the lunchtime addition of the *Post*. But the movies on offer failed to excite. It was mostly franchise fair. More of the *Twilight* saga, the latest Jason Statham violence fest, a vehicle for Justin Beiber which had bored the critics comatose and a romcom starring Adam Sandler, Sarah Jessica Parker and a quartet of meerkats.

But there was a invitation to excitement on page three of the paper. A four column ad for the annual August Fair, up and running on the Downs. The Waltzer, the Dodgems, the white knuckle Bomber, carousels and candyfloss, hot dogs and fried onions. Just what the doctor ordered.

I knocked on Linda's office door.

'Are you busy?'

'I'm devoting the rest of the day to making phone calls and emailing client invoices,' she said.

'Take a break,' I said. 'Come with me to the fair.'

She stared at me.

'On the Downs,' I said. 'When were you last on the Helter Skelter?'

'Probably when I was twelve.'

'Far too long ago. Come on. I'll buy you a toffee apple.'

'Irresistible,' she said. 'How can a girl turn down a toffee apple?'

And with that, we were under way.

We had a terrific couple of hours. As excited as we could only remember being. Daft as a couple of kids.

The August Downs Fair has been running for generations; with a license from the city council to return every year, in the run-up to the August bank holiday. It was the highlight of the summer for Chrissie, until she decided she was too grown up to be out having fun in the company of her parents. So the visits stopped. And today, it was great to be back.

Getting in to the Healey, mid afternoon, I asked Linda if she had to go back to the office.

'Afraid so,' she said.

'Can't the invoices wait?'

'Not if I want the books to balance at the end of the month.'

'I was just thinking…'

I put the key into the ignition. When I looked up again, Linda was staring at me. She looked like she was about to say something, so I waited.

'Okay,' she said. 'What have you been thinking Jack? When all the time we should have been doing.'

I stared at her. She elaborated a little.

'You know what you did? You thought us into this.'

She held up her hand as I opened my mouth to speak.

'Then you thought us on to hold. So what are you doing now? Thinking us into an interim tea time fuck? We are worth more than that. At least I am.'

'I thought some candyfloss and a toffee apple...'

It wouldn't have been an award winning joke, even if I had managed to get to the punch line. As it was, I comprehensively ruined the day. Linda glared at me.

'Jesus Christ Jack. It's bloody simple. Or it should be. You and me and no thinking. It's either the best idea in the world, or it isn't. As far as I'm concerned...'

She stopped mid sentence. She shook her head.

'Never mind.'

'What?'

'Just that. The office. Please.'

The Healey engine turned over and fired. I backed out of the avenue of parked cars and turned onto Downs Road. We drove back to the office in silence. I stopped at the front of the building. Linda climbed out of the car and went into the lobby. I watched her go. Like a wakened sleeper coming out of a dream and confronting reality.

I didn't need to go back to my office. I U-turned the Healey, drove round the Cumberland Basin and headed for home. I switched on the radio. Trisha Yearwood was singing *Two Days From Knowing*.

Another prime candidate for Patrick in his torch song mode.

As for me?... I was complicating something which should be dead simple.

Chapter Nineteen

There were fourteen of us sitting around a table in a meeting room at Trinity Road. DCI Maynard and DS Brown from ST5; Hood and Shackleton; Andy Overton, Julia, two other Inspectors, Tony the video technician and me; two vets and two police marksmen. One of them, DS Allen, got to his feet and picked up a.22 rifle.

'As Andy explained, we hope that he and his team will be able to get to the dogs before anything serious happens and take control with Graspers and Breaking Sticks,' he said. 'But if that's not possible, we may have to shoot the animals. The worst case scenario.'

He held his arms out palms upwards and cradled the rifle.

'This weapon shoots darts by compressed gas. If there are two dogs fighting when we get into the barn, a sedative will be no use. We will have to use a paralysing agent.'

He held a dart up for us all to see. It was about half an inch long.

'13 millimetres,' Allen said. 'Basically it's a ballistic syringe, with the drug loaded in a hypodermic needle. The needle has a barbed collar on it – to make sure that the dart stays in the dog and the full dose is administered. There is a steel ball at the back of the dart and on impact, the momentum of the ball pushes the syringe plunger and injects the drug into the dog.'

He gave us a couple of moments to absorb all that, then sat down again. DCI Maynard continued.

'As soon as the dogs are shot – if that's the way it goes – the vets and the RSPCA inspectors will have to move quickly, to protect the animals and monitor their vital signs. If the dogs are deemed to be too badly injured, they will be killed by a lethal injection.'

He gestured to DS Brown, Overton, Julia and the Inspectors.

'We've done this sort of operation before. Alas, too often. But it does mean we can predict how the people in the barn will react. Some of them will try to leave, but most of them will accept they are in trouble and behave. When we get to Chepstow we'll be joined by a bunch of local police officers. The crowd will be their responsibility. Once in the barn, the dogs will be the priority. The first action for all of us around this table, will be to support the RSPCA Inspectors and the vets.'

He now included Tony and I.

'Concentrate on taking pictures of the dogs. Ignore the people. They'll be dealt with as soon as everything calms down.'

Then he surveyed the whole room again.
'Any questions?'

There was complete silence. DCI Maynard looked at the clock on the wall at the far end of the room. 10.23.

'We leave at half past,' he said.

We left Trinity Road in two vehicles. The four detectives, looking every inch a Countryside Alliance quartet, in a silver-grey Range Rover; the rest of us in a dark blue Mercedes fifteen seater minibus. We picked up another Mercedes in Chepstow, stuffed with local coppers; added three more in plain clothes to our passenger list, then drove to the now familiar lay-by.

We got out of the buses and assembled in front of Maynard. He completed the briefing.

'We're still not sure what time the shindig will start. Ideally, we want to interrupt proceedings after all the punters have arrived. Grab as big a haul as we can. So we'll get into position and wait... There will be a couple of undesirables stationed at the lane end leading to the farm. The two buses will pull up a quarter of a mile short. Then all of you will stay low. Lie on the floor if you have to. Just make sure everybody passing, believes the buses are empty. We'll go on with the Range Rover and deal with the two sentries in the lane. That done, we'll radio back to the rest of you and invite you to join us.'

He pointed at the plain clothes cops.

'You will replace the sentries. The rest of you will follow the Range Rover up the lane, stop with twenty yards to spare and let us drive into the farmyard. Again, we'll deal with any security problems in the yard, then ask you to come on.'

He pointed at the line of uniformed coppers and counted to twelve.

'There are barn entrances back and front. You will go around the back. On my signal open the door and go in. And hold your positions. Don't wade into anything, just don't let anybody out. The rest of us will go in the front door. Remember, the dogs are priority one. Let the marksmen and the vets go to work. Once that's accomplished, you can then set about anybody who's misbehaving. And you have my permission to be as pro-active as you feel is necessary.'

He nodded at Hood, who took an A5 size envelope from inside his jacket, opened it and handed out copies of a photograph.

'Keep a sharp lookout for this yahoo. Lloyd Starratt. He's the chief malefactor. Grab him, any of you; sit on him and don't let him go. I don't care how many size twelve boots have to stand on his neck.'

Maynard looked at his watch.

'Okay, let's do this…'

At just before 1 o'clock, we parked up again. From the front seat of the Mercedes, I watched the Range Rover disappear around the bend in the road ahead. The second Mercedes pulled in behind us. The walkie-talkie on the shoulder of the cop sitting next to me crackled into life.

'Complete radio silence now,' Maynard ordered. 'Get down out of sight. We'll get back to you.'

Three minutes later he did.

'Come on now,' he said.

A few yards along the lane, a couple of heavyweights were sitting side by side on the grass with their feet in a ditch, their hands cuffed behind their backs. The Range Rover was parked, pointing in the direction of the farmyard. The sentries' long wheelbase Land Rover was sitting behind it. The two buses squeezed by and stopped. The plain clothes cops, hefted the heavyweights out of the ditch, escorted them to the Land Rover and shoved them into the back. One of them took up station by the rear door. The other two, moved to the head of the lane and replaced the sentries.

The Range Rover went on ahead and the four detectives did their routine again. Then the rest of us were called into the yard. Two more of Lloyd's associates were in handcuffs. Chained to the wheel spokes of a hay baler.

The barn door facing into the yard was closed but not locked. Maynard gave his final instructions to the police who were headed for the other side of the barn.

'The door on the other side isn't locked either.'

Then he included all of us.

'According to Dumb and Dumber...' He jerked his thumb in the direction of the hay baler. 'There are already twenty-six punters inside. And they're ready to start. So let's–'

A huge roar of noise erupted inside the barn. Maynard yelled at everyone.

'Thirty seconds from... Now.'

We all started counting. DS Brown and the back door cops set off at a run and disappeared around the side of the building. Maynard, Hood and Shackleton stepped towards the double doors. The rest of us closed up behind. Hood took hold of the right hand door hook, Shackleton the left. Everybody counted down. Maynard yelled at Hood and Shackleton and they heaved. The doors swung open. The wall of noise spilled out into the yard. Flanked by the marksmen, Maynard led the way into the barn. The rest of us moved in behind them and fanned out left and right. Across the barn, the rear door opened. Brown and his band of locals dived in from the car park.

That's all I could take in, before the reality of the carnage in the middle of the ring hit home. Tony began filming. I could only watch, rooted to the spot. One of the dogs, dark grey in colour, bleeding from a hole where the flesh had been ripped from its left flank, had its teeth deep into the neck of the other – a huge white beast, which was shaking its head from side to side, desperate to dislodge its opponent's jaws. The dogs rose up on to their hind legs, lost balance and thumped to the ground. The grey dog's head hit the barn floor with a crunch like a hammer splintering wood. It lost grip on the white dog. The white dog rolled over, then stood up, blood streaming out of the wound in its throat. The two were separated by about eight feet. Maynard looked at Overton, who took a nano-second to make a decision. He yelled 'Yes' at Maynard, who raised his right hand and waved an order to the marksmen. The white dog was hit in mid air as it launched itself across the space. A shock wave rippled from its head to its flanks and it lost all control of the attack. It hit the ground inches short of the grey dog, which got to its feet as the dart went into its shoulder, spun around, staggered a couple of paces, fell onto its belly, got to its feet and fell again.

By which time, although the noise level had fallen considerably, chaos was reigning supreme among the punters. Maynard took a police .38 out of a shoulder holster and fired twice into the pile of straw bales to his left. On the other side of the barn, Brown did the same. Three of the punters made the mistake of trying to get through the police lining the main doors. The first was felled by a kick in the groin. Another was punched in his adam's apple. He grabbed at his throat and fell to his knees choking. The third was lifted off his feet by two cops, up-ended and dropped face down on to the floor.

Suddenly everything was quiet. The two vets and Julia and Overton were inside the ring.

George Hood had Lloyd Starratt in a half nelson, his face buried in a straw bale. Lloyd was struggling and yelling something indistinguishable. Hood pulled his head up. With his face full of straw, Lloyd looked like Worzel Gummidge.

'What was that?' Hood asked.

'You have no right to–' was all Lloyd managed to get out. Hood shoved his face back into the hay bale.

Maynard addressed everyone else in the barn.

'Where are the rest of the dogs?... Come on... Somebody...'

There was no response. Maynard called across to Brown.

'Take a couple of officers and go look in the car park. And while you're out there, take a note of all the registration numbers.'

Brown and two of the local cops went

outside. Hood clamped a pair of handcuffs on Lloyd's wrists. He turned Lloyd round, then pushed him back down onto the bales.

'Don't move a fucking inch,' Hood said.

Maynard walked into the centre of the ring. He knelt down beside the white dog, still bleeding from its neck. He looked at the vet tending to the dog. 'He's going to die, he's lost two much blood,' the vet said. 'I'll put him out of his misery.'

He took a hypodermic of pentobarbital out of the briefcase on the floor next to him and injected the beast. Julia stepped over to the dog and watched. Maynard turned away and gave orders to the police officers.

'Get all these people over there next to Starratt. Sit them down. Names, addresses and car registration numbers. Check with the officers in the car park. When you match owners to any dogs outside, arrest them. Find out who's holding the betting money and arrest him too.'

He looked around at all the cops, now busy doing stuff. Picked out one of the Mercedes bus drivers.

'Dobson isn't it?'

'Sir.'

'Right. When you've weeded out the hard cases, shove the rest of the bastards into the buses and lock them in.'

Dobson nodded at the DCI. 'Sir.'

I moved into the ring and stood at Julia's

shoulder. The vet dealing with the white dog got to his feet.

'He's gone,' he said.

A couple of yards away, Overton was discussing the grey dog's prospects with the other vet.

'He has skull damage,' the vet said. 'I don't know how bad it is. X-rays will tell us, but even if the poor bloody creature survives…'

He couldn't finish the sentence.

'Put him down,' Overton said.

Julia asked me if I was alright. I couldn't speak. I shook my head and walked out into the sunshine of the farmyard.

The next half hour or so, was a haze of discomfort and misery. I was sick down a drain in the yard. I found a bottle of water under one of the seats of the Mercedes I had travelled in. Maynard came out into the sunshine and talked into his mobile. I watched as a crocodile of punters was escorted across the yard and on to the other bus. The two men handcuffed to the hay baler looked on, helpless and pissed off. Two more police vans, one of them a blue Ford Transit with grills on the windows, drove into the yard. Maynard now had a sizeable chunk of the Gloucestershire Constabulary's fleet at his disposal.

As I dragged myself back into a reasonable condition, I got fed up with sitting in the yard. I had no desire to go back into the barn, so I took a walk around the real estate.

In the car park, Overton, Julia, Tony and the vets were dealing with the other four dogs on the afternoon's bill. Something else I didn't want to see. Which left me with no choice other than to inspect the green painted ship containers.

The doors on both containers were closed and padlocked. I walked around them. First one, then the other. They were as boring as huge steel boxes could be. But the padlocks were heavy duty items. Big, silver and brand new; by no means your average, across the counter, hardware store kind. Which gave rise to speculation as to what could be inside the containers.

I went looking for a sledgehammer and found one in the unrestored barn; behind an old workbench, amongst the wooden crates, the engine blocks, the broken machinery and the tractor bits.

Despite its weight, the lock on the first container bolt, broke at the third blow of the sledge. I swung the doors open.

And out of nowhere, surged a truck load of brand new possibilities.

Inside the container, there were two battered sofas, a couple of old armchairs, a cheap chain store dining table with half a dozen chairs around it. There was a double door kitchen unit standing in the down right corner, with a two bar electric fire alongside it. And lying on the floor was a metal inspection lamp, the kind a car mechanic uses to hang above a car engine when he's working under the bonnet. Heat and light. Sort of. The left hand wall was lined with bright red, metal framed, bunk beds – eight of them, stretching four by two, along the wall from the doors to the rear of the container. And in the extreme right hand corner, was an area fringed by a plastic shower curtain. There was even a carpet on the floor. Not Axminster by any means, but somebody's careless attempt to turn a crap steel box into a crap steel box with a carpet.

Even with the doors open, the container smelled like a locked up fish and chip shop. With a combination of other odours attached, like damp and sweat and the faint smell of shit.

I stepped inside and walked to the shower curtain. It was hanging from a track drilled into the roof above it. The shit smell intensified as I got closer. I opened my mouth, sucked in air, blew it out and pulled the curtain aside. There was a portable plastic toilet in one corner of the space and a plastic topped table filling much of the rest of it. There were buckets under the table with large bars of cheap soap in them.

Enough was enough.

I pulled the curtain back across the space

and turned round. George Hood was standing outside the container, looking in.

'Jesus Christ,' he said. 'What the hell have you found?'

I joined him in the yard. Shoulder to shoulder, we stared at the second container. Hood nodded at the sledgehammer. Then at me.

'You don't need a search warrant.'

I picked up the sledge. Hood gestured to the padlock.

'Go on. The last thing we want is for Lloyd Starratt to accuse the police of breaking and entering.'

I smashed the lock on the second container door. The interior design concept was a replica of the first. But the carpet was thicker and the furniture a bit less tatty. This was the deluxe version.

Hood called Shackleton on his mobile and told him to join us. He looked at me.

'Don't touch a thing,' he said and stepped into the container.

We had just seen a demonstration of how much Lloyd Starratt cared about animals. Now we were being offered his opinion on how human beings should be looked after. These two containers represented his version of a halfway house. Presumably for immigrants. Probably illegal.

Assuming the latter, it wasn't difficult to work out for whom Lloyd was running this gruesome B & B. And if Dujic and Tudjman were in the people trafficking business, then I had stumbled into something way beyond anything I had experienced.

'Take a look at this,' I heard Hood say.

He was standing in the nearest right hand corner of the container, looking at the floor. I moved to him and looked down too. There was a double plug, plastic electrical socket lying on the floor, with what looked like a two kilowatt cable stretching out of the back of it. Running behind the kitchen unit and up the wall to a junction box, a couple of feet short of the roof. And beyond the box, a yard or so in from the top corner, a grill, about a foot square had been cut into the roof.

'That's how the air, such as it is, gets in,' Hood said. 'And the mains power cable they run from somewhere. Seems to have some sort of hat over the top. You know, like a chimney pot cover. To stop the rain seeping in. Or at least some of it. There's one in each corner.'

Shackleton arrived and stood staring into the containers, as gobsmacked as Hood and I had been. Hood pulled him out of his reverie.

'How's it going back there?'

'Almost done. The punters are in one of the buses. The dog owners and Starratt's four guards are in the Transit. All the registration plates in the car park have been logged. The camera guy has photographed the dead dogs. They're in body bags and another couple of local vets have been called in to take them away. The RSPCA inspectors are discussing what to do with the dogs that didn't get to fight.'

'Where's Starratt?'

'There are four of our men super-glued to him in the barn.'

'Right. Keep him there for now. Give my compliments to DCI Maynard and ask him to come round here. And get somebody to find a ladder.' He pointed to the grill. 'I want to take a look at that from the roof.'

Shackleton set about the business. Hood finished his inspection of the inside of the container. I waited in the sunshine.

One of the uniforms came back with a ladder; as amazed as the rest of us had been, about what he was looking at. Hood propped the ladder against the container and climbed up onto the roof. He called down to me.

'It's like a coolie hat,' he said. 'Raised a couple of inches above the grill. Un-noticeable from down there I'd guess.'

I backed away, towards the un-restored barn, then up to Hood.

'You're right, I can't see it.'

Maynard arrived at my side.

'What the hell is he doing up there?'

Hood climbed back down the ladder while

Maynard took in the scene. After which, they discussed how to wind up the day. Hood explained that he and his boss needed to talk with Lloyd Starratt about a whole bunch of stuff besides the dog fighting and asked for time to do it. Maynard agreed.

Back in the farmyard, the local Mercedes was full of punters and police. All the leading miscreants, save for Lloyd were in the Transit. The rest of the local cops piled into the van that had arrived with it. The three vehicles left for Chepstow. Tony completed his work, photographing the empty barn and the bloody evidence of the fight. It was decided that the four dogs which didn't get into the fray, should be destroyed also. The local vets did the work. The six bodies were loaded into their ambulance and driven away. I joined the Bristol party as they were climbing into the remaining bus. Shackleton, iPhone in hand, walked across the yard towards me.

'I've just checked my emails,' he said. 'The Burgh Island Hotel manager has sent us the info you wanted. You've got it now. Check your inbox when you get back to Bristol.'

In the Mercedes, I sat down next to a window and looked out as the bus pulled away. We left the Range Rover, the four detectives and Lloyd Starratt in the yard.

Chapter Twenty

Back in my office, I read DC Shackleton's email.

The three guests who had stayed in the *Agatha Christie Suite* at the Burgh Island Hotel, during the second week in July 2006, had signed in as Sofie Thornton, Daniel Thornton and Deborah Thorne. The bill had been paid by Deborah. The family were all listed at the same address. In the village of Woodcroft Dean, Chepstow.

There was an email from Linda also. Saying she had a client to see in Southampton. A couple of days work to do. She was driving down and staying over and would be back on Sunday. It was an FYI email. There was no suggestion as to any prospect that Sunday might hold.

I emailed a note to DC Shackleton, thanking him for his help, then sat back in my chair to consider the next move. A drive back across the Severn bridge seemed to be it. On the other hand, a call to 118 118 might be a sensible interim endeavour.

Which was a good decision, given the result. There was no listing for Deborah Thorne, but there was for Sofie Thornton.

Only, when I rang the number, I discovered Sofie Thornton didn't live there anymore. Jamie Warburton did. He was renting the property.

'From Sofie Thornton?' I asked.

'From Ashdown and Noakes,' Jamie said.

'How long have you been renting the house?'

'Since the beginning of July.'

The pattern was just too bloody familiar. Every time I got near to closing the distance between a discovery and what should then prove to be a result, the whole narrative broke down. And I was left with a big hole where there should have been progress. I slammed the phone receiver back into the base. On reflection, Jamie must have considered that seriously rude.

So a drive across the bridge was necessary. Again. With a cast iron ploy to prise Sofie's current address out of Ashdown and Noakes.

But that was tomorrow's task. The clock on the office wall said 5.45. I was out of all sympathy with the day and I had no plans for what was left of it. Except to go home. Or maybe go to see Chrissie and Adam. And Sam.

I called the number in Clevedon. I got Adam's recorded message. I said hello and goodbye. I dialled Chrissie's mobile and received her apology too. Finally, I tried

Adam's mobile. He wasn't answering that in person either.

A quarter to six was late enough for a drink. I fished the bottle of malt out of the filing cabinet and looked at it. Thought for a moment or two about Annie Marshall. Then put the bottle away. Drinking in the office was one thing. Drinking alone in the office with nothing to do, was something else. I recalled the brilliant Tony Hancock solo episode where he spent the whole morning on his own, trying to find stuff to do. A tour de force. But he was a lot funnier than me...

I was saved from further introspection by the phone ringing.

'Sorry, Dad,' Chrissie said. 'Sam and I were out for our tea time walk. Come for supper. Adam will be home soon.'

'I'd like that.'

'Bring red wine. Oh and bring Linda.'

'She's in Southampton.'

'That's a pity.'

An hour later, I was rolling around the hall floor, locked in a wrestling match with Sam. I finally got the better of him. He lay on his side panting. I patted him on the shoulder and got to my feet. He turned his head and looked up at me, thought about getting up, then decided to stay where he was.

Adam had cooked. He delivered his terrine to the dining table and we sat down to eat. Sam strolled into the dining room and sat down to watch.

After a couple of minutes, Chrissie got to the point.

'How are things with you and Linda?' she asked.

'I think we're on a break.'

'Already? What did you do?'

'Why are you assuming it's my fault?'

'Because it probably is.'

I looked to Adam for support.

'Don't involve me in this,' he said and began clearing away the first course.

'Seriously Dad...' Chrissie said.

'I had one relationship for twenty-three years,' I offered. 'Exclusively. Through all the great bits and the good bits and even the best forgotten bits, Emily and I stayed close. It seemed that, no matter how tough it got, there was never space between us. Even when she was having to do the patching up and the healing. Right now, I really have no idea how to begin again.'

'Do you want to? With Linda?'

Yes I did and no I didn't. Linda was right about that. It was as though I had done all the commitment I could possibly do, with Emily. Which, if I thought about it, was nonsense. Just lame and final. Nobody should close down in that way. Yes, you should be positive and selective about the stuff you don't want to repeat. Like open heart surgery, or the deepest of sorrows. But relationships ought to be able to start out well, at least. Linda and I had been involved for a week. And considering we had known each other for fifteen years, I owed the positives on offer, a little more effort.

I don't know how much time I took over that rationalisation, but Chrissie waited. We looked at each other, wondering which one of us should speak first. Adam came in with the beef stroganoff and the conversation was put on hold. Sam got to his feet and waggled his nose, padded around the table and sat slap bang underneath the casserole pot.

'Lie down Sam,' Adam ordered.

Sam considered for a moment, then did as he was told. Put his head down on his front paws and sulked.

The stroganoff was terrific. I stopped thinking and gave myself up to enjoying it. Adam appreciated that.

'You may now re-convene,' he said, as he began clearing the table once more.

'Well?...' Chrissie asked.

'Must try harder,' I said.

'Indeed you must. When is Linda back from the south coast?'

'Sunday, she said.'

'Then make the most of it. And that's an order.'

Adam returned and put a large plate in the middle of the table. On it, a gorgeous, pink wigwam of a dessert.

'Summer pudding,' he said with pride. 'Strawberries, blackberries, raspberries and redcurrants.'

He sat down, picked up a knife, sliced it open and the delicious fruit came tumbling out.

We finished the second bottle of red wine and Chrissie made coffee. When that was done, she gave me the considered, old fashioned, sideways look she had inherited from her mother.

'Why did you call?' Chrissie asked. 'I sensed you weren't on top form when you did.'

'I thought that too,' Adam said.

'I'm sorry. I shouldn't have allowed my misery to seep down the line.'

'Yes you should. Especially if it was misery.'

'Don't worry, I'm not going to whinge. In fact this is something I think you ought to hear. More ammunition for your crusade against Lloyd Starratt.'

I looked at both of them, across the table, then for some reason, down at Sam.

'I went to a dog fight this afternoon.'

They both stared at me in horror.

'A what?' Chrissie asked. As if she needed to be sure she had heard me correctly.

I told them the story. Précised the violent stuff. There were pauses and astonished silences, but I got to the end. Chrissie called to Sam. He got to his feet and moved round to her chair. He looked up at her. Chrissie began to stroke him. He responded and leaned his body against her knees.

Adam slipped resolutely into work mode. 'Will anyone object if I write this story?'

'I'm sure the RSPCA would love you to write it. As far as they're concerned, all intelligent advocates for their cause are welcome. Talk to Julia. And Tony, the video man, has pictures.'

Chrissie looked up and across the table. 'Pictures?'

'Evidence,' I said. 'He recorded the events of the afternoon.' I looked back at Adam. 'And talk to DCI Maynard at ST5.'

Chrissie and I took Sam for his late night walk.

'How are you? Really?' she asked.

'I'm okay. A bit shell shocked that's all.' I looked at Sam, on the end of the lead, nose down and sniffing. 'I wonder if he knows how lucky he is.'

Sam responded by lifting his right leg against a lamppost. We waited for him to finish his business, then moved on.

'What about Deborah? Are you any closer to finding her?'

'No.'

'And the Serbs?'

'No.'

'What about the people on the beach in Devon?'

'For a while, I was doing well with that.'

'Until?'

'I hit another dead end. Messrs Ashdown and Noakes.'

'The estate agents?'

Sam stopped to sniff at a car wheel. I stared at Chrissie. She stared obligingly back. So I told her about finding Deborah's address and then finding her tenant.

'So if Ashdown and Noakes are acting for Deborah, they will have her current address,' Chrissie said. 'Problem solved.'

Not exactly. But Chrissie went on to explain.

'I help out in the student union accommodation office. Just about every estate agent and landlord in the area is listed. Names, addresses, emails. Ashdown and Noakes have a place in Clifton, another one in Bath and a third in Chepstow. If Deborah approached them in something of a panic, because she wanted to get out of her house quickly, they probably asked her if she would be okay with students in the place. Usually the guarantee of a quick let. So she says yes, gives the estate agents her new address, drops off the keys and moves to ... wherever. If Mr Warburton has a short lease and Ashdown and Noakes want Deborah's business ongoing, her contacts will be in the system. Maybe I can find them.'

'Won't they be confidential?'

'Christ Dad, this is the internet we're talking about it. Confidentiality is a long forgotten concept. Only the brave and the heroic have any notion of what that might be these days. People like you.'

She grinned at me.

'Leave it with me.'

Sam seemed to have finished doing what a dog has to do late night. We reversed course and headed back to the house.

Chrissie took off Sam's choke chain in the hall. He sped into the kitchen, sat down and waited for his supper biscuits to materialise. He ate them, slurped away in his water bowl, lifted his head and dripped all over the kitchen tiles. Chrissie wiped his beard, he padded back into the hall, did his customary double 360 and sank to the carpet.

'Do you want to stay over?' Chrissie asked.

Chapter Twenty-One

I fell asleep as soon as my head hit the pillow. With no thoughts of my client, Lloyd Starratt, or Serbs to keep me awake. But I ended up in a nightmare world of ferocious four legged creatures with night vision sites for eyes and relentless stamina.

I woke to find Sam staring at me from six inches away; his head resting on the duvet, his beard flattened under his chin, ears cascading down each side of his face. The moment I opened my eyes he was on his feet. He stretched out his front paws, bowed his head, lifted his bum, hoisted his tail like a flagpole and stretched. That done, he grabbed the duvet in his jaws and hauled it off the bed.

I looked at the bedside clock. 7.40. There were no sounds from the direction of Chrissie and Adam, so I reported for duty. When I got downstairs, Sam was sitting by the front door, on his best behaviour.

The walk down to the sea front was most enjoyable. The sun was up and the tide was high. Sam may behave like a maniac while at home, but in public, butter wouldn't melt. He doesn't molest pedestrians or chase cyclists, he backs his bum into hedges to do what a dog has to do and shows off disgracefully when anyone takes the slightest notice of him. Which is, of course, an ongoing routine, because he's such a stunner.

A shaven headed teenager was sitting on a bench with a girl. She was wearing a ring in her nose and a series of them in her left ear lobe. They were drinking coffee and eating doughnuts. Sam ambled up to the bench, sat down on the path in front of the couple and, a moment later, raised his right front paw. The act was shameful, brilliant and irresistible. The two kids were seduced in an instant. Most of the second doughnut went into Sam.

Back home, he belted round the garden while I made his breakfast.

Adam had gone into Bristol. Chrissie occupied his desk in the study and googled the student accommodation website. Breakfast eaten, Sam settled down in the hall and went to sleep.

The website gave up the information I needed. Sofie Thornton was living at an address on Thackeray Road, in Horfield.

North of Bristol city centre, Horfield straddles Gloucester Road and spreads east a couple of miles towards the M32. It's a busy, organised, self contained part of town. Away from the centre and the big chain stores, it still boasts local shops and trades. I scrutinised the A to Z. Thackeray Road sits in an enclave of terraces inspired by giants of literature. There is also a Shelley Way, a Dickens Close and a Shakespeare Avenue. The houses are tightly packed together. They have tiny gardens, a few paces deep, between their front doors and the road.

Just before 10 o'clock, I parked the Healey a dozen car lengths from Sofie's house. The doorbell rang inside the hall when I pressed the button, but no one answered. I went back to the Healey to wait.

Forty minutes later, Sofie and Daniel walked towards me from the direction of Gloucester Road, carrying bags of shopping. He was almost as tall as she was. They were both dressed in blue jeans and white tee shirts. I got out of the car as they reached the front door of the house. Sofie put down the shopping, swung her bag off her shoulder, dug into it and searched for her house keys. Daniel waited at her side. I stepped into the garden behind them. Fiddling around in her bag, Sofie failed to hear me arrive. Daniel did. He swung round to face me.

'Hello,' he said.

'What?' Sofie asked, over her shoulder.

'He was talking to me,' I said.

Sofie, right hand still in her bag, turned and stared at me. I introduced myself. Sofie continued staring at me; the question 'So?'

etched across her face. She had no idea know who I was. Deborah had kept me a secret too. Which was probably useful in this case. No knowledge of me, meant there should be no conditions attached to this moment.

'I'm Jack Shepherd,' I said. 'A private investigator. Deborah came to see me last week. Now she has disappeared and I need to find her.'

Sofie produced her house key. Spent another moment or two on scrutiny.

'You had better come in,' she said. With a trace of an accent. Probably eastern European.

Inside the house, Sofie and Daniel led the way along the hall and into the kitchen. The shopping bags were dumped on to the table, then Sofie surveyed us both.

'Daniel,' she said. 'Take Mr Shepherd into the living room and keep him company while I make some coffee.' She looked at me. 'Or would you prefer tea?'

'No. Coffee will be fine, thank you.'

Daniel and I sat down in the front room. Me in one of two small armchairs, him in the other. Between us there was a mahogany coffee table about eighteen inches square. A two seater sofa sat against the wall which separated us from the entrance hall. And a fat, analogue television set with a digi-box on top of it, was squeezed into a corner, to the left of the window facing the street. A cosy room, but not one for running around in.

'Who are you Mr Shepherd?' Daniel asked.

I compared him to the photograph. He was six years older and six years taller. He had his mother's eyes and nose. And he was, apparently, totally unimpressed by the man who had invaded his house. He had a picture of Kristen Stewart printed on his tee shirt.

'I am a friend of your friend Deborah,' I said.

'Oh,' he said. 'Do you know where she is?'

That question again. Now coming from an eleven year old.

'She's supposed to be here, you see,' he went on. 'But she isn't.'

'Does she live here?'

'Yes. We were all here, together, for a bit. Then she went away. Mum says that as soon as we see her again, we can all go back to Chepstow. If she doesn't come back, I have to go to the comprehensive school in Lockleaze next month.'

Suddenly he looked depressed.

'And you don't want to?'

'I want to go back to Chepstow.'

Sofie came into the room carrying a tray with two mugs of coffee, a milk jug and a can of Sprite.

'We will,' she said. 'I promise. But while we are here…' She put the tray down on the coffee table. 'You must go to school here.'

She handed the Sprite to him.

'Can you leave Mr Shepherd and I alone for a few minutes Dan? You can have your Play Station in your room.'

'Okay,' he said, cheered up at a stroke.

He left the room. Sofie called after him.

'Just while Mr Shepherd is here.' She turned back to me. 'He's not usually allowed to play during the mornings. I try to get him out of the house as much as I can... Milk?'

'Thank you. Do you know where Deborah is?'

Sofie put down the milk jug and passed me the mug of coffee.

'No. She left here six days ago. She won't tell me where she is.'

'Do you speak to her?'

'Yes. On her mobile.'

Sofie leaned back into the sofa cushion and sipped her coffee. I watched. She was as relaxed as any tense and suspicious person could be and there was a stillness about her. The beach photograph didn't do her justice. It was a 2D holiday snap. In 3D she was both graceful and beautiful.

I decided to concentrate on stuff she could tell me. On her, rather than on Deborah.

'Your accent,' I said, 'Is it eastern European?'

'Yes,' she said.

'Are you from Kosovo?'
'Yes.'
'Which is where you met Deborah, when she was Daniel?'
Sofie swallowed a mouthful of coffee, leaned forward and put the mug back down on the table. Slowly and carefully. Then she looked up at me.
'How do you know this?'
I told her the whole story; everything I had learned about Daniel Thornton and Deborah Thorne. The information about Deborah's parents astonished her.
'Didn't she tell you about them?' I asked.
'No.'
I explained there were a bunch of other characters in this narrative and offered her the names of Starratt, Dujic and Tudjman. She grew more and more uneasy. She wrapped her arms across her breasts and around her shoulders, hugging herself tightly. As if trying to contain some kind of panic attack. I got out of my chair to move to the sofa. She shook her head fiercely and unwrapped her arms.
'No no,' she said. 'Stay there.'
I sat back down in the armchair and waited. With an immense effort, she regained control of her runaway emotions, dropped her hands to her thighs, leaned back into the sofa again and closed her eyes.
'Are you Serb?' I asked.

'My father is. My mother was Albanian. That would not happen now of course. But I was born in 1978, in Mitrovica. We were all Yugoslavs then. Tito was still alive. Now, my birthplace is a symbol of all the wrong that has been done. The River Ibar divides the city in two. The Serbs live north of it, the Albanians to the south. It is madness. But generations will have to die before anything can change.'

'Tell me about Donjica,' I said.

'Thirty-six Albanians were murdered by Serb policemen in March 2000. It is a tiny place. Insignificant. Its misfortune was that the Kosovo Liberation Army had a base in the hills. Without that, only those who lived there and a handful of other people, would know of it.'

'Were you there?'

'No. I was never in Donjica. Daniel was. Two days after the massacre. By accident. His truck broke down as he was driving north from the Macedonian border.'

'So where did you meet him?'

'In Pec. It's in north eastern Kosovo. *Médecines Sans Frontières* had a base there. I was working as an interpreter. Daniel arrived from Donjica. I had never seen someone so shocked and so angry. But that was nothing, compared to what was to come.'

She drifted into silence. She seemed to be miles away. Lost in the remembrance. I waited. Her eyes misted. She blinked. Tears rolled down her cheeks. She sniffed, wiped her eyes with the back of her right hand, then looked at me again.

'We were sent a few miles south, to Lipojane. Another place of no significance. On what you call April Fool's Day, Serb police and paramilitaries entered the village. They rounded up everyone who had not managed to escape. They took the women and children away and assembled the men in the main street. Twenty-two of them were machine gunned to death. Then the Serbs burned the village and forced the women and children to travel south, eventually to the Albanian border. Most of them walked all the way. Word got to Pec from the people who returned to the village. Daniel and I went into Lipojane three days later with an OSCE Team. I talked with a man who had survived. He was not hit by machine gun fire. He lay under the corpses for three hours and crawled out after the Serbs had gone.'

She looked at me, dead centre, now making no attempt to control the tears.

'This happened in my country. My home. I was there. And I still do not understand how ordinary people can turn into butchers.'

'The people who do this are not ordinary,' I said. 'They are criminals, feeding on a residue of centuries of fear and hate. Dujic and Tudjman are living examples. Like you said before. Even after you eliminate them, the situation will take generations to mend.'

'Dujic and Tudjman were in Lipojane,' Sofie said. 'The OSCE Team had photographs of men they suspected of war atrocities. They were passed around the village. Seven people identified Dujic and nine picked out Tudjman.'

'So, who are they?'

'They were policemen. Who saw opportunities. Who rode on waves of prejudice and advanced politically, stole property, made money. All they had to do was learn to kill. I suppose that came easy.'

'Tell me about your relationship with them.'

'I do not have one.'

'Yes you do,' I said. 'And it's frightening you to death. Deborah too.'

I let the pause fill, then tried again.

'Talk to me. Otherwise I can't help.'

She took a deep breath.

'I saw Dujic and Tudjman three weeks after Lipojane. In Pec. I was in a Serb area, for some reason I can't remember. I went into a café. I was drinking coffee when they came in. I could not help it, I stared at them. Once, or perhaps twice, Dujic saw me looking at him. He smiled. And he thought ... well you can imagine. I went home, to the apartment Daniel and I shared. They must have followed. A few minutes after I got there, they knocked on the door. I opened it, then tried to close it again, but Dujic kicked his way in.'

Sofie had come to the difficult bit. I was about to tell her not to go on, but she held up a hand.

'No. I will tell you,' she said. 'Tudjman held me down while Dujic raped me. Then they changed over. And then again. And once more. When they had finished, they left. Daniel came home half an hour later. He got into a rage and then he went quiet. He stayed in his room for maybe an hour. Then he came out and said we had to leave. We did. We packed and we left the apartment. That evening we got a ride on an *MSF* truck into Croatia. We took a boat from Dubrovnik to Pescara in Italy. Two days later we were in London.'

'This was when? June 2000?'

'Yes.'

'When did you come down to the west country?'

'A few days later. We rented a cottage in the village of Aust. Do you know it?'

'Yes. Just this side of the bridge.'

'Then I discovered I was pregnant. I hated it. I was sick with misery. Two possible fathers. Both of them murderers and rapists. But Daniel was wonderful. He kept me focussed and together and gradually I began to look forward to being a mother. Then he asked me to marry him. I could never be an illegal immigrant if I was his wife. He did not ask anything from me in return. I realise now, that he was already planning his gender change. Young Daniel was born in March 2001.'

'So you were now Sofie Thornton, wife and mother?'

'A single mother. Daniel began living as Deborah during the spring of 2003. She moved into Bristol.'

'Why?'

'Deborah had no doubts about what she was going to do. She knew that the next few years were going to be very hard. She did not want to draw Daniel and I into what must happen. And in her future relationship with him, she just wanted to be Deborah. She did not want him to know her as anybody else. Daniel and I moved into the Forest of Dean house when he was two. And regularly, this wonderful lady came to visit us. Daniel fell in love with her. We had lots of holidays together. Not just the one on Burgh Island.'

'So when did Deborah move to Chiswick?'

'After the surgery.'

'Why?'

'She wanted to start over. Somewhere new. Away from the support system she had built up. To really be an independent woman. The call centre job was good for her. A work place she could control. She did not have to present to the public at large. It gave her confidence.'

So the question begging to be asked was, what happened to threaten this carefully constructed new order?

The answer was a trip to the Mall at Cribbs Causeway. Mecca to retail junkies, an abomination to those to whom shopping is less than pure joy. Several square miles of retail sprawl, with pubs, restaurants, cinemas and enough parking spaces for a football stadium crowd. Host to pop concerts and flash mobs.

'Back in April,' Sofie said, 'the week after Easter, Daniel and I were at the Mall. And I saw Dujic and Tudjman, coming out of *Hugo Boss*. All these years later. For a moment, I was convinced I was wrong. How could they be here? These criminals. Dressed in eight hundred pound suits. But it was them.'

'So you called Deborah. She left London and came to Bristol.'

'Yes.'

'And you moved here.'

'Not at first. It seemed best to stay where we were. Out of the way. But things got more complicated.'

Sofie sat upright in the sofa and leaned towards me.

'Daniel should be starting Year 1, at Wye Valley Comprehensive School,' she explained.

Connection made.

'Which has a brand new sports field, courtesy of Lloyd Starratt,' I said. 'There was a cricket match to celebrate his generosity, back in May.'

'Yes,' Sofie said, 'And Mr Starratt was there.'

I nodded. She looked at me for a long time, then dropped bombshell two. 'So were Dujic and Tudjman. Standing among the parents and the teachers and the guests. Joining in the applause for Mr Starratt.'

'Did they see you?'

'Perhaps. But why would they recognise me? A nameless rape victim, long forgotten among countless others. I thought Daniel and I would be safe. Deborah did not agree.'

'So it was then that you moved.'

'Yes. I took Daniel away from his home and his school and his friends. He has been very good about it, but he does not want to be here. I have managed to persuade him this is only temporary. I hope it proves to be the case. I only wish I knew what Deborah was doing?'

A consideration which had obsessed me for twelve days.

'Mr Shepherd, if you can accomplish what you have to do, as soon as you can, I would be delighted.'

'So would I,' I said. 'But, in truth, I've run out of plans and purpose.'

'We should be at home,' Sofie said. 'Daniel should be getting ready for his first year in his new school. But we must wait here.'

Out of nowhere, I remembered something Bill Thornton had talked about.

'Daniel kept a journal during his time in Kosovo,' I said. 'Do you know where it is?'

Sofie looked concerned. She shifted her position on the sofa.

'Do you have it?'

She made a decision and nodded.

'Yes.'

'May I read it?'

She stood up.

'It is in my bedroom. I will get it.'

I followed her into the hall and waited at the bottom of the stairs. She came back down with a brown, leather bound notebook. She handed it to me.

'Please take care of it Mr Shepherd.'

'Of course.'

I turned to go.

'I'll get Daniel,' Sofie said.

'No leave him. Let him play on. Tell him I'll see him again soon.'

'Is that a promise?'

'Yes,'

'You did not say "if I can".'

'It's a real promise,' I said. 'And they come without "if I cans".'

She smiled.

'Thank you.'

Back in the street, I sat in the Healey and talked to myself for a while. In spite of all the work I had done during this investigation, the good people were still losing. This had to be put right. Giving up, wasn't an option. Deborah and the Serbs were around, somewhere. And if Lloyd Starratt was the only lead left, then he would have to do.

My mobile rang. I fished it out of the glove compartment.

Harvey wanted to talk to me.

'Do you fancy a trip to the seaside?' he asked. 'Seriously. A walk along the beach at Weston, followed by fish and chips. I want to offer you a deal Jack. We have some talking to do, but not at Trinity Road. Somewhere out of the way. How about it? I'll drive.'

'I never turn down fish and chips at Weston,' I said.

'Where are you?'

'On my way back to the office.'

'I'll pick you up in half an hour,' Harvey said.

Chapter Twenty-Two

I like Weston Super Mare, even if its baron incumbent is Jeffrey Archer. Happily, it's more famous for its donkeys, which have graced the beach since 1886 and have been worked for the whole of that time, by generations of the Mager family. It's an impressive job record. But then the Weston donkeys are legendary; the quintessence of the British seaside holiday. And a symbol of continuity; like the apes on Gibraltar and the ravens at the Tower of London. If ever the donkeys were to leave the beach...

Harvey parked the Vauxhall at the south end of Marine Parade and we stepped on to the sand, stretching unbroken for a mile and a half, along the front and round the curve of rock at Knightstone. Past the town landmark, the magnificently re-imagined and rebuilt pier pavilion, now defiantly back in business after the violent destruction of the fire.

The sky was cloudless. The donkeys were about their business, the beach was dotted with kids, parents and grandparents engaged in sandcastle engineering and games of cricket. Weston in the sunshine. Unbeatable.

We hadn't talked about anything in particular during the drive from my office and Harvey was in no hurry to launch into anything now. We walked for a while before he got round to explaining what this excursion was all about.

'The conversation we're about to have,' he said, 'must stay on this beach. I'm breaking a lifetime rule here. Only because I want to see justice done and because I'm pissed off that I can't be in charge of doing so.'

I didn't say anything.

'You know me Jack. I don't believe private enterprise has any place in the day to day business of law and order. At best, you're what I can't be, a knight errant. But mostly, you're just a vigilante, albeit with some moral purpose.'

'Well at least there's that,' I said.

'Let me finish this,' he said. 'We don't have Lloyd Starratt anymore.'

I stopped walking. So did Harvey, a step ahead of me. He turned to face me.

'What do you mean you don't have him? Where is he?'

'Back at Southfork I imagine.'

'Jesus Christ Harvey, how did that happen?'

'DCI Benjamin happened. The star of Gloucestershire Constabulary's Major Crimes Unit. He's claimed the people trafficking case. Southfork is on his manor, not mine. And Starratt's done a deal with him. To roll over on the Serbs, if he's not prosecuted for dog fighting and housing illegal immigrants.'

'But you had him, at Trinity Road. All you had to do was put the thumbscrews on him.'

Harvey looked down at the sand and dug at it with the toe of his right shoe. He took a deep breath and looked up again.

'So how did this DCI get Starratt?' I asked.

'Maynard and George had him for an hour and a half. Starratt admitted he was at the dog fight. He couldn't do otherwise. But he said the organisation of the gig had nothing to do with him. In fact, currently the barn wasn't his to control. He had, he said, temporarily leased the place to a company in the Cotswolds, as a storage facility.'

'So how did he explain all the work going on?'

'He said he was in the process of restoring all the buildings and adding an extension to the main barn. With the intention of creating up market, country holiday accommodation. Currently, suffering a minor cash flow problem, he had suspended building operations and let the place.'

'Then why was he spectating?'

'He claimed, he had developed concerns about what the facilities were really being used for and had turned up to investigate. He had not promoted the event. He wasn't the banker. And of course, he was horrified by what he had encountered and hoped we would prosecute everyone involved, with all the machinery of law at our disposal.'

'What does Maynard think?'

'He's pleased enough. He's busted the ring. Nailed everybody else involved, including the banker and the bookie. Starratt is out of the dog fighting business. The RSPCA has permission to examine all his animals and they will conduct their own prosecution regardless. It's not a total bust by any means.'

'Did you get anything else out of him?'

'The interview was suspended and Maynard left. I joined George and we started again. Getting into the stuff about ship containers and suspected links with Serb people traffickers. Obviously Starratt had figured out what he wanted to say. But he got very jumpy and lost track of what he'd rehearsed. We had him scared. We were miles away from dangerous dogs and he knew he was in the mire. Steadfastness isn't one of his qualities. He started to panic. Then there was a knock on the interview room door. I took a phone call from my ACC, who had just taken a call from Gloucestershire HQ. We were ordered to render the utmost courtesy to a DCI who was, at that moment, speeding down the M5. We got glued, screwed and papered over. There was some sort of deal done and Starratt went home on bail.'

'So we're bolloxed.'

'No... Not altogether.'

He looked out to sea, lifted his face to the breeze and allowed it to caress his cheeks. Then he turned back to me.

'Words of one syllable,' he said. 'I am, but you're not. I can't go looking for the Serbs. But you...'

'In my role as Don Quixote...'

'Can feel free to pursue enquiries in your independently resolute fashion. I can't stop you.'

'But DCI Benjamin can.'

'That's your problem. However, your presence in this endeavour so far, is not recorded. DCI Benjamin doesn't know you from a hole in the ground. That's the advantage you have. Use it.'

We started walking again.

'By the way, did you find the woman and child you were looking for?'

'Yes I did.'

'Do they know where your client is?'

'No.'

'Still not getting any closer?'

Harvey looked across Marine Parade, towards Beach Road. We had walked as far as the Grand Atlantic Hotel.

'I think we deserve superior fish and chips,' he said. 'I hear the chef at the Grand Atlantic is from Newcastle. He cooks them in dripping.'

'I won't eat them any other way,' I said.

Friday night, back at home.

I settled down in the living room, with Daniel's journal and a large glass of twelve year old malt.

And I read his words about Donjica.

Kosovo is land of mortar holes and rubble. Donjica is a prime example. Blasted and broken down. A year ago the place flourished, as best it could in this wasteland. Close to 1600 people lived in and around here. A woman I spoke to today told me, that at the last count, there were now barely 350.

Today, 36 of those are bodies. Men, women and children, some of them mutilated beyond all recognition. There was a line of bodies in the village square, in front of the mosque. In a gully, on rising ground above the village, I saw another one, covered with a dusty blanket. When the doctor who was with me, pulled it back, we saw there was no head on the corpse. Just a sickening bloody mess on the neck. I don't know where the man's left arm was ... is ... we couldn't find it. Further up the gully we found a torso. A woman with silver grey hair. The doctor said she was probably in her mid 60s. Then another group of bodies. I didn't count them. I just looked and saw holes in their twisted shapes and dismembered limbs. A man came down the gully towards us and said there were other bodies, further up the hillside.

If the people who did this, truly believe that the butchery of farmers, labourers and villagers, in this nowhere corner of Stimlje province, is the way to the creation of Milosevic's 'Greater Serbia', then may this reality burn their lousy souls.

I walked back to our truck in the village square and went searching for the driver.

The journal chronicled a story of organised violence and brutality. And in trying to act as witness, Daniel had descended into hell. As events unfolded and the pages went by, his notes became less and less structured. The writing more and more distraught. Sentences turned into phrases, then into roars of rage and finally into incoherent, unfinished, distracted, segments of words.

Shortly after his visit to Lipojane, Daniel stopped trying to write altogether.

I closed the book and poured another glass of whiskey.

So how was Deborah, right now? That was the question.

It had been twelve days since she had walked into my office. And I had spent most of that time working in instalments. Deborah was so determined to protect Sofie and Daniel, she had achieved what she said she would. Made my job impossible. I was overloaded with information, but it was all sound and fury. Finding some direction out of the noise, had always been the problem. And even now, it was no easier.

My client was hiding in the city, somewhere. But from what? Or rather, from what now? Dujic and Tudjman couldn't possibly recognise her as Deborah. Could they? And Starratt was now in cahoots with Gloucestershire Constabulary.

And that had become personal. Everybody I had encountered on this case, fervently wanted Lloyd Starratt's bollocks on a skewer. Which certainly wouldn't happen if he gave DCI Benjamin all he needed. Apart from a couple of overnights – at times when he had been brought into a police station for questioning – Lloyd had not spent a single day of his fifty-six years on this planet, behind bars; which had to rate as a monumental judicial oversight.

The phone rang. Deborah was angry.

'Why the hell are you bothering Sofie and Daniel?'

'Doing what you hired me to do.'

'You are supposed to be looking for me.'

'And that's what I'm trying to do,' I said. 'The fact that you're ringing me in such a rage means I'm close. I now know your connection to Dujic and Tudjman. And a team of Gloucester coppers is investigating their UK operation.'

'What operation?'

I ignored her question and ploughed on.

'And that they're using Lloyd Starratt as a conduit. I've seen his five star hospitality suites.'

'This operation, whatever it is,' Deborah insisted, 'has nothing to do with Sofie and Daniel.'

'Do you have anything to do with Lloyd Starratt?'

There was a pause. The mobile connection started to hiss.

'What sort of question is that?'

'Just answer it.'

'No.'

The line interference grew. Deborah raised her voice and shouted above the noise.

'Consider your job over. Take what you feel you're owed out of the safe at Windmill Hill and stop what you're doing. I mean it. No more.'

She disconnected. The line hiss oscillated in my ear. I pressed the off button and threw the phone receiver across the hall. It smashed into the wall, gouged a chunk out of the wallpaper and dropped to the floor, the casing in three bits.

Over and out.

Chapter Twenty-Three

When you're fired by your client, usually the best thing to do is acknowledge defeat and quit the field. But some cases require more backbone. This was one of them. I contemplated driving over to Windmill Hill and collecting a thousand pounds from the safe, but this next move had to be on my money.

Saturday morning, I was on my way to Southfork at 7.45. I crossed the Severn Bridge twenty-five minutes later and by half eight I was on Starratt land. Given his deal with the police, it was safe to assume Lloyd would be at home.

Southfork was a monstrous piece of self indulgence. *Footballers' Wives* meets *Dallas*. Clearly a big fan, Lloyd had commissioned his own version of the Ewing mansion. Huge was a fair description, extravagant certainly; but the building had not so much as one ounce of class. The panelled front door was six feet wide and ten feet high, painted white and studded with black bolts.

I knocked and waited. Nothing happened. I knocked again. Still no response. No one at home. No servant, no mother Aurora, no Lloyd. I took hold of the ornamental cast iron door ring and turned it. The door swung open.

The hall did not disappoint. It was octagonal and dominated by a circular staircase, sitting bang in the middle. There were eight doors, one in each straight of the octagon. The floor was tiled black and white. He had obviously paid the tiler a fortune, but I wondered what the artisan had thought about the commission.

'Anyone at home?'

Still no response.

Discounting the front door, there were seven others to chose from. One of them opened in to a storage room, piled with tea chests and cardboard boxes. Another revealed the downstairs loo, again an example of impeccable taste. Black tiles, a gold bath and gold, swan necked taps. Deeply disturbed, I closed the door quickly. Five to go. One was the door to the study, with of course, the biggest desk Lloyd could have found anywhere. It looked like it was real mahogany at least. Next to the study, was some kind of glory room. Full of pennants, rosettes, and king size trophies for macho sports like 4 by 4 off-roading, truck racing and tractor pulling. That left the kitchen, the dining room and to the extreme left, the door to the living room. I chose to start there.

The white shag pile closed round my shoes and reached up to my ankles. The tan leather furniture suite consisted of a sofa and four armchairs with over-stuffed cushions and big, fan-shaped, shell backs. At the far end of the room, two high backed, wicker chairs sat in front of the French windows looking out across the lawn at the rear of the house.

There was somebody sitting in the chair on the right. At least, there was an arm, hanging over the arm rest and dangling down to the floor. Below the arm, there was a dark stain on the carpet. The stain was dried blood and the hand at the end of the arm was minus two fingers.

Lloyd was roped into the chair, eyes closed; his face as white as the shag pile. And there was more blood, which had seeped out of the bullet hole in his forehead, dribbled down his face and his shirt front. There were bits of skull and skin and brain, sprayed across the chair back behind his head.

I opened the French windows and stepped out onto the lawn, gasping for breath. I bent forward, put my hands on my thighs, dropped my head between my knees and looked down at the grass for a while. The waves of nausea began to wash away.

Lloyd had been tortured and then executed in the same way as Philip Soames. Obviously not by Grant and Copley. This time, the fingers were somebody else's signature. Maybe those whose idea this kind of exercise was originally. Dujic and Tudjman. Who had ultimately decided that Lloyd was a liability. I could see their point. Lloyd had stirred up so much interest in the last few days, he was no longer any use as a low profile associate.

Fortified, I stood in the doorway and looked at Lloyd again. If this was the work of the Serbs, there must be clues to their whereabouts somewhere in this house. I stepped around Lloyd, crossed the living room and the octagonal madness of the hall and went into the study. Five minutes ago, I had poked my head round the door and noticed the desk. Now, inside the study, I discovered something else.

The room was a shrine to Deborah.

There were at least a couple of dozen pictures of her. On the office walls and on the desk. Looking stunning in frocks and heels. At parties and functions. In many of them, on Lloyd Starratt's arm.

I swear I felt my blood run cold. Deborah and Lloyd? In a relationship? No, that was impossible. Surely...

Two photographs set the seal on my minor bout of turbulence. In one, a quartet of people, dressed to the nines was smiling into the camera lens. Deborah, Lloyd, Philip Soames and a man I guessed was his date. In the other, Deborah was pictured, flanked by Philip and Lloyd. I looked at the pictures closely. In the bottom left hand corner of both, someone – presumably Lloyd – had scrawled *Mind Care Charity Ball.* The occasion may have been a one off encounter, but it would have been enough. Even assuming Lloyd knew nothing of Deborah's past, he couldn't have failed to notice that she and Philip had some kind of connection. So later, when Deborah dropped out of sight...

As satisfying as this piece of rationalisation was, it still left me tired and desperate.

The mobile on Lloyd's desk began to ring. I rehearsed my best, gruff Forest of Dean 'yes', then picked up the phone and hit the green button.

The 121 service played a message left three minutes earlier. A strongly accented male voice said, 'We are here, as you asked. Where are you? We give you another fifteen minutes.'

I pressed the red button. Dujic or Tudjman? Fifteen minutes to get where?

I put the mobile back on the desk, left the study and went up the staircase, as fast as going round in circles would allow. At the head of the stairs I took stock. Which bloody direction was I facing?

The first door I tried, opened into the main bathroom. The second, into a pink bedroom with a massive en-suite. A big bath with a door in the side, so there was no necessity to climb up and over, with a seat to sit on. Aurora's room obviously. For a moment I wondered where she was, then swiftly dismissed the consideration and went back on to the landing. The next door I opened was the one to Lloyd's bedroom. An inferno, in shades of red and bronze. I don't think I have stood in the middle of anything so gross.

Still, this was no time to diss Lloyd's design concept. I crossed the room to the huge double casement window and looked out. Dead ahead; beyond the garden, a field with half a dozen horses in it, a stream and another couple of hundred yards of grazing land, was the hedge camouflaging the dog fighting barn. Three quarters of a mile as the crow flies, according to DC Shackleton's iPhone. And from here in Lloyd's bedroom, I could see over the top of the hedge into the car park.

There was a pair of binoculars on the window sill. Big and black, with sixteen times magnification, like the ones battleship officers used in 1950s British war films. Powerful enough to make out the craters on the moon.

I put the binoculars to my eyes and refocussed them. It took up precious time, but it yielded a result. There was a car in the car park. An ostentatious, designer 4 by 4. The kind of vehicle it is always assumed pimps and hit men drive; and in European thrillers, ex-Soviet bloc gangsters.

Whatever, the car park was where I needed to be. And there was a gate at the end of the garden.

When I was running seriously every day, I could do a mile in five and a half minutes, on tracks around the Ashton Court estate. Farm land was another proposition altogether. And the stream wasn't user friendly. It took me ten minutes to get to the hedge behind the car park. I arrived, gasping for air, shirt sticking to my back, socks squelching in my shoes.

The foliage was so dense I could barely see through it. So I stood, chest heaving and listened. Tried to imagine the lie of the land in front of me from this direction. The restored barn and its extension was to my left, the ruin and the containers to my right. I chose the latter and began to crab my way around the hedge. Bits of the ruin came in to focus, then dissolved again into a haze of leaves and branches. I came up against the boundary of the field; another hedgerow running back towards Southfork. And there was a gap here, the branches forced apart by the run of some animal. A deer perhaps.

Through the gap, I could see I was right behind one of the containers. In fact that was all I could see. A corrugated steel wall. I ducked, squeezed through the hedge, stood upright and listened again. To what passes for silence in the country. The swish of the breeze in the leaves behind me, cows mooing a couple of fields away, a confused chattering of birdsong and the buzz of a chainsaw somewhere to my right.

Now what?

I didn't want to blunder into the arms of a couple of angry Serbs. On the other hand, there was obviously no mileage in skulking behind a big steel box. So, up and at 'em then...

I shifted to my left, still squelching in my socks and found myself looking across the yard towards the chaser bin door. To the left of the bin, sat the 4 by 4; big and black, with tinted windows. There was no response from inside it. No sign of any east Europeans with machine pistols. I moved quietly along the length of the container towards the ruined barn and into the space in front of it. I was alone in the yard. Or so it seemed, from the direction I was approaching. I swung round and looked back at the container. The doors were closed and locked. The door to the other box was open.

Inside, two of the dining chairs were occupied. Two men were roped into the chairs and their mouths were sealed with gaffer tape. The man on my right, had a bloody hole in his left thigh. He was unconscious. The other man was awake. As soon as he saw me, he began groaning and shaking his head and bouncing in his chair.

Behind me, a husky voice called out, 'I was under the impression you had been sacked.'

I turned round. Deborah was standing about ten feet away. She pointed over my shoulder, into the container.

'I'd like you to meet Vojislav Dujic and Josip Tudjman.'

There was a gun in the hand she was pointing with.

'A Russian Makarov M57,' she explained. 'Supplied to Serb security forces by the Chinese. I picked it up in Kosovo. It fires eight rounds. There is one in Starratt's head. And one in Tudjman's leg. As you can see, he's the bastard on the right.'

For a moment or two I wondered how Deborah had managed to subdue the pair of them. She read my mind.

'I shot him, Dujic tied him into the chair, then sat in that one and did as he was told.'

She was calm and cool and as collected as anyone I've met. But there was something wrong about her. About the way she was dressed, about the way she stood, about the pitch of her voice. There was no carefully applied makeup, the shoulder length hair was now cut short, her breasts were barely noticeable, obviously strapped up. The pink scarf she was wearing when we first met was gone, no longer in place to disguise her Adam's apple. Her tight Wranglers had been replaced by workaday men's jeans, the Hogan trainers by soft soled, brown shoes.

She wasn't Deborah any more. She was Daniel again.

Daniel, steely eyed and concentrated.

Taking revenge on behalf of Sofie and her son and the butchery he had witnessed in Kosovo. Because it was he who been there at the time. Deborah was later. A new life, a new person. Light years away from the brutal realities of 2000.

I couldn't begin to guess what sort of psychological state Deborah/Daniel was in. But right now, outwardly, Daniel was cold as ice.

I heard him from miles away.

'Of course, you know what they've been doing?'

I nodded. Came back to the present.

'I'd be interested in knowing how,' I said.

Daniel grinned.

'It's very simple. They've been using a route that *MSF* knew all about back in 2000. It's essentially the way Sofie and I came to England. The difference then, was that Sofie had a Croatian passport. She was travelling with a UK citizen. And once into Italy and the EU, we just climbed on a train. The people Dujic and Tudjman are smuggling into the country, begin with Serb passports, at best, and can't get visas because they're on the run. These days, being smuggled into the EU can be less of a risk than waving a forged passport, or being searched, at a European border control.'

Daniel pointed the Makarov at the container.

'Trafficking, as well as smuggling.'
'There's a difference?'
'Trafficking, is a much more evil business altogether. The end of the journey isn't the end of the story. At best, the immigrants go underground and are left to struggle on as well as they can, without papers or work permits, living with relatives. That's a happy ending of sorts. The unhappy ending is, as you'd expect, much worse. Some illegals never get out of the clutches of the people who got them into the UK. They end up living in shitholes, four or five to a room, working as prostitutes, or rent boys, or worse.'

Daniel paused to give all that an opportunity to sink in.

'But it's a risky business to be involved in,' he went on. 'Too many people on the books, as it were. Plain straight forward smuggling is relatively low risk by comparison. The tricky bit is the journey into a EU country. Once that's accomplished, it's a lorry drive to northern France or the low countries, followed by a short, if uncomfortable, ferry crossing. In this case, Brest to Avonmouth. The border agencies aren't too inquisitive about UK road haulage contractors working inside the EU, if the paperwork is in order. And searching a lorry load of fridge freezers is nobody's idea of preferred work. Smuggling is the high end of this business. And much more lucrative in the short term. So they have diversified.'

He pointed at the Serbs again.

'According to Starratt, he came across them when they switched their UK entry from Folkestone to Avonmouth. Working a relatively up-market operation. Smuggling in fellow Serbs; as opposed to desperate Bosniaks or Albanians. Their new clients are one time members of Milosevic's police and security services, who have decided they're no longer altogether bullet proof. Most of them have money. And Dujic and Tudjman are only too happy to take it away from them. Once they get into the UK, they spend two or three days in a halfway house like this; after which they're delivered into an established Serb community. Where only cream and bastards rise. And where they become the pimps and the drug dealers and the enforcers.'

'Lloyd told you all that did he?'

'And then some.'

'But only after you had taken the tin snips to his fingers.'

'That's what Grant and Copley did to Philip.'

'At which point, he agreed to set up this encounter?'

'He called the Serbs from his mobile. I told him to tell Dujic there was a serious problem and they had to talk.'

'About what?'

'His percentage. That he wanted a bigger cut. I knew that was sure to bring them here. Starratt was getting ten per cent, by the way. Of ten thousand per head. A lot of money.'

The sums weren't difficult to do. Eight beds in each container. At one hundred percent occupancy, that was sixteen thousand for three days' hospitality, each time around.

'He said they'd had three successful runs. And they were working on a fourth. Well now, I've put a stop to it.'

'You could have helped the Gloucestershire police to do that.'

'I could have. And those two might have been caught. But then what?... Held in detention for a while perhaps, then deported. Back to Serbia. Where's the justice in that?'

'Is that what you're after?'

'Natural justice is what I'm after, Jack. For Donjica and Lipojane. And for Sofie. Those monsters don't deserve to live. So I'm going to make sure they don't get a chance to.'

Daniel swung round, aimed the M57 and fired. A hole appeared in Dujic's forehead. He screamed, jerked in his chair, fell onto his back and died. Daniel fired again. Tudjman's left eye socket blew out. It didn't bother him. He just didn't wake up.

It was over, in the time it took to pull the trigger, re-sight and do it again. Daniel was a hell of a marksman. He swung back to face me.

'Mission accomplished,' he said.

I stared at him. Then eventually found my voice.

'Now what?'

Daniel sighed. 'It's all done now.'

'Not quite,' I said. 'Tell me about Lloyd Starratt.'

Daniel nodded.

'Okay. You deserve an explanation,' he said. 'Deborah came to Bristol, as she told you, back in April.'

Now, Deborah was somebody else.

'Because Sofie had seen Dujic and Tudjman at Cribbs Causeway. It was after she saw them once again – with Starratt at the cricket match – that Deborah figured out what to do. She asked around about Starratt. Then decided he was her way to the Serbs.'

I stared at Daniel, astonished at his segue into this third person narrative.

'She got an invitation to a charity dinner at the Swallow Hotel. Introduced herself to Lloyd Starratt. And seduced him.'

He looked at the expression on my face.

'Why are you surprised? She's a very sexy lady.'

I dredged up a response.

'That's not why I'm surprised.'

Daniel continued as if he hadn't heard me.

'The trouble was, Starratt had no intention of giving anything away. And the longer the relationship went on, the more experimental it became. It was downhill all the way. To anal sex, games with ropes and handcuffs and just enough violence to get him excited. That's why it was easy to get him into that wicker chair. The promise of a blow job with him tied up in it. Fucking degenerate bastard.'

I didn't want to hear any more of this. I wanted Daniel to stop talking and give me the gun. Instead, he waved it around in the air, like he was amazed at the absurdity of everything.

'In the end, Starratt decided he would get even more aroused if Deborah attempted to strangle him.'

He stopped waving the gun and looked back at me.

'It's called erotic asphyxiation.'

'I know what it's called.'

'He told Deborah he had heard that doing this during orgasm, produced a bigger rush than cocaine.'

'On occasion, it also produces death,' I said.

Daniel nodded.

'And Deborah was seriously tempted. Especially at the moment when Starratt produced his home made ligature. "End the bastard's life" she thought. How easier was it ever going to get? The problem was, she still didn't know the whereabouts of Dujic and Tudjman. Lloyd Starratt was a pig. A sex addict. A slimy, masochistic deviant. But he never talked about his business. Not once.'

'So what did Deborah do?'

'She tried to get out of the relationship. But Starratt was obsessed with her. He went looking for her. Eventually, he remembered the night he had met Philip Soames.'

Fine. But Lloyd was in no position to hire Grant and Copley. Way out of his league surely. Lloyd was big fish in a very small pond. Head of the clan sure, but not even a wannabe gangster. With absolutely no track record as a major criminal.

'He simply wouldn't let Deborah go,' Daniel went on. 'And he was also intoxicated by the cash he was making from his deal with the Serbs. He was beginning to feel like a player. Earning huge sums of money and getting sex the way he liked it. Both were driving him to places he'd never been before. So when Deborah disappeared, he moved heaven and earth to get her back.'

He pointed the M57 at the Serbs.

'He took his problem to those two. They introduced Grant and Copley to him.'

Who in all probability, uncovered the scope of their new associate's sexual proclivities and the unpredictability of the rest of the family. And, under orders from the Serbs, monitored Lloyd's progress. All the while encouraging him to believe he was in the driving seat, as the godfather of organised crime in these parts.

Daniel summed up the final chapter.

'In the end, when the Serbs realised that Deborah was proving impossible to find, they began to imagine all sorts of risks and complications. Which left them with two choices; either pull out of their arrangement with Lloyd, or slip Grant and Copley's leash. They chose the latter.'

'Let's talk about that,' I said.

Daniel shook his head and looked away across the yard.

'Philip Soames' torture and murder was a direct result of the course Deborah set herself on,' I said. 'Therefore she is responsible. Does she realise that?'

Daniel didn't respond. I insisted he did.

'Does she?'

Daniel turned back to me, eyes blazing; in a moment overwhelmingly angry. He pointed the Makarov at Dujic and Tudjman again and yelled at me.

'Those two sub-humans tortured, raped and butchered their way around the former Yugoslavia. Towns, villages, tiny places, dots on the map. People were burned out of their homes, survivors dragged from the ruins and force-marched to the Albanian border. Then the villages put to the torch. All of this inspired and excused by the most monstrous ideological bollocks since the Third Reich. Milosevic gave them means, motive and opportunity. And left a legacy so out of control, we have come down to this. Two ship containers in Gloucestershire.'

Daniel stabbed the machine pistol at the Serbs, like he was using a pointing stick.

'Those bastards gloried in the whole murderous business. Well, the glory days are over.'

He fired again. The bodies of Dujic and Tudjman jerked in response. I took a step towards him. But too slowly. Daniel squared up to me once more and raised the M57.

'No no. Not yet. I haven't finished.'

'Philip's death,' I said, going back a few moments, 'was more than just a piece of collateral damage.'

Daniel nodded in acceptance.

'Yes... You will never know how sorry Deborah is about the death of her friend. Without Philip, she would not have made it through transition. She would not be a woman. She would not be herself.'

'But the decisions she made–'

'All she wanted was to protect Sofie and her son.'

'So why didn't she tell me that? Tell me she was really looking for Dujic and Tudjman. Hire me to find them. Not give me all the nonsense about finding her.'

'Sofie and Daniel, Sofie and Daniel,' he said. 'Nothing ... no one, is more important.'

'Philip Soames sent Deborah to me,' I said. 'She trusted Philip and therefore she should have trusted me. With the whole story.'

'No. That would have meant risking the security of Sofie and Daniel.'

'But I found them anyway.'

'It was not supposed to happen,' he shouted.

I raised the volume level too.

'Deborah lied to me!'

Daniel stared at me. We were both silent. I could hear both of us breathing. I broke the silence.

'Deborah set me up,' I said. 'To do the work she couldn't accomplish. Always intending to exact her own revenge, given the opportunity.'

Daniel was struggling with the reasoning here.

'No ... the revenge ... that was my responsibility... Deborah, you see, was in no position to trust anybody.'

I counted back over the days. And the timeline made sense. Philip disappeared on the Friday. On the following Monday, he failed to turn up at his office. His murder hit the news stands on Monday evening. The next morning, Deborah called me. No longer capable of pursuing her vengeance without help. And she presented one hell of a challenge. Find her. She must have been convinced I would take that on. A much safer bet than trying to talk me into searching for a couple of Serb rapists and murderers.'

'All along, she wanted me to flush out Dujic and Tudjman,' I said.

Daniel nodded.

'And did she always intend to kill them?'

Daniel shook his head.

'No no. It was me who had to do it. Deborah was never in Kosovo. I was the one, the only one, who could dispense justice.'

This was his ultimate rationalisation. And I couldn't find anything to say. Daniel wound the business up.

'Now it's done,' he said. 'And so am I.'

He raised the automatic and pressed the barrel into his right temple. He fired. The left hand side of his head exploded outwards and he fell to his knees. He looked up at me in mute apology and dropped onto his face.

Chapter Twenty-Four

I spent two hours in Lydney, with the Gloucestershire constabulary and a way beyond furious DCI Benjamin.

He didn't believe a word I said. About anything. You know the old saying about banging your head against a brick wall? The best thing about it is when you stop. So I stopped trying to explain and that only made matters worse. In the end however, he had to admit that I wasn't responsible for the collapse of his gold medal bust and grilling me wasn't going to improve the shining hour.

I drove back across the Severn Bridge just before 2 o'clock.

First to Clevedon, where I told the story of the last two days to Chrissie and Adam. He listened with his sub-editor's hat on and went into his study to think. From Clevedon I drove to my office, where I worked out what I was going to say to Sofie. I picked up the phone, told her I would be with her in half an hour, ran through what I had devised one more time, then drove across town to talk with her.

I kept the explanation simple. Sofie cried, softly and gently, weeping for a dear friend, rather than raging at the madness of it all. I sat next to her as she told Daniel that Deborah was dead. He cried too and Sofie held him tight. I stood up to go. I dropped the keys to 15 Windmill Hill and the envelope containing the Burgh Island photographs on the coffee table and let myself out of the house.

From the Healey, I called Annie Marshall. We met in the *Clifton Coffee House*. She struggled, as I had done, with the reappearance of Daniel.

'Deborah was not suffering any gender change complications at all,' Annie said. 'She had done all the hard work. Daniel was way back in the past. She had stopped explaining herself to herself. During the beginning of your new life as a woman, the knee jerk reaction is to try and forget that you have ever lived as a man. And if you persist with that, you struggle. Best to acknowledge the past and move on. Deborah had done that. She had made the biggest decision of her life. She was over it and she was thriving.'

Until a ten year old atrocity came back to haunt her. And hammered into her a deep seated fear of what would happen if she ignored it. To deal with it, she chose the worst thing in the world she could possibly do. Go back into the past and confront her demons. And to kill, she chose to pass as Daniel. Deborah was now. The best time in her life. Kosovo was then, the worst time in Daniel's life and it was he who had to deal with the sequel.

Annie picked up the teaspoon in the saucer in front of her and scooped sugar into her coffee. She stirred the coffee. Almost an absent-minded action.

'It was a complicated scheme she worked out,' she said. 'And supposing you hadn't found Dujic and Tudjman...'

'I was bound to do that, eventually. Deborah knew that Lloyd Starratt's contractors would find me if I went to Windmill Hill. And once that happened, I would have something to work on.'

'Providing you stayed alive.'

'A risk she was prepared to accept.'

'She could have gone to the police. After Philip's murder.'

'Then she would have lost control of the situation. A police investigation would have spooked Dujic and Tudjman into disappearing. And that wasn't the desired end result. Everything worked out as planned – until I found Sofie and Daniel. Which forced Deborah out into the open. And back to Lloyd Starratt.'

Annie picked up her coffee cup.

'As Daniel,' I said.

Annie sipped her coffee, then cradled the cup in both hands.

'It's as though she was three personalities,'

she said. 'The Deborah she presented to you. Cool and organised in jeans and sneakers. The Deborah she lived while out on the town and in her relationship with Lloyd Starratt. Sexual and predatory, in bling and heels. And the Daniel she became again; to kill.'

God knows what courage – or madness – it took to do that. To go back to being the person she had done so much to escape from. I drained my cup of coffee and asked a waitress for the bill.

Outside the *Coffee House* we shook hands.

'Take care Jack,' Annie said. 'And call me. Soon.'

I promised her I would. She turned away from me, crossed the road and set off along Victoria Street. I watched her until she disappeared into the throng of Clifton village shoppers, then I walked to where I had parked the Healey.

Back in my office, I put all my notes on the case into a folder, labelled it 'Thorne' and filed it in the middle drawer of my filing cabinet under 'T'. Actually, straight after the last 'S' – Philip Soames.

The phone on the desk rang.

'I'll be back in Bristol in time for brunch tomorrow,' Linda said.

'It's a date,' I said.

'A date? You sweet old fashioned thing.'

There is always a story which comes after the end of a story. Events and their consequences, roll on into sequels. Life doesn't wrap stuff up in tidy conclusions.

The Gloucestershire Constabulary held on to Deborah's body for three days. Bill and Elizabeth Thornton were informed of the death of their daughter. I remembered, like it was yesterday, every occasion during my years on the force, when I had to stand on someone's doorstep, ring their doorbell and ask 'May I come in?' Breaking the worst news of all, is never routine, even to the toughest case hardened investigators. I called the Thorntons myself to offer my condolences, which were received with grace. And Sofie, the daughter-in-law they had never met, called them. She and Daniel went to visit and Deborah's funeral service was held in Ringsmere.

Adam, Chrissie, Sam, Linda and I headed east too. We loaded ourselves into Adam's Espace and took a charabanc trip to Suffolk a few days later. The welcome was wonderful. Auntie Joyce baked. And Uncle Sid unveiled his latest piece of work.

The publishers hope that this book has given you enjoyable reading. Large Print Books are especially designed to be as easy to see and hold as possible. If you wish a complete list of our books please ask at your local library or write directly to:

Magna Large Print Books
Magna House, Long Preston,
Skipton, North Yorkshire.
BD23 4ND

This Large Print Book, for people
who cannot read normal print,
is published under the auspices of

THE ULVERSCROFT FOUNDATION

... we hope you have enjoyed this book.
Please think for a moment about those
who have worse eyesight than you ...
and are unable to even read or enjoy
Large Print without great difficulty.

You can help them by sending a
donation, large or small, to:

**The Ulverscroft Foundation,
1, The Green, Bradgate Road,
Anstey, Leicestershire, LE7 7FU,
England.**
or request a copy of our brochure for
more details.

The Foundation will use all donations
to assist those people who are visually
impaired and need special attention
with medical research, diagnosis
and treatment.

Thank you very much for your help.